A
DANGER
TO
HERSELF
AND
OTHERS

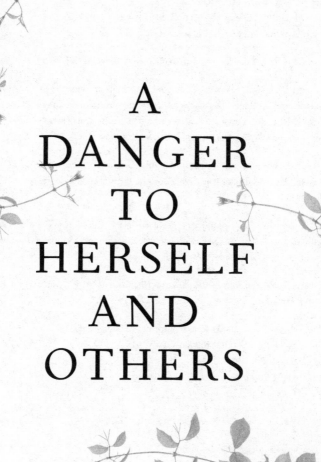

A
DANGER
TO
HERSELF
AND
OTHERS

Alyssa Sheinmel

sourcebooks
fire

Published by Sourcebooks Fire, an imprint of Sourcebooks, Inc.
P.O. Box 4410, Naperville, Illinois 60567-4410
(630) 961-3900
Fax: (630) 961-2168
sourcebooks.com

Library of Congress Cataloging-in-Publication Data

Names: Sheinmel, Alyssa B., author.
Title: A danger to herself and others / Alyssa Sheinmel.
Description: Naperville, Illinois : Sourcebooks Fire, [2019] | Summary: After her best friend, Agnes, goes into a coma as a result of a game of Truth or Dare, rising senior Hannah's secrets begin to escape while she is locked in a psychiatric hospital.
Identifiers: LCCN 2018010683 | (hardcover : alk. paper)
Subjects: | CYAC: Psychiatric hospitals--Fiction. | Friendship--Fiction. | Mentally ill--Fiction. | Jews--United States--Fiction.
Classification: LCC PZ7.S54123 Dan 2019 | DDC [Fic]--dc23 LC record available at https://lccn.loc.gov/2018010683

Printed and bound in the United States of America.
WOZ 10 9 8 7 6 5 4 3 2

PART ONE

inside

one

When I first got here—when they brought me here—a man with blue pants and a matching shirt, both of which looked like they were made of paper, asked me questions. As I answered, he took notes, balancing a clipboard against his left hip and holding a pen in his right hand. I'm left-handed, so that's something we didn't have in common.

"What's your name?" he began.

I considered saying: *What's in a name? A rose by any other name would smell as sweet.*

I was sitting; he was standing. The clipboard was level with my forehead, and when he cocked his hip, the clipboard swayed dangerously close to my face. He smiled tightly. His teeth were yellow and crooked. He said, "Don't be difficult."

Do you find Shakespeare difficult?

"What's your name?" he repeated.

I closed my eyes. I suppose your name is the first thing that ever really belongs to you, but when you think about it, it's not *yours* at all. Your parents chose it. A million people might have had it before you. Maybe even a specific person, if you were named after someone. My name begins with an *H* for my mom's late aunt Hilda because that's something Jewish people do, carrying the dead around with us almost from the instant we're born. Plenty of people name their children after a relative who's passed away, but as far as I know, we're the only ones who *require* it. And my mother told me we're absolutely not supposed to name our children after someone who's still alive, though I've never actually seen her go to temple so I don't imagine she's an expert on the rules. Nonetheless, Mom insisted I be named in honor of Hilda, who died while my mom was pregnant, and to whom my mother was apparently really close. Mom told me once that she never considered actually calling me *Hilda*. She thought the name sounded too old.

So: *Hannah.*

A sweet name. A good girl's name. Even more traditional and old-fashioned than Hilda, when you think about it. I mean, I don't think there's a *Hilda* in the Bible.

Hannah is nothing like *Agnes.*

Hannah wanted to play games that *Agnes* thought we were getting too old for.

No, not getting *too old,* Agnes said. *We've* been *too old for these games for years now. We're going to be seniors in a couple months!* But she was laughing, so I knew I'd be able to make her play.

Back to the man with the clipboard.

We both knew he didn't really need me to tell him my name. Someone must have told him before I got here. He scribbled something on my file. The corner of the board dug into his belly, and I wondered if it hurt or if he was numb beneath his paper clothes. I couldn't see what he was writing, but I guessed he wasn't smudging the letters because he wasn't a lefty.

Maybe left-handed people should be taught to write right to left instead of left to right. (And in languages that already read right to left, right-handed people would get to write in the opposite direction, too.) It'd be more fair that way. In kindergarten, my lowest grades were always in "penmanship"—not that they were real grades back then. Where I go to school you don't get A's and B's and C's until seventh grade. Anyhow, comparing my penmanship to the right-handed kindergarteners wasn't remotely fair when you think about it. I was the only lefty in my class. My teacher had to procure special left-handed scissors for me, but I could never make them work. I ended up using the right-handed scissors instead. I read somewhere that every year, twenty-five left-handed people die using products designed for right-handed people.

Maybe even scissors.

The man with the clipboard led me up the stairs (two flights) and down a hall to this room. I wanted to ask about Agnes. I wanted to know whether Jonah was with her. She'd been in the hospital for nearly a week by the time they brought me here, plenty of time for Jonah to come. Maybe he was holding her hand. Maybe he'd lean over and kiss her forehead. I never saw them *really* kiss. Jonah said Agnes was shy about doing stuff like that in front of me, even though she and I were roommates and best friends.

Agnes's parents arrived less than forty-eight hours after Agnes was admitted to the hospital. I was sitting by her bed when they got there. After that, the doctors wouldn't let me back into her room because I wasn't *family*. At the time, I assumed that since her real family had arrived to sit at her bedside, the doctors didn't feel the need to bend whatever rules they'd bent so that Agnes wouldn't be alone. Though she was in a coma, so it was impossible to say whether or not she knew she wasn't alone. Agnes was still in the ICU when her parents arrived, and the hospital only allowed visitors into the ICU two at a time, and Agnes's parents almost never left her.

With Agnes gone, I spent a few nights by myself in our dorm room, where we'd been living together since the summer program started nearly two months before. I took taxis back and forth to the hospital each day. (I considered checking into a hotel closer to the hospital, maybe the same hotel where Agnes's parents were staying, then decided against it.) But they never let me back into Agnes's room.

I can still picture how she looked the last time I saw her—that is, before her parents arrived: one tube going down her throat, tape over her lips to hold it in place. An IV stuck into her left arm that was attached to a plastic bag full of liquid (medication? fluids? nutrients?) hanging on a hook above her bed. She'd told me once that she hated needles; at least she'd been unconscious when they stuck her this time. Her blond hair was only a shade or two darker than the white sheets on her bed.

By the time they sent me here, Agnes was out of the ICU, but she was still in a coma, still had that tube taped to her mouth. They said it wasn't safe to move her to a hospital closer to home in her condition.

When the doctors asked me what happened, I told them. Light as a Feather, Stiff as a Board. Never Have I Ever. Truth or Dare. When they arrived, Agnes's parents asked me what happened, so I told them, too. And of course, I told the police when they asked.

Agnes's mother had never heard of Light as a Feather, so I had to explain how the game worked: One person lies on the ground while everyone else gathers around, putting their fingers beneath her and chanting *light as a feather, stiff as a board* until the girl (or boy, but in this case, girl) in the middle levitates. Mrs. Smith looked so alarmed that you'd have thought she actually believed the game was some sort of satanic ritual that caused its players to float through the air.

I explained that you can't really play Light as a Feather with only two people. That of course no one really *levitates*—the group simply lifts someone and sets her back down. I told Mrs. Smith that wasn't what had happened to Agnes. I said we switched to Never Have I Ever—each of us trying to trick the other into confessing a secret—but that got boring, so eventually we started playing Truth or Dare.

I explained how Truth or Dare worked, in case Mrs. Smith didn't know that either. (You take turns asking each other *truth or dare*. If you pick *truth*, you have to honestly answer whatever question you're asked. If you pick *dare*, you have to do whatever task you're given.)

The day after that, they brought me here.

I didn't put up a fight, didn't kick and scream and protest my innocence like people do in the movies. I came calmly and quietly because I knew this was all a misunderstanding that would get sorted out once Agnes's parents had some time to calm down. They were probably still in shock, too upset to see straight. After all, their daughter had just fallen out of a window two floors off the ground. But soon they'd realize that if I'd actually done anything wrong, I'd hardly have been sitting at Agnes's bedside (more accurately, in the hospital waiting room, since they wouldn't let me in to see her anymore), where it would be easy to find me. They needed someone to blame, and I was the only available scapegoat. Their daughter was my best friend. Playing the scapegoat was the least I could do under the circumstances.

This room is eight feet by seven feet. I don't mean feet as in twelve inches, I mean the number of steps it takes me to get from one end of the room to the other. I've had plenty of time to count. Maybe I should've been counting the days instead of my steps, so I'd know how long I've been here, but it's hard to keep track when every day is almost exactly like the one before it. The only furniture is the narrow bed where I sleep and another bed on the opposite wall. The only light, other than the fluorescent beams overhead, comes from a tiny, square-shaped window on the wall opposite the door. The window is off-center, so it's slightly closer to the bed I sleep in. At night, a tiny strip of light comes in under the door because the lights in the hallway stay on twenty-four hours a day. The overhead lights must work on a timer. I don't know exactly what times they go on and off, but suffice it to say, they let me know when to wake in the morning and when to go to sleep at night.

The walls in here are made of oversized bricks. Not tile, and not rocks or stone, but some kind of manufactured material, complete with fake divots and imperfections like someone thought it would look less institutional that way, like that would help whoever was stuck in this room forget what kind of place this is.

Someone—maybe the same someone who picked the oversized bricks—thought it was a good idea to paint the walls green. Maybe they thought this place would feel more natural that way, but the only natural way for a wall to be green is if it's covered in ivy or moss, and ivy and moss don't grow here and even if they did, they aren't *this* color green, this industrial vomit green that vaguely reminds me of the never-used classrooms in the basement of my school where they supposedly discovered asbestos in the walls. The classrooms we actually use are above-ground and asbestos-free, painted yellow and blue and even purple because someone's parent read that the color purple was good for your brain.

There's fog here, but it never rains. I stand on my tiptoes to look out my small window and wait for the few plants and trees I can see to dry out and die.

two

Too old for these games. Too old for these games. Too old for these games.

I hear the words over and over, like a song I can't get out of my head. It's Agnes's voice I hear, not my own. Like she's in the room with me. I can practically see her flipping her long blond hair over one shoulder. Her hair is thinner than mine, but less unruly. Plus, mine is brown. So much more ordinary than Agnes's hair. At least, that's how Jonah must've seen it.

On the other hand, Jonah said once that my brown hair paired with my light green eyes made me pretty in a *striking* sort of way. He didn't say it like it was a good thing. More like it was merely something he'd noticed.

Too old for these games.

You're never really too old for games. The games just change. You'd think someone with a name as grown-up as Agnes would've understood that.

Come on, Agnes. It'll be fun.

I'm not sure we have the same idea of fun, Agnes said. But she was smiling, so she must have been having at least a little fun.

Light as a feather, stiff as a board. Light as a feather, stiff as a board. Light as a feather...

When I say the words out loud, they echo off the ugly brick walls like a beacon, bringing Dr. Lightfoot along with them. That's not her real name. Her real name is Priya Charan (she introduced herself to me when we met, obviously), but I call her Lightfoot because she wears ballet slippers, and they *tap tap tap* across the linoleum floor with every step she takes. And I don't mean stylish ballet flats, the kind you can get at J. Crew, the sort that Audrey Hepburn made famous and fashionable. I mean, this doctor literally wears ballet shoes. They're not even nice ballet shoes, like the kind professional dancers wear. These are the sort of plain slippers parents give to little kids taking their first ballet class.

These slippers have no laces and no soles. They have no sharp or heavy parts. They can't be used as weapons. Dr. Lightfoot wears them because they make her feel safe around girls like me.

Which, I have to tell you, is absurd. Not because I wouldn't try anything (I can't make any promises—who knows what being trapped in a room could drive a person to do?), but because Dr. Lightfoot always brings a clipboard with my file clipped to it and a pen with her, just like the man who asked my name when I arrived here. Maybe it's the same clipboard. I asked to see my file the first time she came to see me, and she held it out in front of her so I could only see the first page.

Now *those* items—the clipboard, the pen, even the heavy file—could be useful, if you were interested in that sort of thing.

Which is why Dr. Lightfoot never comes to see me alone.

"Who's that?" I asked on the first day. Or maybe it was the fifth day. Or the tenth. Like I said, I haven't been keeping track. Anyway, it was the first time Dr. Lightfoot made an appearance, so I'm guessing it was at the beginning of all of this.

"That's my colleague Stephen," she answered, gesturing to the enormous man standing in the doorway with his arms crossed like a bouncer at the hottest club back home in the city. When Dr. Lightfoot is here, the door stays open, but Stephen is so big that he blocks any light that might come in from the hallway, along with any chance of seeing my fellow inmates (patients? prisoners?) who might be walking in the hallway. Or any chance of them seeing me.

"What's he doing here?"

"Observing," Dr. Lightfoot answered. "He's a student."

I sighed. It's not like I thought they'd have the best doctors in the world at a place like this, but I'm surprised they put someone as incompetent as Lightfoot in charge of my case. It's bad enough that she keeps me locked in this room all day, which definitely wouldn't be good for my sanity if I were actually mentally ill. But even I know that doctors like her are supposed to gain their patients' trust. Which is pretty hard to do when her answer to one of the first questions I ever asked was a bald-faced lie.

It was true that Stephen was observing, but it was a lie that he was here to learn something. He was here to keep an eye on me. He was here so Dr. Lightfoot wouldn't have to be alone with me.

Because I've been labeled *a danger to herself and others.*

Another phrase that floats through my head. Though not in Agnes's voice. Agnes wouldn't have said that because no one ever said that about me before they brought me here. And by the time they brought me here, Agnes had a tube stuck down her throat, so she couldn't have said anything anyway.

I don't hear this particular phrase in anyone's voice because I never heard it at all. I saw it written on the first page of my file when Lightfoot held it out to me.

My name was typed at the top of the page: *Hannah Gold.*

Beneath that was my date of birth, my address in New York, my medical history (strep throat at eleven, tonsillitis at thirteen).

And beneath that were two bullet points:

- *Hold for observation.*
- *Patient may pose a danger to herself and others.*

"So that's why I'm stuck in this room?" I asked. "Because you think I'm dangerous?"

"You're in this room for your own safety." I was already sick of Lightfoot's dull, monotonous voice.

"And the safety of others," I added. Lightfoot didn't respond.

Patient may pose a danger to herself and others.

I always hated when people said *maybe, maybe not* in answer to a question. What an absurdly redundant, completely unnecessary expression. Maybe *is* maybe not. There's no reason to say both. Saying I *may* pose a danger to myself and others is also saying that I may *not*.

I sigh and pace the room in perpendicular lines. Just because I'm stuck in here is no reason to forgo exercise. I will not get fat.

My muscles will not atrophy down to nothing. These people will not keep me still and pump me full of food like they do to the girls with eating disorders down the hall. Or anyway, the girls I imagine are down the hall. I haven't actually seen any other patients yet, but sometimes I hear doors opening and closing, hear muffled female voices rising and falling as they approach then pass the door. More than once, I've heard one girl or another yelling, though the walls are too thick for me to make out exactly what they're yelling about. Maybe they don't want to take their medication. Or maybe they're complaining about the locks on the doors. (I assume all the doors have locks like mine.) Or maybe they're protesting being here at all. They didn't come here calmly and quietly like I did. Of course, the other patients are here because there's actually something wrong with them. I'm only here because of a misunderstanding, so there's no need for me to panic.

Anyway, the sounds I hear make it clear that at least some of the other patients here (all girls, judging by their voices) aren't left alone in their rooms like I am. I stand between the beds and do a few sun salutations. When I was little, Mom used to bring me to the yoga classes she frequented to help keep her belly flat.

Maybe being stuck indoors will be good for my skin. Maybe when all this is over, I'll emerge with a preternaturally youthful complexion, like those kidnapping victims who are kept in underground bunkers for half their lives and emerge with non-sun-damaged skin after their rescue. Maybe my perfect skin will be a sign of my survival, a show of solidarity with those kidnapped girls, like a uniform—we were all held indoors against our will.

Not that I intend to be here that long. Like I said, this is all just a misunderstanding.

Eight steps. Turn. Seven Steps. Turn. I'd prefer to keep to the walls and circle the room like it's a tiny little track, but the beds get in the way.

Dr. Lightfoot never uses the second bed. I don't mean *uses* like sleeps in it or anything, but when she comes in here to talk, she brings a plastic folding chair with her and sits in the center of the room with her back to the vacant second bed while I sit on the first, the one in which I sleep. Maybe Lightfoot doesn't sit on the bed because she doesn't want to make our interactions feel too casual. After all, we're not two friends catching up. We're not roommates in a college dorm. She's not my new Agnes.

Agnes never knew that I was hooking up with Jonah. Don't let the biblical name fool you. *Two* biblical names: Hannah and Jonah. We were doing some pretty non-biblical things. Or actually, completely biblical things, when you think about it.

I gaze out the window. Dusk and dawn look the same here. The fog is rolling through. There are redwood trees as far as I can see, and when the fog gets thick, it condenses on the needlelike leaves and drips onto the roof. It sounds like rain, but it isn't.

It's not true that I can only see a few plants from here. We're actually in the middle of a forest.

I was lying before.

three

Here's what I remember about this place from when they brought me here (I haven't left the room since, so I only know what I saw that day):

This building is three stories high, and I'm on the third floor. There's no elevator, or anyway, they didn't bring me up in one. I trudged up the stairs behind Clipboard-Man. The walls in the stairwell are the same vomit-green brick that they are in here.

When we reached the second-floor landing, I heard shouting. Almost the kind of sound you'd hear coming from a classroom of unruly kids or a group of teens hanging out in the cafeteria. (I assume this place has some sort of cafeteria.)

First floor: admitting, arrivals, emergencies, offices.

Second floor: cafeteria, classrooms (or something like that).

Third floor: a long hallway of closed doors, behind which I guess are all patients' rooms. I wonder if any of the rooms are different inside. Like, depending on what you got sent here for.

There could be a basement, I suppose, but I don't think they have basements in California because of earthquakes. Also, the building is kind of built into the side of a mountain, so in order to have a basement they'd have had to carve a hole into the hill. That seems like a lot of trouble to go to for a place like this.

I can tell this isn't the sort of building that used to be something else. You know how hospitals become boarding schools become jails become high-end condos because they have *good bones*? Not this place. This building was designed to be exactly what it is. What other use could there possibly be for a long, rectangular, three-story stone box built into the side of a mountain?

My window faces the woods, but I'm pretty sure the windows on the other side of the building face the Pacific Ocean. I'm not positive, but I think I smell salt water sometimes.

I want to know whose idea it was to build this place here. The building may be ugly, but the location seems better suited to a high-end resort where rich people from the big city spend thousands of dollars to relax and unplug, seemingly oblivious to the fact that millions of people relax and unplug for free.

But then, putting this facility someplace beautiful probably makes it easier to convince parents like mine to allow their children to be sent here. I imagine mothers telling their daughters: *It's so lovely in the Santa Cruz Mountains. It'll be like you're on vacation.*

Right.

There are certain allowances that have to be made if you don't leave a room.

Allowance 1: Bedpans.

They offer me a chance to go to a bathroom down the hall

a few times each day, but there's also a bedpan in the room *just in case*. I actually prefer using it because at least that way I get to decide when I perform my bodily functions. I know a bedpan is supposed to be humiliating, but I have to disagree. There's something oddly luxurious about not having to leave the bed to pee. And about the fact that someone else has to take your waste away. You don't even have to flush it yourself.

Allowance 2: Food.

My meals are brought to me on a tray three times a day. I guess it's the same food the others eat—whatever they serve in the cafeteria for the girls who aren't *a danger to themselves and others*. It's safe to assume that no one here gets to choose when they eat; mealtimes are probably strictly adhered to whether you're in a room or in the cafeteria. This morning, they brought me Honey Nut Cheerios, or what was probably some generic off-label version of Honey Nut Cheerios. I wanted to tell them that I hate honey, but it's not like there's a menu to pick from. Jonah had Cheerios for breakfast nearly every morning this summer, though we always suspected that the dorm cafeteria stocked the generic off-label brand, which Jonah thought was ridiculous considering how much our parents paid to send us to that summer program. Maybe the food in this place is supplied by the same company that supplies food to the dorm I'd been living in before I came here. But having the same cereal we'd eaten on the outside doesn't make this place seem any more normal.

Wherever he is, Jonah is probably still eating Cheerios for breakfast.

Allowance 3: Clothing and bathing.

There's no closet in this room. No furniture at all other than the two beds. They bring me a change of clothes every other day. The cloth is paper thin, and the pants are held up by a short string that I have to double knot above my hip bones. I think the clothes are specifically designed so that you can't use them as a weapon. The string on the pants is so short that you couldn't even wrap it around your neck to strangle yourself. I suppose you could wrap the legs of your pants around your neck and tie them tight if you really wanted. But then you'd be found naked from the waist down, and that might be worse than staying alive in this place.

Then again, the pants are so thin they'd probably rip into tiny, useless pieces before you could do any real damage.

Once a day (or so), a (female) orderly brings me a bucket of water and a washcloth so I can give myself something resembling a sponge bath. The orderly doesn't look away. Maybe most patients wash themselves with their clothes on, but I strip naked and scrub myself clean, just to show them I'm not ashamed.

Dr. Lightfoot tells me that I'll probably get to take a shower soon. But she never explains the delay, and I'm not about to ask. It's too obvious that she wants me to, and anyway, it's easy enough to guess that it has something to do with my being *a danger to myself and others.*

There are other allowances, of course. But let's call those the big three.

four

A little background.

I was born seventeen years and approximately one month ago (like I said, I don't know exactly what day it is) in New York, New York, to a pair of adoring parents, Byron and Margaret Gold. I'm an only child, and my parents brought me with them to the sorts of places and events that other parents hired babysitters for: going to the theater or to fancy restaurants, on luxurious vacations during which I always got my own private hotel room, no matter how young I was.

I came to California in June of this year for summer school. Not the kind of summer school for delinquents who won't graduate without extra credits, but the kind for kids who are so smart and so studious that they choose to spend their vacations living in dorms and taking classes at one of the most prestigious colleges in the country in order to get a head start. If I'd been allowed to complete the program this summer, I'd have accumulated nine credits to put toward my college education. And I haven't even started my senior year of high school.

After I was brought to this place, my parents came to visit me. I'd been in California for more than six weeks, but so much had happened that it may as well have been six months. My mother had a perfect tan from spending her weekends in Southampton back in New York. Her hair had been highlighted recently; the strips of blond were still bright and yellow, not the brassy color they always faded to after a few weeks in her naturally brown hair.

She hugged me, and I smelled her perfume and shampoo.

"It's only temporary," she said. "Just until everything…passes." Maybe she would've cried if she hadn't gotten her semiannual Restylane shot into her tear troughs a few days prior. (I recognized the telltale shadowy bruises beneath her eyes that meant she'd had a recent trip to the plastic surgeon's office.) For days after her injections, she's scared to cry, or laugh, or sleep on her side—anything that might affect the way the filler sets under her skin.

My parents' lawyer tried to keep me from getting sent here in the first place, but eventually he gave up, saying that we had no choice but to *let this thing play out* for now. He's the kind of attorney who usually deals with wills and estates—family law, that kind of thing—but my parents are good clients, and he's authorized to practice law in both New York and California.

I nodded calmly. I'd never had a temper tantrum, not even as a baby—a fact all three of us were proud of—and I didn't want to break my streak. Anyway, like my mom said, this was only temporary. (*Let this thing play out. Just until everything passes.*) Plus, I knew my parents had made plans for a trip before any of this happened. They were going to spend the last two weeks of August in Europe, even though my mother had always said that's the worst time of year to travel on the continent.

My mother is the kind of woman who says things like *on the continent.*

My father wrinkled his nose, as though he could tell—despite the fact that I'd stashed the bedpan beneath the bed—that I performed all my bodily functions in this room, which is almost the same size as my mother's walk-in closet in Manhattan. (I've counted my steps in that room too: nine long by six across.)

"I'm fine, Dad," I said. I let my lower lip quiver a tiny bit. Just to show him that no matter how much I was trying to be strong, no matter what had happened to make them send me here, I'd always be his little girl. I fingered the plastic bracelet on my wrist, the one they'd given me when I arrived, with my name and an identifying set of numbers, the kind they give to hospital patients.

He put his arm around me and squeezed. I knew he was proud of me for being so brave, for taking this on with such maturity. (My parents have always praised me for acting grown-up. The inside joke in our little family is that I was born mature. Mom's voice, full of pride: *Hannah was even a mature baby!*)

"I'm glad you're getting to see more of the West Coast," Dad answered finally. Maybe he thought this was the kind of place where they take us on field trips. Maybe he thought I'd already waded through the tide pools in Monterey, admiring the flora and fauna.

I didn't bother correcting him. I knew how much he liked the idea. The mature thing to do was to let him keep that thought if it comforted him.

California was why he'd wanted to send me to summer school in the first place. I'd never lived anywhere but New York, and with college applications just around the corner, good ol' Byron thought I should audition living away from the Upper East Side. (Though he said he and Mom would miss me terribly.) I wonder if now he wishes he'd kept me closer to home. If he wishes he hadn't put such a premium on *broadening my horizons*. (A phrase I've heard in his voice for years.)

He kissed the top of my head when he left, even though he hasn't been more than two inches taller than me since I turned fifteen. Mom didn't kiss me at all. At five foot seven, I tower over my mother, who's only five foot three. She always marveled at my height, wondering where I'd gotten it from, as if she couldn't believe that someone who grew up to be so tall had ever actually lived inside of her. Once, she and I were out to lunch with a friend of hers, and Mom said that the hospital must have mixed me up with some other baby, there was no way she could have given birth to someone who ended up this size. I pointed out that we had the same green eyes, and I clearly share her husband's hair and eyebrows.

"But where'd you get all that height?" she countered with a smile, and I couldn't come up with a clever response.

"You two are so lucky," Mom's friend said. "You're more like best friends than mother and daughter."

Mom beamed.

Before they left me alone in this room, I said, "I like California,

Dad." He smiled and I smiled back. Whether or not it was the truth hardly mattered since I was stuck inside. This room could be anywhere and the only thing that would change would be the view through the small window.

In case you're wondering, though: I don't particularly like California. In fact, I think the whole state is weird. And not in the way that so many New Yorkers think it's strange—too laid back, too culturally shallow, too much driving, too many cars, too much space. Too dark at night. Too much sky. (*I* don't think those things, but I've heard other New Yorkers say them.)

To me, the weirdest thing about California isn't only that the ocean is on the other side, but that north can feel like south, and south can feel like north, and east and west don't feel quite right either. The university's campus is what they call "on the peninsula," which (as far as I could tell) means near Silicon Valley. You could go north into the city—not *the* city (Manhattan), but San Francisco—and the temperature would probably drop precipitously. But then *farther north*, up in Napa Valley (where I went on vacation with my parents years ago), the temperature might rise ten, twenty, thirty degrees.

And here—up in the mountains along the water with the too-tall trees and foothills and valleys—the temperature is cooler than it was on campus, even though this place is miles *south* of the peninsula. On top of all that, there's a severe drought, but the fog is so thick that each morning it condenses into water that drips off the roof, and there's frost on the window even though it's August.

It's like California doesn't have to follow the laws of nature.

five

Lying on the bed, I can only see a skinny strip of sky out the window, so I shift my attention to the ceiling. It's one of those pockmarked ceilings, full of dents and drips, like gravity tugged at the plaster before it had time to dry and harden. At least, unlike the walls, it's white. If I concentrate on the ceiling hard enough, I don't notice the springs in the cheap mattress digging into my spine.

After a while, I stop staring at the ceiling and shift my gaze to the walls instead, studying every manufactured crack and divot.

Then I look up again. This time, I stare at the lights: two long, skinny fluorescent bulbs under a plastic cover. What will happen if the bulbs die while I'm here? Will they send someone in with a ladder and a fresh set of bulbs? Maybe they wouldn't trust me with a maintenance worker in the room. There'd be too many items that could be used as weapons: the glass in the bulbs, the screwdriver they'd need to take the cover off the light fixture, the metal hinges on the ladder, to say nothing of the ladder itself. They'd have to take me outside while the bulbs were changed, even if it was just into the hallway.

Footsteps. The sound of the door opening. I don't have to take my eyes off the ceiling to know that it's Dr. Lightfoot, *tap tap tap*ping in her ballet shoes. Then Stephen, in his heavy, black boots, too warm for this climate (not that I've been outside lately), peeking out from under the hem of his scrubs. I've gotten used to the rhythm of their steps: they check on me every morning, and then come back in the afternoon for what Lightfoot refers to as our "session."

But this time there's a third set of steps. *Slap slap slap*. Bare feet.

I turn my head, keeping my back flat against the mattress. It has a vinyl cover like the ones in the dorm. Though this mattress is even thinner than those were.

There's a girl standing behind Dr. Lightfoot and Stephen. They took her shoes—must've had laces—but not her clothes. Not yet. She's still wearing real clothes: boot-cut blue jeans and a white, scoop neck T-shirt. She curls her light-brown toes against the linoleum floor. Her long, dark hair falls around her face like a sheet, but I can see her eyes are almost black, and a few freckles dot her cheeks like scars.

The girl hugs a bundle to her chest. It takes me a second to realize it's a set of the same paper clothes that I'm wearing. Dr. Lightfoot and Stephen must be waiting for her to change. She shivers like she's cold, but I can see that her upper lip is coated in sweat.

"You guys don't exactly put a premium on privacy, do you?" I mutter finally.

"What was that?" Dr. Lightfoot asks.

"Nothing," I say, but the girl must have heard me and understood because she walks over to the bed on the other side of the room and turns her back to me. She seems to realize Dr. Lightfoot and Stephen can see her profile that way, and she shifts slightly, so we all have more of a diagonal view. She takes off her shirt first and lifts the paper one from the bed. Stephen clears his throat before she can put it on.

Slowly, the girl reaches back and unhooks her black, cotton bra. Even from here, I can see that this place's no-underwire policy is going to be a bigger problem for this new girl than it is for me. She's fit, but her soft parts—her chest, her belly, her bottom—are softer than mine.

I look back at the ceiling. Agnes was shy the first time she changed in front of me too. We giggled about it later, after it became clear that being shy in front of your roommate was more trouble than it was worth.

"You're awfully quiet today," Dr. Lightfoot says.

"I'm not a big fan of change," I answer, and Dr. Lightfoot shrugs as if to say: *Don't tell me you thought you'd have this room to yourself forever. What did you think the second bed was for?*

I shake my head. I'm not going to be here forever.

I can't be that much of a *danger to myself and others* if they're giving me a roommate. Unless she's part of my therapy. Or my punishment. Whichever is the real reason I'm here.

"We'll check on you later," Dr. Lightfoot promises, the way a parent promises to check on a little kid after lights-out. Does she think I miss her when she's gone? The door locks automatically behind them with the magnetic click that I've almost gotten used to. No Stephen planted in the doorway in case I try something. Maybe they think I'm safe now. Or maybe this girl isn't as valuable to them as Dr. Lightfoot is.

Maybe they just want to see if I'll do better with her than I did with Agnes.

In fact, this girl could be a test. She might not be a patient at all. She could be an intern, a doctor-in-training. Going undercover could be one of her requirements. They could be watching us secretly right now to see how I'll react.

I sit up and look around the room. Since I've been here, I've checked for signs of surveillance: cameras, microphones, a recording device stuck under the bed like the "bugs" in spy movies. I've had plenty of time to make multiple searches, and I've never found anything. You'd think a place like this would be wired with cameras everywhere, so they could keep an eye on us at all times, but then again, maybe they don't want to risk someone else getting a hold of the tapes and seeing how they run things here.

They have other ways to watch us: Multiple times a day some attendant/orderly/nurse pops in for a "room check." (That's what they say as they open the door, in an insufferable, high-pitched, singsongy voice: *Room check.*) The girl perches delicately on the second bed, her back stick straight, her posture perfect. If you were standing in the doorway, her bed would be on the right side of the room, directly in front of the door. The bed on which I sleep (I've refused to think of it as *my bed*) is on the left side. Though, if you were standing beneath the window, her bed would be on the left side of the room, and the bed where I sleep would be on the right.

Let me put it this way: If I'm right about where the ocean is relative to this building, then her bed is on the south side of the room. That doesn't change, no matter which direction you're facing.

"I'm Hannah," I offer finally. I swing my legs over the side of the bed. I roll my shoulders down my back so that I'm sitting up straight too. If she's a test, I'll be so polite they'll have to give me an A. (I've literally never gotten a grade below a B+.)

"Lucy."

Lucy sounds even sweeter than *Hannah*.

"What's your last name?" I ask.

"Quintana," she answers.

"Gold," I offer, even though she didn't ask. "Welcome to my room," I say, calling it mine for the first time.

The day we moved into the dorm back in June, Agnes got to our room before I did. She was sitting on one of the desk chairs when I arrived.

I can still hear her voice saying the first words she ever spoke to me: *You must be Hannah.*

She stood and held her hand out in front of her for me to shake, but I leaned in for a hug instead. Her hair fell perfectly straight down her back, and when I put my arm around her, my fingers brushed against the soft strands. It was the kind of hair that dozens of girls at my school in the city paid thousands of dollars for, between colorists and straightening treatments and flat irons and special brushes. Later, I found out that Agnes used Johnson's Baby Shampoo and nothing else—no conditioner, no product. She didn't even have to use a blow-dryer. Her hair was naturally perfect.

I haven't picked a bed yet. Agnes gestured to the two bare, narrow beds on either side of the room. Each bed sat beneath an enormous window, and sunlight streamed in, so bright that Agnes hadn't bothered to turn on the overhead lights. The windows were open wide because the dorm wasn't air-conditioned, and the sounds and scents of the campus drifted inside: shouts from our future classmates, eucalyptus leaves, sunscreen.

I didn't think it was fair that I'd get first dibs just because my parents drove me here faster than yours did.

My parents didn't drive me here. I took a cab from the airport.

You flew here alone?

I shrugged like it was no big deal, but I could tell Agnes was impressed. Maybe she'd never been on a plane before. (I found out later that she had, but only twice.) She was wearing a white T-shirt over denim shorts. Her skin was fair but dotted with freckles in odd places (not across her cheeks like Lucy's): a smattering on one cheek, on the back of her left hand, behind her right ear. She was wearing pink lip gloss; coral would have looked better with her complexion, but there would be plenty of time for me to teach her that.

Lucky for you, I do believe in first dibs. You got here first, so you should get to choose your bed.

But that's not fair! When Agnes was upset, her blue eyes got so wide she looked seven instead of seventeen. *We should at least flip a coin.*

I shook my head, my smile still wide on my face. I already knew I wanted Agnes to be my new best friend.

Your choice.

Agnes hesitated, and in the end, I agreed to flip a coin. I wonder if she ever regretted having been so considerate.

Now, Lucy turns to face the window, though there's even less of a view from that side of the room. She's several inches shorter than I am. She probably won't be able to see out the small square of glass even if she stands on her tiptoes. The beds are bolted to the floor, so she won't be able to drag it over and stand on top of it in hopes of getting a better look.

I saw a movie that took place in prison once, and when a new inmate arrived, they all went around the table in the cafeteria and took turns saying what they'd done—or been found guilty of doing—to get sent there. They talked about what their lives had been like on the outside. Just like new roommates getting to know one another. Just like Agnes and I did not so long ago.

Agnes sat on her second-choice bed (I won the coin toss) and told me she was from a small town near Fargo, North Dakota.

I've never met anyone from North Dakota.

I thought people from New York knew people from everywhere.

I shook my head. Almost everyone I knew was from New York. *Why'd you think that?*

Isn't that where everyone goes when they want to escape where they came from?

I smiled and shrugged. Personally, I never thought about New York as an escape—it was where *I* was from, after all—but I knew plenty of people from other places saw it as a destination.

Agnes asked, *What's New York like?*

My smile grew wider. *You'll find out when you visit me someday.*

What makes you think I'll visit you?

Can't you tell we're going to be best friends?

We've known each other for less than thirty minutes. What makes you so sure?

Agnes laughed before I had a chance to answer, as if she could already tell that anything I might say would be clever enough to deserve it.

I narrow my eyes and study Lucy's face. Even through her veil of hair, I can see that her eyes are red. She was probably crying when they admitted her downstairs. Maybe (unlike me), she put up a fight when they sent her here.

Maybe they had to wait for her to calm down before they could bring her upstairs.

six

Despite the lack of prison-like confessions, it doesn't take long to find out what Lucy did to get sent here—only until our next meal, which she finishes before I'm on my second bite, then immediately sticks her fingers in her mouth and throws up into the bedpan she pulls from beneath her bed.

(So much for my theory that she might be a medical student.)

"Aren't you supposed to be secretive about that?"

Lucy wipes her mouth. I can see a barely chewed crust of bread in her bedpan. "What's the point?"

"I don't think they clean those all that thoroughly," I say, as she curls over the bedpan for a second time.

"Looks cleaner than the gas station we stopped at on the way up here," Lucy says when she finishes. She drops the bedpan onto the waxy linoleum floor, and some vomit splashes over the side. She nods at some crackers wrapped in shiny plastic on my tray. "You gonna eat those?"

I shake my head. They don't give us food that requires a fork and knife. It's a lot of soup and cereal and sandwiches. Lucy grabs the crackers from my tray like she's stealing something. She lifts her thin mattress and slides them onto the plastic platform beneath it. For later, I guess.

I leave more than half my sandwich untouched on my tray. I can feel Lucy staring at it.

"You want?" I offer with a smile.

She shakes her head so slowly that it looks like it hurts.

Patient may pose a danger to herself and others.

We pile our plates—paper, flimsy, useless—by the door for the orderly to take away. Lucy leaves her bedpan there too, like she's daring them to ask her about it.

Lucy lies back on her bed. I feel a tug of possessiveness as she stares at the ceiling.

Don't be silly, Hannah. Dozens of girls probably lay on the beds in this room and memorized every crack and cranny on the ceiling long before you got here. I imagine the perfectly reasonable words in Agnes's voice.

Lucy says she's from Oakland, and she's studying ballet. (That explains her perfect posture.) I wonder if she ever tried to starve herself in addition to purging, but of course, I'm too polite to ask. (I read a book once about a girl who vacillated back and forth between anorexia and bulimia. Maybe Lucy does, too.)

"Lightfoot's shoes must drive you crazy." I point at my own feet. We're not even allowed socks. They give us these flimsy cloth slippers. You can barely walk in them. You have to sort of shuffle just to keep them on. I only wear mine when I'm cold.

34

Which is all the time because they pump AC into this place like they're trying to keep us fresh.

Lucy doesn't answer. She rolls over so her back is to me, hugging her pillow.

I get up and start walking, counting my steps. I'm not sure eight feet (steps) by seven feet (steps) is enough for two people. The room I shared with Agnes wasn't much bigger and look how that ended.

The walls seem to shake in time with Lucy's sobs (she's not calm and quiet like I was), but then this is California, earthquake country: the ground beneath your feet can be unreliable here. I press my fingers against the vomit-green stone (the color suddenly seems appropriate), to make sure it's still solid. But it's impossible to tell with all those manufactured imperfections.

"I miss my boyfriend," Lucy says finally, like I asked for an explanation.

The back of my neck tingles.

The first time Jonah called Agnes his girlfriend, we were walking back from American Studies class. I asked if he wanted to grab some lunch, and he said he was meeting his girlfriend.

You're welcome to join us, he added quickly.

No thanks, I said. *I'm not exactly third-wheel material.* It's not as though I didn't know he and Agnes were together.

Jonah grinned. He knew he looked irresistible when he grinned. *No,* he agreed. *You're not.*

We started hooking up a week later.

Lucy wipes her eyes. "What do you have to do to get phone privileges?"

I shrug. "I don't know." Lightfoot hasn't said a word to me about any kind of privileges.

"These places all work the same way."

"How many of *these places* have you been?"

Lucy doesn't answer. Instead, she recites: "Gain a pound, get an hour online. Gain two pounds, get twenty minutes on the phone."

Does she think I have an eating disorder too? I walk back across the room and sit on the edge of my bed (it's simpler to call it that now that there are two of us), keeping my back straight like she did.

"I don't think this place works like that." If this place rewarded good behavior with privileges, surely I'd have earned some for having come so calmly and quietly.

"I'm never going to make it if I can't call Joaquin." Lucy rolls onto her back and starts biting her nails, then laughs. Her throat must be scratched raw from years of making herself throw up because her laugh doesn't sound like anything I've heard before.

"Figures this place would be different." She practically spits the words *this place*.

I'm tempted to ask why exactly it figures, but I don't want Lucy to know that I'm not sure of the answer. Instead, I lie on my side, facing her. She clutches her pillow like it's her boyfriend. She even sort of kisses it. As if anyone would want to kiss her so soon after she threw up.

Jesus Christ, they put me in here with a real crazy person. Now Lucy isn't the only one who wants phone privileges. I'll call my parents and demand a private room. I'm under eighteen. They can't stop me from contacting my legal guardians.

For the first time, a slim ribbon of doubt snakes its way through my brain: *Can they?*

Up until the day I arrived here, my parents and I spoke every single day for more than seventeen years. But my parents weren't the ones who chose to send me here, to a place where (apparently) I have to earn the privilege of talking to them.

Lucy rolls away from me again, and I stare at my new roommate's back. I can see the knobs of her spine through her paper-thin shirt, and I watch the muscles—a sign of the years she's spent dancing—ripple beneath the surface of her skin when she moves.

It's actually not all that different from staring at the ceiling.

seven

"I'm afraid you can't call your parents."

Dr. Lightfoot drags her plastic folding chair into the room for our next session. It's white and cheap-looking, and unlike our beds, it isn't bolted to the floor. She unfolds the chair, but she doesn't sit. Neither do I.

"Of course I can call my parents," I counter. "They're my *parents.*" I emphasize the word, but it's not enough to make Lightfoot understand how close we are.

Mom used to say she couldn't understand parents who left their children behind when they went on vacation or complained that they needed a break from their kids.

Other families aren't like ours.

I add, "I'm a minor. You can't keep me from them. It's against the law."

It's probably also against the law to keep me in this room for days on end. Well, against the law if I'm a patient. Probably not if I'm a prisoner.

"Your parents understand that isolation is the best course of action for you right now."

No, they don't, I think but do not say. Somehow, Dr. Lightfoot must have talked them into believing it. I study her mousy face. She could be some kind of sadist, taking advantage of the fact that no one on the outside takes the complaints of patients on the inside all that seriously.

Or maybe she just knows I'm not stupid enough to complain. Not when I know full well that when the good doctor types up her report for the judge, she might hold my complaints against me.

I glance at Lucy, lying on her bed with her back to the room. She didn't budge when they brought us water and soap this morning. Maybe she didn't want to get undressed in front of me, didn't want to give me a second chance to see all the flaws she's worked so hard to eliminate. Her long, almost-black hair is starting to look greasy.

"I'm hardly isolated," I say finally.

"I meant isolation from the familiar. You'd be surprised how powerful it can be when you need to reset."

Reset. Like I'm an appliance that needs tinkering, a frozen laptop that needs to be rebooted. I don't think Ctrl + Alt + Delete is going to cut it here.

"My parents will insist on talking to me eventually." Once they get back from Europe, probably.

"It's not up to them."

Lucy shifts, and the metal frame beneath her mattress squawks. I'm tempted to point out that conducting therapy with another patient present is surely a violation of doctor-patient confidentiality, but I don't want Lightfoot to think I have anything to hide. Anyway, she probably doesn't care about protecting my privacy.

"Doctors' orders can't supersede parental wishes." I try to sound official and adult. I've watched enough hospital dramas on TV to know that in emergencies—like when a patient has cancer, or is in a coma and can't make decisions on her own—treatment plans aren't up to the doctors alone. They have to ask permission from the patient's guardians or spouse or next of kin.

Of course, the hospitals on television don't look like this place: on TV, the doors don't stay locked, the furniture isn't bolted to the floor, and people who are perfectly capable of walking don't use bedpans.

Come to think of it, the hospital where Agnes went didn't look anything like the ones on television either. It wasn't bright and white and clean. The linoleum floors were brown (a good color for masking bloodstains, I suppose) and marked with black lines from gurney wheels. In the ICU there were no private rooms, and the lights never went out, not even in the middle of the night. I asked if Agnes could have more privacy if we paid extra, but they said not in her current condition—the doctors and nurses needed her where they could see her. There were curtains around the bed, but they were kept open. The only time they were closed was when the doctors examined her. The doctors made me wait outside even though I explained that I'd seen her undressed plenty of times before. The curtains were pink and frayed, marked with shadows of old stains. Even the *curtains* weren't like the ones on television.

Now, Dr. Lightfoot pauses before answering. After a moment of (what I assume to be) thinking about how much to tell me, she says, "That doesn't apply in cases like yours." She tries and fails to tuck some of her stringy dark-brown hair back into its bun, settling for hooking the rogue strands behind her ears.

"Cases like mine?" I echo.

"Yours isn't a voluntary confinement." She shifts her weight from one foot to another. She puts a hand on the back of her chair but doesn't sit, as if to underline that this conversation isn't part of our daily session.

"Of course this isn't *voluntary*. I'd never choose to be sent to a place like this."

"We need to wait until my evaluation is farther along before making any changes to your treatment plan."

Further, not farther, I think. They could at least give me a doctor who knows basic grammar. It's not exactly comforting that my fate is in her hands.

"It's not like I'm awaiting trial here." I imagine my unspoken question floating in the air between us: *Am I?* My parents' lawyer—I guess he's technically my lawyer, too—said I was only here for observation.

Finally I say, "What about my side of the story?"

"You can tell your side of the story anytime." Dr. Lightfoot straightens, holding her pen above her clipboard like this is the moment she's been waiting for.

"I mean to someone who matters." To the judge. To my parents. To our attorney. (Not that he'd do me much good. He'd probably say this thing is still playing out.)

I close my eyes. *You can't imagine what it's like growing up in a small town,* Agnes said during one of our many late-night heart-to-hearts. *How trapped you feel. Well, how trapped I feel. Plenty of my friends want to stay there forever, and that's fine for them, but for me—my whole life is waiting to get out. Not knowing if you ever will.*

What do you mean? College is only a year away. You'll get out.

Agnes rolled onto her side to face me. The room was dark, and we were each lying in our beds. Jonah snored softly beside her. By then, he spent most nights in our dorm room. He slept with his mouth slightly open, like a baby.

College is temporary—you still go back for the holidays, over the summer. I'll always be trapped until I call someplace else home.

In his sleep, Jonah's fingers wrapped around Agnes's hip bone. Maybe he was dreaming that he was falling and his girlfriend's hip was the one thing keeping him safe.

You'll get out, I said. *Girls like you don't stay in one place for the rest of their lives.*

You think so? Her voice was hopeful.

I know so.

Her blue eyes widened. *When you say it, I actually believe it.*

Except Agnes is stuck in one place now. They said it wasn't safe to move her.

Not in her current condition.

Apparently, they don't think it's safe to move me either.

43

Slowly, I shake my head. I stand up.

"I have to be back in the city by September seventh." The first day of school. First semester senior year grades are important for college applications. "What's today's date?"

I take a step forward, and Dr. Lightfoot flinches. I'm a few inches taller than she is. "Let's not focus on dates. Let's focus on your treatment."

"What treatment? I've barely done anything but talk to you since I got here."

Lightfoot smiles the way you'd smile at a small child who doesn't understand the ways of the world. My parents didn't look at me like that when I *was* a small child. "Talk therapy is part of your treatment."

I narrow my eyes. *Treatment* can go on a long time. *Treatment* can go on forever.

Agnes's voice: *I'll always be trapped.*

Now it's my own voice I hear. It singsongs like I'm taunting myself from deep inside: *You'll get out, you'll get out, you'll get out.*

Quick as a snake, I grab Dr. Lightfoot's flimsy plastic chair and throw it against the wall as if I throw it hard enough, I could make a hole to crawl out through. Instead, the vomit-green stone breaks the chair into three pieces that land with a crash.

When you say it, I actually believe it.

eight

They gave me a sedative after the chair incident and told me if I
didn't get into bed on my own, they'd have to restrain me.

Have to. As if they didn't have a choice in the matter.

I didn't like the idea of being tied up, so I lay on my back and
closed my eyes. The sedative made it easy.

Jonah was from Washington State. He spent his weekends
hiking through the mountains instead of studying for his SATs,
and he still got a near-perfect score. He said fresh air was good for
your brain. I said there were plenty of brainiacs in New York, and
no one ever called our air fresh. I almost smile at the memory,
but my muscles aren't cooperating.

It wasn't anything as corny as love at first sight when Jonah
and I met. The day we moved into the dorm, I left Agnes in our
room to unpack her things while I explored. Jonah stuck his head
out his door when he heard me walking by.

I'm Jonah, and I can't unpack anymore. His voice was low and
deep. When he smiled, his hazel eyes narrowed. It made him
look like a fox.

When he shook my hand, I felt this strange sort of tug in my belly, like a string pulled taut.

I'm Hannah, and I haven't even started unpacking yet, I said. It was a lie. My suitcases were empty and stowed beneath my bed, my clothes folded neatly in the dorm room's small dresser drawers.

He repeated my name, and his eyes met mine. I could feel my pulse speed up. I pulled my hand away like I was scared he'd feel it, too.

You haven't unpacked at all? he asked.

I shook my head. *Nope. But my roommate's putting her things away as we speak.*

How will you decide who gets to put what where if you're not there to supervise?

That's some pretty serious sentence construction.

Jonah smiled like a fox again.

Anyway, I explained, *she got here before I did. So she got to decide where her things would go first.*

That's a little cold.

I shrugged. *Fair's fair.* I paused. *But maybe you should stop by our room later. Two twelve. In case she uses up all the closet space and we need someone to mediate.*

Or break up a fight.

I shook my head. *Nah, we're not the kind of girls who fight.*

How do you know? Didn't you just meet her? The summer program hadn't given us our roommates' names ahead of time. They didn't want us looking each other up on Facebook or

Twitter or Instagram. Like they were worried it would spoil the surprise of seeing whom the school's computer algorithm had decided we should live with.

Well, I'm not the kind of girl who fights with her friends.

Sounds like your roommate is a lucky to be living with a girl like you.

Jonah shook my hand a second time before letting me go, and I felt that tug in my belly again. *I'll stop by later*, he said. *Just in case. Your roommate might be a fighter, even if you're not.*

I nodded. *Good idea.*

It's not that Jonah was the handsomest boy at summer school. Most all the girls agreed that honor lay with the tall, raven-haired, French exchange student named Bastien. But Jonah carried himself like no one ever told him that he wasn't the best-looking, the smartest, the tallest. As the summer went on, his light-brown eyebrows turned blond in the California sunshine.

And then he chose Agnes over me.

∴

I wasn't there when Jonah and Agnes met. He told me later that he'd come by our room looking for me, but found her instead.

You were right, he said.

About what?

I didn't need to worry that you two might fight. Agnes wouldn't hurt a fly.

She's a sweet girl, I agreed.

A sweet girl, Jonah echoed. He said the words like they were exotic. Like he'd never met someone so sweet before.

I suppose it was my fault. I was the one who told him to visit our room. I wonder what might have happened if he and I had spent more time together before he met Agnes. I could have stayed in his room with him and helped him unpack. I could have shown him that I could be a sweet girl, too.

I didn't find out that they were a couple until after they became one. It wasn't as if Jonah asked Agnes out for a date, and we giggled while she got ready and then winked at each other behind his back when he came by to pick her up. It was much more subtle than that. One day, I noticed that he sat closer to her on the couch in the common room than he did to me. When I came back from class, he'd be studying quietly at my desk while Agnes studied quietly at hers. He always moved before I had to ask, though. He was polite about it.

Then one night, he showed up after we'd turned off the lights and climbed into bed beside Agnes like it was the most natural thing in the world. Agnes must have left the door unlocked so Jonah could get in. It was obvious she was used to being close to him; she barely stirred when he slid between the sheets. It was like watching a celebrity couple go from denying rumors that they're together to suddenly announcing their engagement: you knew it was coming—all the signs had been there—and yet it still surprised you.

Jonah saw me watching him in the moonlight, and he winked at me, as if we were in on some shared secret. I rolled over to face the wall and pretended to sleep. I heard the sounds they made: every time one of them shifted in the bed, every time they kissed (Jonah must have woken Agnes after I turned my back on them), every time Agnes tried to stifle a giggle so she wouldn't wake me up. She was considerate—sweet—even then.

nine

Agnes and her parents were really close. Not close like my parents and me, but close. She talked to them every day.

Day one: *I really like my roommate, Mama.*

And later, what amounted to daily reports of our progress:

Hannah and I went to the movies.

Hannah and I discovered this amazing sushi place on University Avenue.

Hannah and I…

Hannah and I…

Hannah and I…

Maybe Agnes's parents decided they didn't like me weeks before we met. Maybe after all those phone calls, they thought of me as some big city girl putting big city ideas in their daughter's head. After a couple weeks, Agnes switched from saying *Hannah and I* to saying *Hannah says.*

Hannah says I can visit her in New York for Thanksgiving.

Hannah says I should apply to Barnard.

Hannah says everyone *has the latest iPhone.*

Hannah says I should buy some new clothes for college interviews.
It's not as though I put the words in her mouth. Besides, accusing someone of attempted murder is a bit of an overreaction to disliking your daughter's roommate.

Especially when what happened was so obviously an accident.

Or anyway, they can't prove that it *wasn't* an accident, and isn't that the important part? You know, *innocent until proven guilty* and all that. *Beyond a reasonable doubt.*

"What's the status of the investigation?" I ask the next time Lightfoot's ballet shoes *tap tap tap* into my room and Stephen takes up his position by the door.

"Think of this less as an investigation than as my chance to get to know you." She stands in the center of the room (no folding chair this time), shifting her weight from one foot to the other. Her papery clothes—blue, unlike Lucy's and mine, which are green, maybe to match the walls—make noise when she moves. She blinks like she's not used to wearing contact lenses. I bet they told her not to wear glasses around patients like me. Someone who may be a *danger to herself and others* could use the metal and glass to gouge her eyes out.

I wonder what this place's policy is for patients who need to wear glasses. Are those patients forced to wear contacts too? Maybe they're allowed to wear glasses when they're alone, but are required to take them off when Lightfoot comes to call, sitting through their therapy sessions with fuzzy vision.

Lucy is at lunch with the other girls who have cafeteria privileges. (My meal was brought to the room, as usual.) Ever since she arrived, she's been allowed out for things like that, maybe as a reward for staying with her potentially dangerous roommate without complaining, or maybe because they want to watch her eat so she can't throw up as easily. Lucy also gets to leave the room for her sessions with Dr. Lightfoot, and yesterday they let her use the showers down the hall. I guess patients who throw chairs are expected to stick with sponge baths.

"How can you *get to know me* like this?" I ask. "You need to spend more than an hour a day with someone to really know them."

"I'm sorry you feel that our interactions are so limited."

I hate how she makes it sound as if the amount of time we spend together is a matter of opinion, like we're having additional interactions I'm not aware of.

Also, how can she *get to know me* while I'm stuck in this place? This is hardly a normal environment. I know she thinks I need *isolation from the familiar* and all, but people are influenced by their environments and being stuck in this room is enough to drive a perfectly sane person mad. Not that I care whether Lightfoot gets to know me at all. I'm here because of a misunderstanding. I'm here to *let this thing play out.* I'm here *until everything passes.*

I press my bare feet against the linoleum floor. I'm so bored that maybe soon I'll be lying facedown with my head hanging off the bed, memorizing the floor the way I memorized the ceiling and the walls before it.

The edges of Lightfoot's lips curve slightly. "You do have a point—this isn't a normal environment for you." They probably taught her to smile like that in medical school. Her professors must've demonstrated: *Smile like this. Let them see that you're sympathetic to their plight, but not too sympathetic.* I imagine Dr. Lightfoot practicing in a mirror until her jaw was sore.

"We're also interviewing the people who spent time with you before you came here, to get a more fully fleshed picture."

I don't like the expression *fully fleshed*. An image flashes in my mind's eye: a flap of flesh falling open to reveal white skull bone. I swallow.

"What have you discovered?" Everyone in the dorm knew how close Agnes and I were. Agnes joked we were joined at the hip when we walked to class, to lunch, to the gym, always together. We were best friends, even though we'd known each other for less than two months.

"That your relationship with Agnes was very…unusual."

She says the word like it's a euphemism.

"We got really close really fast." I shrug. "I've always been like that. I've had a dozen best friends since kindergarten."

She jots something down on my file, snapped carefully to the clipboard. I narrow my eyes. Since when is there anything wrong with making different friends? It's not as though it's a symptom of anything other than a gregarious nature.

"Yes," Dr. Lightfoot agrees, "I've confirmed that you've had a number of intense friendships."

I want to ask, *With whom have you confirmed it?* but she'd probably list my proper grammar among my symptoms. *Hannah Gold is anxious to show off her intelligence.*

I can't help that I'm smarter than my doctor.

"You don't seem very troubled by what happened," Dr. Lightfoot adds. "You haven't asked how Agnes is doing."

"Maybe that's because I didn't think you'd tell me. You won't even let me talk to my parents." I nearly stamp my foot on the ground, but it wouldn't make much of an impact without real shoes.

"Maybe it is," Dr. Lightfoot echoes, and I realize my error. I shouldn't have said *maybe*.

But I'm right: She still doesn't tell me how Agnes is.

Someone must have made Lightfoot suspect that my friendship with Agnes wasn't as loving as I say it is. Maybe one of the girls in the dorm noticed Jonah and me standing close, or the way he and I shared blankets on movie night when Agnes was back in our room studying. I chew my cheek. Whoever this nosy girl was, she probably called up the good doctor and used words like *intense* and *unusual* to describe my friendship with Agnes instead of *close* and *joined at the hip*.

I shake my head. None of that proves anything. Even if they know about Jonah and me—even if they want to shame me for betraying the sisterhood and all that—it doesn't mean I'm so deranged that I would hurt my best friend to have a clear shot at her boyfriend. But how can I make them see that when I'm trapped in this place with no one but Dr. Lightfoot to listen?

My mother is against solitary confinement in American prisons. She believes it should be considered "cruel and unusual punishment" and therefore unconstitutional. But she couldn't—didn't?—stop them from putting me in here.

Suddenly, despite the AC on full blast (as always), I feel hot. Sweat springs up on my palms and the back of my neck. I glance around the room feverishly, as if I might notice something I haven't seen before. Another window. A trap door. A way out. But the room looks exactly as it's looked every day since I arrived.

I want to curl my hands into fists, but I don't because Dr. Lightfoot would probably note that in my file, too.

Wait. One thing in this room has changed. The wrinkled blanket on Lucy's bed, a stray blackish hair standing out in stark contrast to the white sheets. I have Lucy now, the girl with the sweet name who misses her boyfriend. The girl who got sick because she was trying to have the right kind of body to be a dancer. Just then, Lucy squeezes her way past Stephen, who's all but blocking the door as usual. Even if I'm trapped in this vomit-green room, it's not technically solitary. Not anymore. Lucy may not be a test in the way I first suspected, but she is *here*. She has her own private sessions in an office downstairs and eats in the cafeteria. Surely someone will ask how things are going with her roommate. There may not be a camera in here, but they're still watching us—listening, keeping track, room checking.

Lucy *has* to like me.

Luckily, I know how to become someone's best friend. It's a skill I've honed since kindergarten.

They may not have meant for Lucy to be a test, but I can still pass with flying colors.

Lucy could be the way out that I'm looking for.

ten

"So how long have you been dancing?"

They haven't come to give us breakfast yet, but the lights are on, and I can tell Lucy's awake from the way she's breathing.

"Since I could walk," Lucy answers. She rolls over onto her side so she's facing me, but she doesn't open her eyes.

She's going to make me work for her friendship, and that's okay. It's not like there's anything else to do here. I have all the time in the world (well, as long as they're keeping me here) to show the powers that be what a good friend I am. Incapable of hurting so much as a fly. Certainly not *a danger to herself and others.*

"That's like me and reading."

Lucy opens her dark-brown eyes. "Don't tell me you've been reading since you were a toddler."

"Of course not," I agree with a smile. "But I carried around books the way other kids carried their baby blankets and stuffed animals. I *wanted* to be able to read even before I could make out letters and words."

Lucy nods. "Yeah, that's like me and dancing," she agrees.

"I was so little when I started dancing en pointe that we had to special order toe shoes in my size."

"It sucks when your body won't cooperate with your dream." It's a risky thing to say, but Lucy doesn't argue. Instead, she stretches her arms overhead, her unsupported breasts shifting beneath her shirt. She's begged them to let her wear a bra, but they've ignored her requests.

"Everyone kept telling me that there were successful dancers who were exceptions to the rule. Big boobs, big butt, blazing a new trail for ballerinas everywhere." She sighs. "I didn't want to blaze a trail."

"You just wanted to get where you were going."

"Exactly." She rolls onto her back and gazes at the ceiling. I wonder if she sees the same shapes in the divots and cracks that I saw—a rabbit, a clown, a tree—or if she's making her own shapes. Maybe she sees a cat, a prince, a mountain. "Not that it matters anymore."

"What do you mean?"

"I'm not going to be out of here in time to make my audition."

"What audition?"

Lucy looks at me witheringly, as if the answer is obvious, as if there's only one audition that matters for girls like her. "For the San Francisco Dance Academy. My audition is on September fifteenth."

"You might get out by then," I offer, even though I have no idea how many days or weeks away that is.

"Even if I do, I'll be so out of shape. It's not like they let me practice."

I look around our seven by eight room. Not much room for pirouettes in here.

"I have to be out by September seventh," I confide. "To get back to school. College applications aren't due until the winter, but first semester senior year grades are essential to get into a good school."

"So you know what I'm talking about."

"Yeah."

"Except thousands of kids get into college each year, and there are only five slots for girls in next year's class at the dance academy."

She's testing me. She wants to know if I'll say that *it's plenty hard to get into college, thank you very much* or if I'll be adequately impressed that she's vying for one of five slots, and—before she got sent here—she actually had a real chance to make it. I'm tempted to tell her this isn't my first rodeo. I've made a lot of best friends over the years. I know what to do. I'm good at it.

"Wow, five slots," I say. "You must be really talented."

"I am." She doesn't say it with ego or even with pride. She says it plainly, like it's a simple fact. Lucy is different from the girls I'm used to.

But I need a new best friend, and she's my only option at the moment.

"You must be a good student," she adds, "if you're that anxious to get back to school."

"I am." I try my best to mimic her tone. Just a simple fact.

"God, don't they know they're ruining our lives by keeping us here?"

I nod, genuinely surprised. I didn't really expect the other girls in this place to have lofty goals and ambitions like mine.

The click of the magnetic lock makes both of us shift our gazes toward the door. Breakfast. They leave our trays inside the room, then let the door swing shut. The lock clicks back into place. The sound is loud enough that it would wake you if you were asleep. Maybe they designed it that way on purpose. I turn my attention to the food.

Off-brand Cheerios (plain, not honey nut this time), thin paper towels, and plastic spoons. They've already poured the milk, so the O's are soggy.

Lucy takes a bite and gags. "Whole milk," she moans. "Who drinks whole milk anymore?"

"Gross." I shove my tray aside, then notice that Lucy is eating despite her disgust, so I do the same.

"Sucks that we're stuck in here," Lucy manages between spoonfuls.

"Sucks," I agree.

eleven

The first time Lucy leaves the room today is to take a shower, a *real* shower, not one of those sponge baths I take. She's gone for twenty minutes. At least, I think it's twenty minutes because while she's gone, I pace the room, counting my steps, and each step takes about a second, and I get up to 1,182 steps, which is nearly twenty minutes. She comes back in fresh green clothes with her hair wet, smelling like shampoo.

I must look envious because she tells me it wasn't that great. "There were three other girls in there and no curtains or stalls. It's one big open space with spouts hanging down from the ceiling. Plus, an attendant was watching us the whole time." Lucy bends so her hair is hanging upside down. She runs her fingers through it. She makes it look like a dance. The shampoo smell gets stronger.

I remember how Lucy turned her back to change in front of Dr. Lightfoot and Stephen and me. She probably hated being naked in front of four more people.

I shrug. "My stylist says I wash my hair too much." I'm careful to use the present tense—my stylist *says*, not said, *wash*, not washed. "You know the less you wash it, the less you need to?"

Lucy shook her head. "I always got so sweaty and gross in class. I had to wash it every day."

I don't answer right away. Let her think I never had to do any physical activity to stay slim and trim. But then I remember I'm trying to befriend her, so I say, "Yeah, that makes sense."

∴

The second time Lucy leaves is lunchtime. When the attendant brings my meal, he holds the door open for Lucy.

I wonder if Lucy's right about phone privileges. Maybe if she gains enough weight, they'll let her call Joaquin. It takes four steps to get from my bed to the window. I stand on my tiptoes to look outside. I can't have been here a month. If it had been a month, the days would be getting shorter. The sun would be setting earlier. It would be dark out.

Then again, it's only lunchtime. No matter the time of year, midday is when the sun is at its peak.

When Dr. Lightfoot opens the door, I don't turn right away. I won't ask her what month it is or how long I've been here. I don't want her to know how much I care.

But I really wish I knew how many days are left between now and September seventh.

People lose track of the days of the week all the time, even on the outside. My mother forgot my eighth birthday. When I asked her about it, she said she thought August seventh was the follow-ing week. So if I ask Lightfoot the date, she might not consider it a symptom or a weakness. But that would be giving me the benefit of the doubt, and I don't think the benefit of the doubt is given to people in places like this.

Dr. Lightfoot speaks before I can make up my mind. "It's pretty out there, isn't it?"

Now, I turn. "I've seen prettier views."

It's the truth. I've seen the sun glittering on the Mediterranean through an enormous picture window at a glamorous hotel. I've seen the Swiss Alps in winter, covered in snow so white it makes clouds look gray. I've seen Machu Picchu and a great white shark leaping from the waters around South Africa.

My parents love to travel.

"Like where?" Lightfoot asks. I wonder if they taught her that in medical school too: *Ask your questions casually to get the conversation going. Get your patient to open up about something seemingly innocuous, impersonal. Before you know it, she'll be crying in your arms about the time her parents left her alone in a hotel room all night when she was four years old while they gambled their way across Monte Carlo.*

No such luck, Lightfoot. I didn't mind being left alone. I slept like a baby. I practically still *was* a baby.

But I have to come up with something to start winning the doctor over. I wish Lucy were here, so Dr. Lightfoot could see how well I'm interacting with her. But then, even if Lucy were here, the doctor would be too busy asking me questions—trying to get me to open up, let her in, to do the work of therapy—to see what a good friend I can be.

She has to see me being a good friend. Just hanging out. Like in the cafeteria.

Which means I have to earn some privileges. Clearly being calm and quiet (with the exception of the chair incident) hasn't gotten me anywhere. Lightfoot wants me to dig deeper in the talk therapy part of my *treatment*. She wants to feel that she's *getting to know me*.

Fine.

"Venice," I answer. "The view from our hotel room in Venice was prettier than this."

"I've never been."

"I've been lots of places. Only child, you know. My parents took me with them everywhere." I pause, then decide to offer her something more, so she can write that I *opened up today* in her notes. "I used to hate being an only child," I offer.

Lightfoot still doesn't have her chair, and she sort of sways as she stands in the center of the room, her scrubs wrinkling audibly when she moves. She's nothing like Lucy, who's so graceful that she moves without making a sound even in these paper clothes.

"I used to beg my parents for a little sister." It's a lie, but Dr. Lightfoot doesn't know that. She probably thinks that all only children beg their parents for siblings who never come.

Lightfoot presses her lips together. I imagine she's trying to choose a follow-up question: How did you imagine your life would be with a little sister? Did you dress up baby dolls and wish they were real girls?

64

Silently, I answer: No, I didn't play with dolls. No, I didn't imagine a life with a little sister. Eventually, I had real friends to play with.

Finally she asks, "What did your parents say when you asked for a sister?"

"Oh, you know, they said the usual stuff that parents of only children say. *You're all we need. We love you so much.* Even the occasional, *You're enough of a handful on your own.*" I smile a little, and Dr. Lightfoot smiles back, oblivious to the lie.

I wasn't a handful. I was perfectly behaved. My parents' friends complained about their children's tantrums. My parents marveled that I never gave them any trouble.

Once, when I was five years old, we were having dinner with another couple whose babysitter canceled at the last minute. (My parents didn't bother with babysitters.) We were going to a good restaurant, and my parents had to pull strings to change the reservation from five people to seven. The place didn't have a children's menu, so the other couple had to beg the chef for pasta with butter, and then the kids wouldn't even eat that.

As for me, that was the night I tried oysters for the first time. When I asked for seconds, my father beamed proudly. The other couple stared at us incredulously. Did they feel inadequate, like my parents were superior parents? Or did they think I was simply a superior child?

"I was excited, you know, about having a roommate. It was one of the reasons I wanted to go to summer school."

That's not exactly a lie. I didn't have any anxiety about sharing my space—about negotiating who got to play her music when, or waking up in the middle of the night because of someone else's tossing and turning, that sort of thing. And Agnes certainly didn't. She had two little sisters and hadn't had a room to herself since the first one arrived when she was two years old. Agnes used to complain that her parents weren't the only ones who woke up for feedings three times a night.

When I have kids, I'm only having one, she told me.

I'm never having kids, I answered.

Agnes looked as though the possibility of not having children hadn't actually occurred to her before. *Even better,* she said. *I already practically raised my sisters. It's not like I'd be missing out on the experience.*

You've already missed out on so much.

What do you mean?

I mean, like a childhood of your own. Your parents had you taking care of your sisters your whole life. You had to play grown-up instead of being a kid.

Agnes didn't say anything, but the expression on her face said it all. She'd never been so angry at her parents before, never before resented her sisters for being born.

Now, I tell Dr. Lightfoot, "We loved staying up late, telling each other secrets. Trying to keep our eyes open even after we were half asleep because there always seemed to be more to say. Agnes and I used to turn on the lights to try to make ourselves stay awake longer." I pause. "You can't do that here, though."

I gesture toward the fluorescent lights on the ceiling with

their preordained schedule. There isn't actually a light switch or an electrical outlet anywhere in this room.

"No," Lightfoot agrees. "You can't do that here." She blinks when she speaks. Her contacts must be bothering her.

Planted in the doorway, Stephen clears his throat. Unlike Dr. Lightfoot, he wears a watch. (Another thing that could be used as a weapon if a patient moved quickly and was ambitious enough.)

I smile. "Guess our time is up."

She nods. "It is. But that was some really nice work today, Hannah. Thank you for opening up to me."

"Thank you," I answer. Stephen holds the door for Dr. Lightfoot. When it clicks closed, the magnets that lock it in place sound a little less loud than they did the last time I was left in this room alone.

I smile again, this time for real. It was so easy when I was five, to manipulate my parents' friends into being ashamed of their own children, into thinking I was so much better.

It's still so easy.

twelve

The next day, when the attendant comes to open the door of my room—*our room*, a good friend would say this room belongs to both of us—at lunchtime, he isn't holding a meal on a tray. He gestures for me to leave the room with Lucy.

And just like that, I've earned my first privilege.

The hallway looks exactly how I remember it when they first brought me here: the same vomit-green walls and scratched, gray linoleum floors. Lucy walks a few steps ahead of me, the attendant a few steps ahead of her. We walk toward the stairs. I hear voices as we descend. We stop on the second-floor landing.

I was right, by the way. The cafeteria is on the second floor.

The landing opens into a large room, though the ceiling is no higher than it is upstairs, creating the illusion that the room is smaller than it probably is. There are long tables with benches attached on either side. (No chairs to toss.) The walls are made of that same oversized brick but instead of green, they're painted a sticky, fake sky blue. Baby-boy blue for a room full of girls except for a few male attendants, most of whom are as muscular as Stephen, leaving no question as to why they're here. The floors are the same drab gray. Lucy takes off for a table on the right side of the room, and I begin to follow but the attendant stops me.

"This way," he says, leading me to the left side of the room.

"There's assigned seating?"

"You can sit at any of the tables on this side of the room." He leads me to an empty bench. There are two girls already sitting on the other side.

I wonder if they used to be considered *a danger to themselves and others* too.

I sit. The attendant backs away, planting himself at the foot of our table. He's here to keep an eye on us. On me.

They bring us our food. It's the same sort of thing I got in the room upstairs: lukewarm chicken noodle soup (too cool to burn our fellow patients if we wanted to), packets of crackers, and a sandwich (no forks, no knives, not even plastic ones). They hand out flimsy paper napkins, incapable of giving so much as a paper cut.

The cafeteria smells. Not only because of the food—it's so bland it doesn't give off that much of a scent to begin with—and not just because some of us still don't have shower privileges. (Even those of us who do aren't exactly given baby powder and deodorant to stay fresh.) Really, the cafeteria smells like Girl with a capital *G*, some odor coming from inside us that can't be helped, like if you lock a bunch of us in a room, it does something to our hormones or pheromones or some other bodily-mones that creates an unmistakable scent. Even the cafeteria at my all-girls' school in the city smelled like this from time to time, but there, the scent commingled with perfume and expensive shampoo and real food until it was barely perceptible.

This is not what I had in mind. I wanted to sit next to Lucy. I wanted them to see us laughing and giggling. I wanted them to see me encouraging her to eat, but not too much, not so much that she'd have to purge later. How can I do that when Lucy is across the room?

The girls across from me eat their food silently. I wonder whether Lightfoot put them on medication to keep them quiet. I notice that each of them has clean hair. Unlike me, they have shower privileges.

A girl sits down next to me. I smell her before I see her. Her hair is thick with grease, and her skin is marked with acne. No shower privileges here. No trance either.

"Whatcha in for?" She elbows me. Then she grins. "Just kidding."

I look across the room at Lucy's table. The girl beside me follows my gaze. "You're obviously not one of *them*." I raise my eyebrows. "I'm not calling you fat or anything. But they make the girls with eating disorders sit together."

So that's why I couldn't sit with Lucy. At the eating-disordered tables—three tables in all, with no more than five girls at each table—there are attendants stationed at either end. On this side of the room, the attendants aren't quite as on top of us. (The attendant who walked us down here has moved, so that he's standing in between our table and the next, keeping an eye on both.) It's easy to tell the anorexic girls from the bulimic ones. When an anorexic girl refuses to eat, one of the attendants places a can of Ensure on the table in front of her. The bulimic girls eat quickly, then stare at their plates in disgust. Some of them are wearing real pajamas, not paper pajamas; apparently that's another privilege I have yet to earn.

"Seems to me it'd make more sense to spread them out."

"Why's that?"

"So they could see what normal eating looks like."

The girl beside me snorts, picking up her flimsy spoon and bending it. No matter how much she twists it, it doesn't break. Indestructible plastic, another precaution against sharp edges. "Yeah, 'cause this is so similar to how we all eat at home."

Can't really argue with that.

"True," I say, and I smile, in case the attendant is watching. Maybe this entire outing is some sort of test. Maybe he's going to report back to Lightfoot this afternoon.

I look around. There are five girls at Lucy's table across the room. Four at ours. There are two empty tables directly in front of this one, and then a table with five girls. Four on one side; one on the other, facing us. The four with their backs to us look like they have clean hair—shower privileges. Even from behind, I can tell they're laughing.

The other girl looks like she hasn't showered in weeks, though she's wearing real pajamas. When she speaks, the four girls across from her nod along in agreement.

"Hard to miss her, isn't it?" says the nameless girl beside me.

I nod, but I don't lower my gaze.

I know how to spot a queen bee when I see one, even in a place like this.

One of the trance girls across from me speaks up. I guess Lightfoot hasn't medicated her into silence after all. "I heard she's been here for over a year." She doesn't even have to turn around to know which girl we're talking about.

Beside-Me nods. "Family history on both sides."

"History of what?" I ask.

Beside-Me shrugs. "Mental illness. Violent behavior. Criminal records. You name it, she has it."

"She has it or her parents do?"

"Does it matter?" Beside-Me asks, and again I have to admit that she has a point. Of course, she was *just kidding* when she asked me why I was here. It doesn't actually matter. Perhaps it matters to the staff—the way they seat us and separate us. But it doesn't matter to *us*. Whatever we did, it was enough to get us sent here either way. That's all that does matter.

Three tables away, Queen Bee sits up straight, but not in the perfect-posture way that Lucy sits. No, she lifts her chin to watch the girls across from her hang on every word she says.

"If she's been here so long, you'd think she'd have figured out how to get shower privileges by now."

The other trance girl glances at QB over her shoulder. "She gets what she wants when she wants it." She sounds positively awestruck, like she's talking about a celebrity who turned greasy hair into the hot new trend. The cliques here aren't all that different from the ones in a high school cafeteria, when you think about it. The girls with eating disorders are like the jocks. The girls at Queen Bee's table are no different from the girls at

73

hundreds of high schools across the country, determined to stay on their popular friend's good side, lest they get banished to a loser table across the lunchroom.

Maybe if you put a bunch of teenagers together, it always ends up like this.

"She has the orderlies wrapped around her finger," Beside-Me adds, lowering her voice to a whisper. "I heard she even got one of them to sneak her a *cell phone.*"

Out in the real world, Queen Bee would probably be considered a freak: mentally ill, unwashed, dressed in pajamas in the middle of the day. But in here, the other girls look up to her. In here, she's powerful.

Of course, she's been here for a year or more. With power like that, she probably doesn't *want* to go home.

I look around at the ugly blue walls. There are rows of fluorescent lights on the ceiling like the one in the room upstairs, but this room still isn't as bright as the room upstairs. Perhaps because the cafeteria is so much bigger (I wonder how an attendant would react if I got up and walked across the room, counting my steps), the fluorescents have more ground to cover. The windows in the cafeteria are every bit as small as the lone square of glass in my—our—room, but these are all in a row, a dozen of them. With bars over them.

I can't imagine wanting to stay here a second longer than I have to.

Then again, that girl wasn't sent here because of a misunderstanding like I was.

thirteen

The attendants line us up like first graders to bring us back to our rooms. It's noisy in the stairwell and the hallway, but gets quieter as each pair of roommates disappear inside their room. The hallway is long, with eight rooms on each side, enough for thirty-two girls if it's two girls to a room, though it looks like some of the girls don't share a room. I hadn't realized how thick the walls between our rooms must be. I've heard sounds coming from the hallway (sound travels more easily through the metal door) but not from the adjacent rooms. I wonder what kind of sounds are muffled by the walls each day and night. Screams? Moans? Laughter?

Our room looks smaller than it did this morning. They've barely shut the door behind us before I'm counting my steps.

"What are you doing?" Lucy asks, but I don't answer.

Eight steps across, seven steps long. It's the same size. So why does it feel different?

Lucy sinks onto her bed. "Sucks they make me eat with the E.D. girls."

"Edie girls?" I echo.

"Eating disordered. Like that's the real reason I got sent here."

She doesn't say what the real reason is, and I don't ask. Instead, I say, "Ask Dr. Lightfoot to let you sit with me." It'd be better for me that way.

"Lightfoot?"

I sit on my own bed, twisting my greasy hair around my fingers. "That's what I call her. 'Cause of her shoes."

Lucy shudders. "I hate her shoes. Some days I want to rip them off her feet and put them on to show her what they're really for." Lucy stands and kicks off her slippers, then turns in her bare feet: once, twice, three times. Her hair spins out around her head. She lifts her arms overhead, using them to propel herself around before stopping with a smack of her bare foot. "If I had the right shoes, I could keep going."

"Wonder what she'd say if you asked to borrow them."

"'You're not here to dance, Lucy.'" Lucy's high-pitched, singsongy voice sounds nothing like Lightfoot's.

"That's the worst impression I've ever heard."

"You think you can do better?"

I cock my head to the side, considering. "No," I deadpan. Lucy bursts out laughing, and so do I.

When we finally stop, I gaze at our metal door. I wish the walls were thinner. I wish they could hear us.

∴

Later: Lights out, under the covers, not even the slimmest bit of moonlight coming in through our tiny window. Too much fog. Despite the darkness, I yank my (thin, smelly) pillow out from under my head and cover my face with it.

The words fill my head: *Light as a feather, stiff as a board. Light as a feather, stiff as a board.*

If Lightfoot had told me how Agnes was doing when the subject came up the other day, I'd be able to picture her in the hospital more accurately.

Light as a feather, stiff as a board. Light as a feather, stiff as a board.

But it's impossible to imagine her because I don't know whether her eyes should be open or closed.

Light as a feather, stiff as a board. Light as a feather, stiff as a board.

I don't know whether she's still in the coma. I don't know whether the tube is still taped to her mouth.

Light as a feather, stiff as a board. Light as a feather, stiff as a board.

I don't even know whether she's in a private room or whether she has a roommate.

Light as a feather, stiff as a board. Light as a feather, stiff as a board.

Her mother is probably sitting at her bedside, holding her hand.

Light as a feather, stiff as a board. Light as a feather, stiff as a board.

Before I was brought here, her father told me that they wouldn't leave California until Agnes could leave with them.

Light as a feather, stiff as a board. Light as a feather, stiff as a board.

He said it would be hard, with their younger daughters back home. Maybe he and his wife would take turns going back and forth.

Light as a feather, stiff as a board. Light as a feather, stiff as a board.

Of course, they weren't going to leave Agnes alone, he said. Even if the doctors weren't sure she could tell they were there at all.

Light as a feather, stiff as a board. Light as a feather, stiff as a board.

I wait to hear Agnes's voice telling me, *We're getting too old for these games,* but instead, I hear laughter. I peek out from beneath my pillow and glance over at Lucy's bed, invisible in the darkness, but I can hear her breath, steady and calm. She's fast asleep.

Besides, it wasn't one girl's giggles that I heard but a whole gaggle of them. And not only girls. Boys, too.

Eighth grade. Rebekah's fourteenth birthday party. She called it her first ever boy/girl party, oblivious to the fact that referring to it like that made her sound younger than fourteen.

Rebekah with a K. She used to introduce herself like that, as though knowing how she spelled her name would affect your pronunciation. As though she thought the *K* made her cooler, more interesting, less the plain Jane she so clearly was.

Rebekah with a K. Three—no, four, counting Agnes—best friends ago. Her parents' apartment was on 94th and Park, but during the party there were no parents in sight. It was a Saturday night, after all. They had their own places to be. I think her housekeeper was there, silently cleaning up after us, clearing paper plates soaked through with pizza grease, sliding coasters beneath our drinks so we didn't ruin the heirloom coffee table.

The drinks were soda and juice, by the way. Rebekah was a good girl. Her parents didn't even lock the liquor cabinet before they left the apartment that night. They didn't worry about their little girl sneaking sips of alcohol.

I wore a tight, black, off-the-shoulder top and skinny blue jeans. I was still so flat-chested then that I didn't need to wear a bra. Not like Rebekah. You could see her bra peeking out from under her tank top. It was February, but she insisted on wearing a sleeveless shirt. She thought it was sexy.

I have to look sexy tonight, Han, she insisted, using a nickname no one else ever used because it sounded so absurd. Or maybe the absurdity was Rebekah's little-girl voice saying the word *sexy* without a hint of irony.

I had helped her with the guest list, but the whole point of the party was to invite Gavin Baker, the boy Rebekah had a crush on for more than year.

You can't invite April, I told her.

But she's my best friend! I raised an eyebrow. *Was my best friend*, Rebekah corrected.

Rebekah and April Lu had been inseparable before I came along.

April Luuuser, I used to call her, which always made Rebekah giggle. At first, Rebekah dropped April like the bad habit she was, but as the party got closer, she faltered. April had been at every birthday party Rebekah had ever had. Even her first birthday, when Rebekah was too young to have any sway over the guest list. She and April had been in the same Mommy and Me class, and their mothers were friendly.

Gavin isn't interested in the kind of girl who hangs out with April Lu, I insisted, and that shut Rebekah up.

All Rebekah wanted was a birthday kiss from Gavin Baker. She'd never kissed anyone before, and she wanted Gavin to be her first. I promised to help. Even after April showed up at the party. (Rebekah took me aside and said she just *had* to invite her in the end. I said I'd still keep my promise.)

The couch in Rebekah's parents' living room was an antique, covered in ancient floral brocade and miserably uncomfortable. I slid to the ground dramatically.

We should play Light as a Feather, I suggested, tapping the floor beside me.

Rebekah's eyes lit up. I'd told her that games were part of my plan to make sure Gavin kissed her. Start with Light as a Feather, Stiff as a Board and then move on to more advanced games like Spin the Bottle and Seven Minutes in Heaven.

Most of the boys and even a couple girls had never heard of Light as a Feather, so I explained how it worked, just like I did for Agnes's mother.

One girl lies in the middle of the room and the rest of us crouch around her. We slide our hands beneath her and chant the words light as a feather, stiff as a board *over and over again.*

So we just lift her? Gavin asked. I rolled my eyes. Even Rebekah's fantasy crush was dull.

You'll see, I answered mysteriously.

Since Rebekah was the birthday girl, I insisted she go first. We pushed the coffee table aside and arranged ourselves around her. There was some giggling about where the boys would go. If they stood in the right (or the wrong) places, they could use the game as an excuse to touch her butt, maybe even graze some side-boob. I noticed that Gavin didn't try to put himself in any of those places.

Rebekah with a K. Since I was most familiar with the game, I stood by her head. I placed my fingers beneath her shoulders, one hand on either side of her neck.

When Rebekah fell, her stick-straight, light-brown hair spread out beneath her. She landed with a soft thump at my feet, nothing like the crack when Agnes landed. Rebekah fell onto a carpet so thick and so plush it was probably softer than the mattress beneath me now.

Still, the girls screamed. The boys bent down to help her up.

Give her some air, I shouted. Rebekah rolled onto her side. I crouched beside her and put my hand on her shoulder.

You okay? I asked.

Rebekah blinked. Her face was bright pink and there were tears in her eyes.

I helped her up, held her hand to lead her to the bathroom, and closed the door behind us. I brushed away her tears. I knew she wasn't crying because she was hurt—she hadn't fallen far, and like I said, the carpet was soft. She was crying because her party was ruined, and even though I assured her everything would be okay, we both knew there was no way Gavin was going to kiss her, not with a bump on her head and mascara running down her cheeks. April knocked on the bathroom door, offering to fix Rebekah's makeup, but Rebekah shouted *No*, she wanted me to do it.

I never should have invited her, Rebekah whispered to me fiercely.

When we finally emerged, no one wanted to play games anymore. Gavin put his arm around me.

Accidents happen, he said. *It wasn't your fault.*

I leaned into his embrace for just a second, then quickly spun away. Rebekah looked at Gavin longingly, but her eyes were still teary and her cheeks were blotchy, and there was a tiny piece of tissue stuck to her upper lip from when she'd blown her nose.

Beks is tough, Gavin added with laugh, making a fist and knocking the top of his own head with his knuckles.

Rebekah, I corrected, though I suspected she wouldn't have minded Gavin giving her a nickname.

I slept over at Rebekah's that night. When I closed my eyes, I saw her long hair hitting the ground beneath her. My fingertips were still warm from brushing away her tears. Her breath in the sleeping bag beside me was steady and even, just like Lucy's breath across the room.

It wasn't my fault.

Accidents happen.

fourteen

"I was measuring the room," I volunteer after breakfast the next morning.

Lucy looks up from her bedpan. "What?"

"Yesterday, when we got back from lunch, I paced the room. You asked me what I was doing, remember?"

Lucy shrugs. "Sure."

"I was counting my steps to see if the room was the same size it'd been before we left."

Lucy cocks her head to the side like it makes perfect sense that I think the room could have changed size while we were gone. "And was it?"

I nod. "But it felt smaller."

"Optical illusion. You'd gotten used to it in here before they took you downstairs."

I don't like the sound of that. I don't want to get used to anything about this place.

I get up and begin pacing. At first, I don't notice that Lucy is walking alongside me, but when I look down, I see her feet next to mine.

"Nine feet by eight feet," she pronounces. "Every time."

I shake my head. "Eight feet by seven feet."

"Nine feet by eight feet," Lucy counters.

"Eight by seven."

"Nine by eight." Lucy folds her arms across her chest.

For the first time, I notice that she's shorter than I am. Her legs aren't as long, so her strides are shorter.

Lucky Lucy. The room is a tiny bit bigger for her than it is for me.

By the time Dr. Lightfoot arrives for my next session (morning? afternoon? who can keep track?), Lucy and I are each standing on one leg, holding the other leg out in front of us, trying to see how much bigger my feet are than hers.

Lucy makes it look like a dance. I look like someone who's trying yoga for the first time.

"What's got you in such a good mood?" Dr. Lightfoot asks as she steps inside. Today, her smile looks like genuine, not like one of those fake, medical-school smiles.

Still, I don't answer her. I don't want her to know that I care how big this room is.

So I sit on the edge of my bed and wait quietly.

Stephen steps aside so he's not completely blocking the door, and Lightfoot goes back into the hall. For a second I think this means Dr. Lightfoot is going to lead the way to her office for therapy, another privilege I've earned like lunch in the cafeteria. It occurs to me that I don't know if Stephen he spells his name with a *V* or a *PH*, but all this time I've been picturing it with a *PH* because I don't like that spelling and I don't like him.

I'm halfway off the bed when I realize that Stephen isn't stepping aside for me but for the doctor. She returns with her flimsy plastic chair.

I guess that's supposed to be some kind of peace offering. Her way of telling me she trusts me around furniture that's not bolted down, even if she doesn't yet trust me enough to do sessions in her office or without a guard blocking the door like she's the president and he's her secret service detail.

I sit back down, trying to keep my back straight the way Lucy does.

Dr. Lightfoot blinks as she sits. Her contacts must be bothering her again.

"It's nice to see you in such a good mood." She smiles again, another real smile.

"It helps being able to talk to someone else."

She nods, glancing at the file on her lap. *My* file. "I hear you sat next to Annie at lunch yesterday."

I nod. That's Beside-Me's real name. "We had a nice talk."

"Did you?"

"It wasn't all that different from lunch at the cafeteria back home." I gesture vaguely out the window, which I'm pretty sure faces east.

Dr. Lightfoot looks pleased with my answer. Maybe after a few more friendly lunches, she'll finally come to the conclusion that I want her to: *This was all an enormous misunderstanding.*

Hannah Gold doesn't belong in a place like this.

Hannah Gold wouldn't hurt a fly.

Behind the doctor, Lucy shifts on her bed. I smile at Lucy to show the doctor I don't mind sharing my space.

Instead of smiling back, Lucy playfully sticks her tongue out at me.

Dr. Lightfoot asks a question that I don't answer because I'm scared if I open my mouth, I'll burst out laughing. I don't want the doctor to think I'm not taking our session seriously.

"Cat got your tongue?" Dr. Lightfoot asks.

"Not exactly," I manage finally.

"I asked if you'd like to eat lunch in the cafeteria for the rest of the week."

"Yes," I answer, even though I have no idea what day of the week it is, so I don't know how many days *the rest of the week* constitutes.

"It must be nice to have a chance to change up your routine a bit." She says it as if she's not the one keeping me on a tight schedule.

"Actually," I begin, "I was thinking as long as I'm in here, I might as well be productive. Maybe my teachers could send over a summer reading list or something."

"You *are* doing something productive," the doctor answers. "You're talking with me."

Lucy lies back and holds her book above her face. Some romance novel. Not the kind of book my teachers would assign.

"I meant something that would be productive in the outside world. You know, to keep me on track for when I go home."

Dr. Lightfoot shakes her head. "I want you to stay focused on the work we're doing. Schoolwork would distract you."

"I can concentrate on more than one thing at once. How do you think I managed to be a straight-A student in calculus *and* history *and* French *and* English?" Lightfoot doesn't return my smile.

"I don't want you to use your schoolwork as a way to distance yourself from what we're doing here."

"Well, which is it? A distraction or a distancing technique?"

The doctor doesn't answer. Good. I caught her in a lie. The truth is, she doesn't care if I'm distracted or distanced. Schoolwork is simply another thing she gets to hold over me, another privilege I have to earn like lunch or showers or therapy in other rooms.

Tough luck, Dr. Lightfoot. I'm not going to let being trapped in here turn my brain to mush.

Every college I apply to is going to want me.

Maybe I'll even decide to get a postgraduate degree.

Maybe I'll become a psychologist so I can prove Dr. Lightfoot's techniques are absurd.

Maybe I can get her license revoked for keeping a person like me in a place like this.

fifteen

Here's something they never tell you in books and movies about being imprisoned or institutionalized or trapped (books I'm not allowed to read and movies I can't watch now that Lightfoot controls all my media access): Being locked up is absurdly boring. The monotony is enough to drive a sane person crazy.

Which is why Lucy and I decide to form a book club.

Okay, I know I just said they don't let me read, but bear with me. They don't let me read the books I *want* to read. Academic books that I could turn into an independent study project for extra credit when I get back to school or great literature like *Fathers and Sons* that would give me a head start on the Russian literature class I was going to take on Tuesday nights at NYU starting in September.

Then again, maybe it is September by now.

They do let us read terrible books from a library they claim exists somewhere in the building. I'm pretty sure the "library" is nothing more than a closet with cast-off books from the nursing staff. There's surely no wise librarian curating the list and organizing the books alphabetically or thematically or even by color to make the shelves look nice. I bet there aren't even shelves. It's probably just a pile next to the cleaning supplies.

The books are all paperback—no heavy hardcovers with sharp edges here. Not one is longer than three hundred pages. (I guess even a paperback could be considered dangerous if it's thick enough.) The pages are dog-eared, and the spines are bent, and the covers are creased.

At home, I keep my books in pristine condition. I never crack a single spine, and I underline in pencil only, with .5 millimeter extra-fine lead. My bookshelves are arranged chronologically: Novels I read in school are grouped together by the class I was taking when I read the book and the year I took the class.

Sixth grade: *Little Women, The Diary of Anne Frank*

Seventh grade: *To Kill a Mockingbird, A Midsummer Night's Dream, Clover*

Eighth grade: *Jane Eyre, Romeo and Juliet*

Ninth grade: *Wuthering Heights, The Great Gatsby, Beloved*

At my school, tenth grade is when they start letting you select elective English classes. There's a section on my bookshelves for the class I took on short stories in tenth grade (that's when my school lets you pick elective English classes): *The Complete Short Stories of Ernest Hemingway, The Stories of John Cheever, The Stories of Bernard Malamud;*

a section for women's literature: *Pride and Prejudice, The Woman in White, The Yellow Wallpaper, Their Eyes Were Watching God;*

a section for Latin American lit: *A Hundred Years of Solitude, Kiss of a Spiderwoman,* Jorge Luis Borges's *Collected Fictions.*

And now I've gone from all that to reading some bodice ripper that turned on a member of the nursing staff.

But it's better than nothing. A book is a book, and reading a book is superior to staring at the ceiling for the zillionth time. And talking about a book is better than talking about when the linoleum floors were last washed or how long it's been since I wore pants with an actual zipper. (Both conversations Lucy and I have had.)

So, like I said, we decide to form a book club. We pass each book back and forth between us—first me, then Lucy—reading one chapter each and then discussing it. We dissect these narratives like they've never been dissected before. Lucy folds the page to hold our place while we talk and then hands the book back to me so I can read the next chapter.

"Do you think the writer intended for the wrinkled sheets to be a metaphor for—"

"I don't think the writer intended anything to be a metaphor for anything."

When Lucy reads, her mouth twitches, a tick that lets me know she's concentrating.

An attendant pokes her head in the door, trilling, *Room check*. We roll our eyes and giggle. (Good. Let them see us laughing together.)

"I wish I had a pencil so I could write down my thoughts." (They don't let us have anything to write with.)

"Why? In case we get tested on it later?"

We dissolve into another round of giggles.

Jonah used to say that fresh air was good for your brain. He promised we'd go to Santa Cruz before the summer was over so that we could spend the day at the beach.

I'm going to teach you to surf, he declared once while we lay in bed. (Agnes was in class.)

I didn't know you surfed. The sun streamed in through the open window above my bed, so bright I had to squint.

Jonah grinned, his eyes narrowing irresistibly. *I don't, but I'm pretty sure I'll pick it up quickly.*

And then you're going to teach me?

Yup.

I rolled over onto my stomach and propped myself up on my elbows. *What makes you think I'm not going to pick it up quickly and end up teaching you?*

Jonah grinned again. *Don't get cocky, city girl.* He put his hand on the back of my head and leaned in for a kiss.

Now, I'm surrounded by mountains and sky, but the window doesn't open and they don't let me outside. I imagine my brain atrophying in the recycled air-conditioned air while Jonah is out hiking Mount Rainier, his brain getting stronger with every step he takes.

It's like being trapped on an airplane, the air in here.

Of course, Jonah might not be hiking through Washington State. He might be a few miles away, stationed at Agnes's bedside, waiting for her to awake from her coma (if she's still in a coma), breathing air every bit as cold and recycled as the air in here.

After Agnes's parents showed up at the hospital but before

I was sent here, I went back to the dorms, but I didn't see Jonah. He must have been in class or at the gym or in the library. Maybe he'd gone to Santa Cruz for the weekend, so he could learn to surf before we went there together. I never had a chance to tell him what happened. I never had a chance to say goodbye.

But maybe Agnes's parents called him after I was gone. He could have driven straight from the beach to the hospital. Maybe when he showed up, there was still sand stuck between his toes and his hair was wet and dark with salt water.

Maybe he feels trapped beside Agnes, just like I'm trapped in here. Maybe he finally wants to break up with her, but he can't figure out how to go about it because she's still unconscious and he's a good guy so he has to stay at her bedside to comfort her even though she might not be able to hear him.

Maybe he's silently brainstorming all the ways he could break up with Agnes before she wakes up. He could do it through her parents (also stationed at her bedside), leaving them to convey the message once their daughter wakes up. He could leave a letter, but he wouldn't because no one writes letters anymore. I imagine Agnes waking up to a slew of text messages on her phone, mostly from people wishing her well, but one from Jonah ending their relationship.

The image is almost enough to make me laugh out loud.

I know what you're thinking: How good of a guy can Jonah possibly be? He cheated on his girlfriend (Agnes) with her best friend (me).

And okay, yes. He did. But he felt really bad about it.

It didn't start right away. I mean, it wasn't as though he and Agnes got together and he immediately turned to me. It was more gradual than that. He hated his roommate, so he spent a lot of time in our room, even when Agnes wasn't there. So we ended up spending a lot of time together. Plus, he and I were in the same American Studies lecture on Tuesdays and Thursdays, and we sort of fell in step walking to and from class.

All right, I admit it: I flirted with him. But I *had* met him first. I *had* liked him first. I couldn't help it.

I didn't tell Agnes that I liked him before they got together. Maybe if I had, she would have turned him down. Jonah's voice: *A sweet girl*. Sweet enough to turn her back on a boy her best friend liked? It doesn't matter. In the end, I got to be with him anyway. Not that I would have wanted to be with him after she turned him down—a last resort, a consolation prize. The way things turned out, I knew I wasn't his second choice because he got to be with Agnes, but he chose me too.

At first, on our walks to and from class, he didn't flirt back. I honestly thought he didn't like me—spoiled girl from the big city, nothing like Agnes, the good girl (*sweet girl*) from the heartland. The perfect companion for a boy who'd grown up in the shadow of Mount Rainier, hiking and camping every weekend.

But then one Tuesday after class, halfway between our classroom and the dormitory, Jonah took my hand.

He didn't say anything, so I didn't either. I was scared that if

I acknowledged it, he'd let go. It didn't last that long. Just a few steps together—maybe the length of a city block—and then he gently dropped my hand.

He did the same thing on Thursday. And again the following Tuesday.

But the Thursday after that, he squeezed my hand tight and tugged me to follow him behind the campus athletic center.

He pushed me up against the wall and stood with his face over mine, so close that I had to tilt my head up to see him.

He kissed my neck first, along my collarbones. He ran his hands over my hips and around my waist, his touch featherlight, like he was barely touching me at all. I was scared that if I moved or said anything, he'd stop, so I kept perfectly still, waiting for him to kiss me—not my neck, not my ears, but my mouth.

Finally, when I'd begun to think it wasn't going to happen after all, his lips met mine.

It was the middle of the day. The sun was bright overhead. We were behind the gym, but we were hardly hidden.

Still, we didn't stop.

The next time Jonah came to our room when Agnes wasn't around, I knew it wasn't because he hated his roommate.

Or anyway, it wasn't *just* because he hated his roommate.

But he never broke up with Agnes. He said he couldn't do that. He said she wasn't strong like I was. It would hurt her too much. I didn't argue because if I argued he might stop, and I didn't want to stop.

So like I said, he was a good guy.

sixteen

Okay, I know: He never actually said that he wanted to break up with her. But he didn't have to. I mean, if he really wanted to be with her, he wouldn't have been cheating on her with me. So obviously he *wanted* to break up with her, but Agnes was the kind of girl (*a sweet girl*) whom a guy would go out of his way not to hurt. So we had to keep our relationship a secret.

By now, Jonah probably knows I'm here. But he can't come visit me because it would look too suspicious. But if he's at the hospital with Agnes's parents, I'm sure he's dropping careful hints so they'll realize I would never have hurt Agnes. He's probably subtly explaining what a good friend I was, what a good person I am, how much I care about Agnes. After all, I never told her what was going on between Jonah and me either.

Lightfoot probably wouldn't let Jonah see me if he showed up here anyhow. Maybe it'd be like something out of a movie: He'd storm into Lightfoot's office (wherever it is, I've never been there) and insist she let him see me. He'd bang his fist on her desk, stomp up the stairs to the third floor, shake the door until the magnets that hold the locks in place disconnected. Then he'd rush inside and take me in his arms and kiss me.

No. That's the kind of fantasy Lucy would have. She's the sort of girl who wants her boyfriend to save her. I'm not the damsel-in-distress type. And anyway, Jonah isn't my *boyfriend*.

Plus, I wouldn't want him to see me here. There's no mirror in this room, so I haven't actually seen my reflection since I arrived. (Unless you count the occasional glimpse in the window when it's darker outside than it is inside. Which isn't often, given the automatic lights going on and off around dawn and dusk.)

But reflection or no reflection, I know I look terrible. I haven't had a proper shower since I got here. There's only so much a sponge bath can do. Before they brought me to this place, I washed my hair with expensive shampoo that lathered like bubble bath, then soaked it with conditioner for sixty seconds, and blew it out straight with a blow-dryer every day.

I should get shower privileges.

Just in case.

∴

"This stinks," I complain the next time Dr. Lightfoot comes for therapy.

"What do you mean by that? That you're frustrated by your current situation?"

"No." (Except yes, of course I'm frustrated, who wouldn't be frustrated, you don't need a degree in psychology to know that human beings don't like being locked up.) "I mean that these clothes *stink*. They smell." I press my nose against my shoulder and gag. Maybe Lightfoot is resigned to the stench after years of working with patients who don't shower regularly, but I'm not.

"Don't they bring you fresh clothes every other day?"

"Like that's enough to make a difference," I scoff. The smell is coming from inside me. They changed my sheets while I was at lunch the other day, but my hair is so greasy that the pillowcase already smells again. I reach up and run my fingers through my hair, struggling to untangle the knots. They don't allow us hair ties or rubber bands, so I can't even pull my hair back and try not to think about how dirty it is. I'm beginning to understand why in old movies they always shaved prisoners' heads, or at least cut their hair short. "You say you don't want me getting distracted from the work we're doing." In my head, I underline the word *work* to show her that I'm taking our sessions seriously. "But how can I concentrate when I feel this gross?"

Dr. Lightfoot nods. She opens her mouth, and I brace myself to swallow my anger when she explains that I shouldn't be worried about my appearance, that our focus isn't on the way things look but instead on the way things truly are. Maybe making me dirty is part of her method—break me down and take away my humanity, so she can build me back up again the way she thinks I should be.

But much to my surprise, Lightfoot says, "I can certainly see how that would be distracting." She crosses and uncrosses her legs. I bet she took a body language class in med school. I bet they told her exactly which position they thought would make her patients most likely to open up to her: *Spine not too straight* (that makes you seem unapproachable), *but don't slouch either* (that makes you seem bored). *Don't fold your arms across your chest* (that makes you uninviting), *but not too open* (or your patients might take advantage).

"I'll arrange for you to have a shower," she says, tucking her feet beneath her chair.

Lucy isn't here. She's has art therapy now. (Mondays, Wednesdays, and Fridays, she says. How she keeps track of the days, I don't know.) If Lucy were here, I'm pretty sure she'd be staring at Lightfoot's feet. Today's she's wearing a fresh pair of ballet slippers. Black, instead of pink. She points and flexes her toes.

Her movements don't look graceful the way Lucy's do.

"You're granting me shower privileges?" I try not to make it sound like a question, but I can't keep my voice from going up an octave at the end of the sentence.

Dr. Lightfoot smiles as if to clarify: *I'm granting you one shower. Behave yourself and maybe I'll grant you another.*

"You're doing good work, Hannah. I appreciate the way you opened up to me today." About being *dirty*? "Keep this up, and there might be more privileges in your future."

Some of the other girls have all their meals in the cafeteria: breakfast, lunch, and dinner. (I've learned this from Beside-Me-Annie at lunch.) Like Lucy, they have art therapy, where they weave potholders and baskets, though they aren't allowed to take their crafts back to their rooms. Some of the girls—like Queen Bee—have grounds privileges, supervised walks around the hospital property.

And now, Dr. Lightfoot is dangling these privileges out in front of me.

My plan is working: She's seen what a good friend I am to Lucy. She's heard how nice I am to the other girls in the cafeteria.

It's only a matter of time before she sends me home.

I wait until Dr. Lightfoot stands and turns her back to me so she can refold her chair before I roll my eyes.

Didn't they teach her not to turn her back on her patients in medical school?

seventeen

The water is lukewarm and comes out in a trickle, but I don't care. I close my eyes and imagine that it's hot, hot, hot, and the showerhead is the kind you can adjust to feel like a massage between your shoulders.

I open my eyes. I'm standing in a stall without a door or a curtain, one of eight stalls in this room. (Four on one side, four on the other. Lucy must have been exaggerating when she said there were no stalls.) A female attendant sits on a bench that's bolted to the floor in the center of the room. She's wearing scrubs, but she took off her shoes when she led me inside, so now water drains beneath her bare toes. The tile on the floor and the walls are light brown, as though whoever designed this place knew it would be better to pick a color that already looked dirty. The dividers between the stalls are yellow and nailed into the walls. The stall is so narrow that I bump my elbows into the dividers when I lift my arms.

When I hold out my hand, the attendant gives me shampoo, then soap. (No conditioner.) I shampoo my hair twice to make sure I get all the grease out.

What kind of person applies for a job supervising teen girls in the shower? Maybe she's just desperate for work. I honestly don't care. I'm just glad to be clean again.

Though it does make me wonder why anyone would work here. What made Stephen take his job, protecting a therapist from girls who've been labeled *a danger to themselves and others*? Maybe he applied to work someplace else—at a prison, perhaps, or a mental institution for adults. Maybe he only took this job after those other places turned him down. Or maybe those other places were farther from wherever it is that he lives, so he chose this place because the commute is better. Or maybe his girlfriend works in the kitchen, and he took the job to be close to her.

I decide he must have taken this job because he couldn't find work anyplace else. It's too hard to imagine anyone coming to this place by *choice*.

I wish I could shave my legs, but I don't think the attendant would give me a razor. I practically had to beg for that second helping of shampoo.

Lucy must hate this, being naked while an attendant stares at her. Though when Lucy showers, there are other girls here too, so maybe the attendant can't focus her gaze on my roommate like she can on me.

"Where are the other girls?" I speak loudly to be heard over the sound of running water.

"What?"

"How come I have the whole place to myself?" I gesture to the other stalls. "Seems like an awful waste of space."

"You haven't earned group shower privileges yet."

I turn my back and close my eyes, letting the water trickle over my face. What makes them think I'd *prefer* it if there were other girls here to steam up the room and squeal that the water is too hot or too cold?

I open my eyes. The metal showerhead is covered in rust. This water isn't nearly warm enough. My skin is covered with goose bumps.

If this room were full of other girls, I might be able to soap myself all over without thinking about being stared at.

It might mean my plans are working and Lightfoot thinks I'm improving.

Less *a danger to myself and others.*

Water drips into my right ear. I shake my head hard to get it out.

I lift my arms—careful not to bump into the sides of the stall this time—and let the not-hot water trickle down my sides. At home, I take showers so hot that I emerge from the bathroom bright pink. At home, I have fluffy towels and a fluffy robe, and the tile beneath my feet is bright white and scrubbed clean by our housekeeper twice a week.

At home, it doesn't smell like a janitor came in overnight and overturned a bucket of bleach and left it to soak into the floor instead of actually cleaning.

At home, I have three different shampoos with three corresponding conditioners to choose from: mint, coconut, and lemon. Sometimes I mix and match the scents to see what smells best.

At home, after my shower, I rub moisturizer all over myself until I'm as slick and slippery as a dolphin.

At home, I shower in a *shower*, not in a stall so narrow that I can't hold my arms straight in any direction but up and down.

At home, it doesn't feel strange and lonely to shower alone.

In *this place*, there is a raggedy towel waiting for me when I turn off the water, then the *slap slap slap* of my wet bare feet down the hall toward the room with the magnetic lock and the bulimic girl waiting on a bed with a mattress so thin you wake up feeling seventy instead of seventeen.

A group of four dry-haired girls wrapped in towels follows another attendant down the hall in the opposite direction. They're on their way to shower together. I turn my head and watch them go.

This place makes you wish you were showering in a room full of girls instead of on your own.

This place makes showering with other girls seem more *private* than showering alone.

Stay in *this place* too long, and how can you help going crazy?

But crazy people don't get to go back to school and earn the straight A's they need to get into Harvard and Yale and Stanford.

And crazy people don't get to hand in their college applications not just on time but early, because crazy people don't get to control their own schedule.

Crazy people are told what to do by doctors and caretakers for the rest of their lives.

I've got to get out of here.

One way or another.

eighteen

"September eighth," I announce when they close the door behind us after lunch the next day.

"What?" Lucy asks.

"Today is September eighth."

"How do you know that?"

"Annie told me."

"How did she know?"

I shrug. "Maybe they granted her calendar privileges."

Lucy giggles, but I don't feel like laughing. September eighth means I've been here for a month. It means Dr. Lightfoot is taking her sweet time with me, completely oblivious to the fact that she's ruining my life.

It means I've missed the first day of school.

Okay, sure, plenty of kids miss the first day of school.

Maybe their camp session didn't end in time or maybe their parents signed up for a tour of Italy without realizing that it overlapped with the start of the school year. People miss school for circumstances beyond their control. Maybe they were visiting someplace tropical that got hit with an unseasonably early hurricane and all the flights were canceled and they couldn't get home for another week or two. I started kindergarten two weeks late, and it never kept me from being a straight-A student.

But fall semester of senior year is different. Those are the grades that colleges look at, the grades they scour for weakness, searching for any reason not to admit you.

My school has a strict attendance policy: miss a quiz without an excused absence and you get an F. One F is enough to drag down your entire GPA. And teachers love giving pop quizzes your first week back from school, to see how much you suffered from *summer slide*, words they repeat like they're referring to a disease, the sort of thing mosquitoes carry for which there's no inoculation.

I look at the pile of romance novels at the foot of my bed. I was supposed to spend this summer earning college credit, the furthest thing from summer slide imaginable. I'm supposed to be back home, starting Chaucer and Dickens with my English class. Instead, I've read these awful books so many times I can practically recite them. Maybe that'll be the next phase of our book club: testing each other on how much we've memorized.

When Lightfoot comes, I can't help myself. I don't want her to know how much I want out, but I need to ask: "How much longer am I going to be here?"

I hold my breath, preparing for her answer. One week, two, and I can still make it home in time to make up for lost time and maintain my GPA. Three weeks, four, and my GPA will slip, but I can still get into my second-choice schools, right?

Any longer than that, and I can kiss even my safety schools goodbye.

Any longer than *that*, and they might actually hold me back for a year.

Lightfoot crosses her legs in her folding chair, her papery clothes crinkling beneath her. "I know you're concerned about school," she begins.

"Of course I'm worried about school!"

"But I want you to keep your focus on where you are today, not on where you'd rather be."

I shake my head. I can't possibly focus on where I am now any more than I already have. I've memorized every nook and cranny of these god-awful green walls. I know every bump of paint on the ceiling and every crack in the gray linoleum floor, and I've read every book they've given me at least twice. How much more focused could a person be?

"Don't let this…" Lightfoot pauses, searching for the right phrase, "*derail* your progress. You're doing so well. I'm going to send you to group shower in a few days, and perhaps you'll be able to begin art therapy soon."

I smile. Privileges like that are just a hop, skip, and a jump from being sent home, right?

"So maybe I won't miss that much school after all?"

Lightfoot shakes her head. "I don't want you focusing on that. We have a lot of work to do."

"But you said so yourself, I'm doing so well."

"Hannah, a date hasn't been set for your hearing yet."

"Why not?" Agnes's fall was five weeks ago. (Now that I know the date, I know that too.)

Lightfoot shrugs like it's no big deal, as if to say *Backed-up legal system and all that.*

"Can't you call the judge?" I ask.

"What would you like me to say?"

I press my lips together, biting them from the inside so she won't see. *Tell him they need to set the date of my hearing! Explain that this stupid misunderstanding is ruining my life!* I'm so mad I can barely look at her.

I hear my mother's voice, lamenting a legal system that kept inmates awaiting trial at prisons like Rikers Island. *Kids!* she said to me once, her voice full of passion. *Under eighteen! In gen-pop.*

She said *gen-pop* (which I later learned meant the general population of the prison, as opposed to separate facilities for minors) like she was familiar with the lingo, but the truth was, she'd only read one article on the subject.

I wonder if she'd be pleased that at least I'm here with other minors.

Lightfoot blinks. She shifts in her seat, dropping her hands and gripping either side of her folding chair. She's scared I'm going to try to grab it again. I look up and see that Stephen isn't standing with his arms crossed like usual. He's crouched, his arms out in front of him, ready to move, ready to pounce, like I'm a wild animal who might try to escape her cage.

No. I will not lose my privileges. I need Lightfoot to be on my side, so that when we finally meet with the judge, she can tell him that (in her expert medical opinion) I'm *perfectly normal*, that Agnes's parents were taking out their anger over what happened to their daughter on me, and the other girls in our summer program were talking trash about me because they're nothing more than silly little girls who live to create drama out of something perfectly innocent. Maybe Lightfoot will even write a letter for my college applications explaining what happened and praising me for persevering despite the difficult circumstances. I could write my admissions essay about how I overcame this hardship, how I intend to help others who were wrongfully accused.

In fact, if I play my cards right, this could even look *good* on my college applications.

I relax my lips and open my mouth, letting out a heavy sigh so Lightfoot will think I've accepted the situation as it is. One finger at a time, Lightfoot releases her grip on her chair. I don't look at Stephen, but I hear him clear his throat and his boots squeak against the linoleum floor. He must be moving out of his crouch.

"I haven't diagnosed you yet, Hannah," Lightfoot says. That's the second time she's said my name in the last five minutes. Another trick they must have taught her in school: *Use your patient's name to establish intimacy, to make her think you're on her side.* "It's not in your best interests to rush this process."

It's not in my best interests to be diagnosed at all, because diagnoses are for sick people and I'm perfectly healthy.

Doesn't Lightfoot understand that being in here is more likely to *derail* my progress than the other way around?

Across the room and behind Lightfoot's back, Lucy's mattress squeaks as she shifts on her bed. She's holding a book above her head, but she's not reading. She's listening.

September eighth.

Her audition is a week away.

It's not too late for Lucy.

nineteen

"We're getting you out for your audition," I whisper after lights-out.

Even though it's dark, I can see Lucy sit up in her bed across the room. "How are we going to manage that?"

"I didn't say I knew how, I said we were getting you out. Making the decision is Step One."

"What's Step Two?"

"That's figuring out how."

"Okay." Lucy sounds skeptical but intrigued.

"Remind me what your schedule is. When do you have art therapy?"

"Mondays, Wednesdays, and Fridays."

I shake my head. Kids at summer camp probably aren't forced to spend that much time doing arts and crafts. Not that I would know. I never went to camp. "What exactly does weaving a basket have to do with curing bulimia?"

"I don't know. It's supposed to be meditative. Like I can't think about fat and dancing when I'm doing it."

"Does it work?"

"Of course not." Lucy laughs. "Maybe they think it's enough to keep my hands occupied so I can't stick them down my throat."

"How do you get to and from art therapy?"

Lucy shrugs. "I don't really pay attention. They come get me, and I go downstairs."

I nod, considering. "Is it just you or are there other girls?"

Lucy shrugs again. "It varies."

That makes sense. The other girls here probably gain and lose their privileges just like I do. Which means some days they have art therapy privileges and some days they don't.

Which means sometimes the group walking to art therapy is small, maybe only two girls plus the attendant escorting them. It would be impossible to slip away without being noticed if there were only a couple of girls in the group. And we have no way of knowing when it will be a large group and when it'll be small, short of breaking into Lightfoot's office to find a log of who has which privileges when. (Which would just add another difficult step to an already difficult plan.)

I hear Lucy shift in her bed, lying back down. "Look, I appreciate the sentiment, but I think this plan of yours is going to have to end with Step One. They keep too close an eye on us to—"

"Lunch!" I interrupt gleefully.

"Lunch?"

"Lunch," I repeat. "I can't believe it took me this long to come up with it."

"This long? It's been, like, three minutes."

"Three minutes too long." Being stuck in this place must be slowing me down.

"How is lunch going to help? I have to sit with the E.D. girls. They keep a really close eye on us. Every meal is a chance for them to keep the bulimics from bingeing and the anorexics from starving."

"Anorectics," I correct.

"Huh?"

"I read that it's anorexic when it's an adjective—you know, an anorexic girl—but anorectic when it's a noun—a person is *an* anorectic."

"What are you talking about?"

"Just making sure my brain hasn't totally atrophied."

"Your brain isn't a muscle. It doesn't atrophy."

I hadn't thought of it that way. The notion is vaguely comforting.

"Anyway," Lucy prompts, "what's your great lunch plan?"

"They keep a close eye on you while you're eating. And when they pick us up and lead us downstairs, right?"

"Right."

"But afterward, they kind of just...*herd* us back upstairs. I mean, they tell us to get in line, but they don't take attendance or anything."

"They're probably hungry for their own lunch by then."

I shrug. I don't feel sorry for the people who work here. Okay, yes, I know nurses and hospital workers are overworked and underpaid, and it's probably not exactly fun dealing with ungrateful, unstable girls day after day after day. Back home, my mother volunteers at New York Presbyterian (planning fundraisers and recruiting donors; she doesn't actually interact with patients), and she sided with the nurses when they went on strike to get higher pay and shorter hours. My mother passionately defended the nurses over dinner in our dining room (not home-cooked—delivered, of course, because Mom's too busy to cook) while my dad and I nodded along.

When Dad had the gall to play devil's advocate—"But aren't they putting the patients at risk by striking, patients who have no control over how much the nurses get paid?"—Mom got up and walked away.

Dad apologized and within five minutes, we were nodding along again. My parents always said that the recipe for a healthy marriage was *staying on the same page.* (I hear those words in my dad's voice.) Even if staying on the same page sometimes means simply nodding along in agreement.

I didn't know then what I know now. Nurses and orderlies hold the keys (or magnetic key fobs) that open and close doors. They can eat and drink when they please, rather than at a predetermined assigned time, and they get to choose their meals (sushi? pizza?) and use knives (steak! a whole chicken breast!), instead of having nothing but a flimsy spoon to scoop up bite-size noodles and tiny meatballs. So no, I don't feel sorry for them, no matter how long their hours or how low their pay.

I haven't had a cup of coffee since they brought me here. Not that I was a big coffee drinker before. I didn't rely on caffeine to keep me functioning after a sleepless night or rush to the coffee shop around the corner after school to order a skim latte extra foam or anything like that.

But I *could* have, if I wanted to. Whether I ate or drank, and what I ate or drank, and when I ate or drank was entirely up to me. I could have gotten a milk moustache or burned my tongue by taking a sip of cappuccino without giving it a chance to cool off.

Here, they serve us soup and hot chocolate at room temperature, so there's no chance we might hurt ourselves or anyone else (*danger to herself and others*) with it.

When I get out of here, I'm heating all my soups to boiling and burning my tongue every chance I get. I'm drinking hot coffee out of a heavy ceramic mug, not a plastic cup like this is some sort of ongoing frat party.

"Hannah?" Lucy sounds concerned. She thinks I've gone silent because I've realized my plan isn't going to work after all.

I shake my head and my father's voice (*stay on the same page*) disappears, along with the phantom scent of coffee and the weight of the hot ceramic mug in my hands. Back to Step Two of our plan.

"After lunch, some of the girls don't go back upstairs. The ones with grounds privileges head down, right?" Like elementary school children heading outside for recess after a meal.

"Right," Lucy agrees. The single syllable sounds different than when she said it before. She's getting excited. She knows this could work.

"They trust us to know which direction we're supposed to go."

"They don't trust us as far as they can throw us."

"Okay, bad choice of words, but you see what I'm getting at, right?"

Lucy's long hair rustles as she nods. "There's only one problem."

"What's that?"

"Once I get outside, how the hell am I going to get to San Francisco?"

I hope Lucy can see my teeth in the darkness so she knows I'm grinning. "That's Step Three. I have a plan for that too."

twenty

When I wake up the next morning, I say out loud: "Today is September ninth." I can't lose track of the days again, at least not until the sixteenth. Not if this plan is going to work.

Before we fell asleep, I asked Lucy, *Do you know Joaquin's cell number by heart?*

Of course I do, she replied with urgency, as though she would never have relied upon her cell phone to keep such an important piece of information.

(I rolled my eyes. It was dark enough that Lucy couldn't see.)

Teach it to me.

I made her repeat it over and over again until I could recite it back, like a little kid learning how to spell his name for the first time.

His number is the second thing I tell myself after I wake up: "Joaquin's number is 510-555-0125."

This goes on for days:

Today is September tenth. Joaquin's number is 510-555-0125.

Today is September eleventh. Joaquin's number is 510-555-0125.

Today is September twelfth. Joaquin's number is 510-555-0125.

Today is September thirteenth. Joaquin's number is 510-555-0125.

Today is September fourteenth. Joaquin's number is 510-555-0125.

Today I wake up and say, "Today is September fifteenth. Joaquin's number is 510-555-0125."

Today is Step Four.

We didn't want to put the plan into motion too far ahead of time. What if word got out somehow? What if we gave Joaquin too much time to think about it and he lost his nerve? (*That would never happen*, Lucy insisted. *He would do anything for me*. More eye-rolling when she couldn't see.) What if we gave ourselves too much time to think about it and *we* lost *our* nerve? What if something went wrong?

The less time, we agreed, the better.

So we waited until today. September fifteenth. The day before Lucy's audition. It was scheduled long before they sent her here: 4 p.m. on September sixteenth.

Plenty of time, I promised last night while Lucy slid into a perfect split between our beds, stretching in preparation for tomorrow.

It'll only take you a couple hours to get from here to there, right?

Depends on traffic.

Yeah, but even with traffic, you'll have plenty of time to get there.

We don't know exactly what time lunch lets out.

We can assume it's sometime after noon but before two, right?

Right.

Now, I remind her, "You know, I won't have time to hear back from him. You're sure he'll do what we tell him to do, even coming from a number he's never seen before?"

"He'd do anything for me."

(I look up at the ceiling so she won't see me rolling my eyes again. Her voice goes all earnest and sappy whenever she talks about Joaquin.)

∴

Step Four takes place at lunch, in the cafeteria. (We've been on our best behavior to make sure we didn't lose any privileges.) I have to do this step by myself, since Lucy is stranded across the room with the other E.D. girls.

When the attendant gestures that I can take a seat, I don't choose my usual table with Trance-Girl and Beside-Me-Annie.

Today, I head straight for Queen Bee and her minions.

Queen bees have never been particularly interesting to me. They're all alike: relishing their little bit of power, holding it over the girls around them. Queen bees are boring because they're already exactly where they want to be—at the top of the high school (or mental institution) food chain. Nothing like the best friends I've made over the years.

I sit beside QB, to show that I'm not like the four girls who sit across from her every day. No, not four girls. Today there are only three.

"What happened to...?" I gesture vaguely in front of me. I don't know any of their names.

The girls opposite me don't answer. One redhead, one blond, and one girl whose short curly hair is even darker than Lucy's. The missing girl was another blond, but her hair was so light it was almost white, even lighter than Agnes's hair, not like the yellow-haired blond sitting across from me now. Each of the girls is strikingly pretty, just like the girls in QB cliques in the outside world.

But their eyes are milky—soft, like a photograph taken out of focus. Meds have made their pupils enormous, despite the bright fluorescent lights above us.

"Cara got sent home yesterday."

QB's voice is deep, several octaves lower than mine or Lucy's. Even sitting down, I can tell she's taller than I am. She looks like maybe she was an athlete before they sent her here. But trapped in this place, unable to exercise, her bulk has gone soft.

Nothing like in those prison movies, where men work out in the yard, counting the days until their release, until they can take revenge on whoever it was who sent them there.

QB's brown hair is matted into dreadlocks; I wonder when it was last washed. The smell coming off her is powerful. Maybe that's the real reason her minions sit across from her.

QB's eyes are sharp and crystal clear.

"Good for Cara," I answer finally, as though I knew her name all along. Queen bees assume that the people around them know not only their names, but their friends' names too, as though their friends are the supporting cast in the reality show of their lives.

QB shrugs. "It's not like she got well."

"No?"

"No way. They just loaded her up with meds and sent her on her way."

Briefly, I wonder why Dr. Lightfoot hasn't tried that approach with me. Maybe—despite the near-solitary confinement and strict meting out of privileges—she isn't quite unethical enough to medicate a perfectly healthy person.

Of course, she'd say that she hasn't medicated me because she hasn't diagnosed me yet.

But QB has been here for months, and she doesn't look the least bit medicated.

I say, "Still, it's better than being stuck here forever."

QB raises her eyebrows. "You think so?"

"Maybe out there she can go to a real doctor, someone who'll give her the right meds for whatever's wrong with her, instead of just stuffing her full of pills to keep her quiet."

Another thing all queen bees have in common: disdain for those who have power over them. Out there, it could be the principal who caught them sneaking a smoke behind the school or the childhood friend who knows they wet their bed until they were eleven.

In here, it's the doctors.

"Yeah," QB agrees. "They only care about keeping us under control."

"You look like you've managed to sidestep their efforts." (All QBs want you to be in awe of their wiles.)

"Yeah, well, don't think they haven't tried. But mine is the kind of diagnosis that can't exactly be medicated out of you." She looks at me meaningfully, and even though I'm not actually intimidated, I break her gaze as though I am. She wants me to know that whatever she has is serious, worse than whatever I have. She wants me to be scared of her. As though being sicker than I am means she's more powerful than I am.

Maybe in here, it does.

I glance around us, biting my lip so she'll think I'm nervous. "Don't worry," QB offers. "The attendants don't watch this table too closely."

I exhale like I'm relieved.

"I heard that you…had stuff."

"What kind of stuff?"

"A connection to the outside world." I raise my eyebrows and drop my voice into a whisper. "A cell phone."

She scoffs. "That's the least of what I have."

I consider all the things they don't allow us in here—not cigarettes and beer, the things adults keep from teenagers outside—things like chewing gum and good novels, pencils and paper and SAT II prep books.

But I can't get distracted. I'm here for Lucy, not for myself.

"I need to send someone a message. That is, if you really have a cell phone."

In the outside world, queen bees expect to receive something in exchange for whatever they give you: an eye for an eye, a tooth for a tooth, a ticket to a sold-out concert in exchange for an invite to their birthday party. Sometimes it's enough to confide *why* you need their help; a good queen bee collects knowledge to use against you later, should the need arise.

I'm counting on the fact that in here, merely proving to me that she is queen bee will be enough for this girl.

I'm right.

twenty-one

I feel the weight of the phone on my lap as QB slides it onto my thighs. She turns from me to her lukewarm vegetable soup and starts slurping it loudly.

I look down.

The screen glows back at me, confirming the date: September fifteenth.

It tells me the time: 11:48 a.m. (They feed us lunch at 11:30? What are we, toddlers? Whatever. At least it's better for Lucy. It'll give her more time to get to her audition.)

I open the messages folder. It's empty. QB erases everything she sends as soon as she sends it. Clever girl.

I could text my parents. (They'd be back from Europe by now.) Or Jonah.

With a start, I realize I don't actually know his number. Not that I didn't memorize it or that I forgot it, but that I never knew it at all—he never gave it to me. I guess it didn't seem necessary. We lived in the same dorm. He was never far away.

I could text Agnes. (She might still be comatose, but maybe her parents keep her phone beside her bed, so friends and family can reach out, check in. But not if she's back in the ICU. They don't allow phones in the ICU, right? Anyhow, I don't know her number by heart; it's stored safely in my own cell phone, which I haven't seen since they admitted me.) Maybe I could reach out to my attorney, get some answers. (But I don't know his number either.)

I shake my head. I'm texting Joaquin. That was the plan. That's what I'm here for.

I hide my hands beneath the table and angle myself, so it looks like I'm leaning over my bowl of soup. Carefully, I dial Joaquin's number: *510-555-0125.*

Hi, Joaquin. I'm Lucy's roommate at the institute. (I asked Lucy if I should use some sort of euphemism instead of calling this place what it is, but she shrugged. "He knows where I am," she said. "He doesn't hold it against me.")

Maybe Joaquin will wonder what I did to get sent here. Maybe I should explain that I'm not eating disordered like she is.

"What are you, writing a novel?" QB asks. "You better hurry up."

I lift my head and follow QB's gaze. An attendant is making his way toward our table. Guess they can't ignore QB's table entirely.

Lucy can still make it to her audition. She needs your help. Send.

Pick her up at 12:15 p.m. tomorrow. Send.

Don't write back. Send.

QB reaches to take the phone back, but I hold fast. I need to delete all this before she has a chance to see it.

"He's coming," QB says. Under the table, she tries to twist the phone from my grip. Her hands are hot.

I shake my head. At school, queen bees always have the teachers and administration wrapped around their fingers. If she knows what we're planning, she might turn Lucy and me in, just to make herself look good.

"Now," QB says firmly.

My palms are starting to sweat.

If I drop the phone, everyone will hear.

The attendant will see.

He'll confiscate the phone.

He'll read the message.

Lucy will get in trouble.

I'll get in trouble.

QB—as QBs always do—will get away with it. She'll claim it was my phone, not hers.

Delete.

I slide the phone onto QB's lap. She slides it up her shirt and tucks it away. Apparently, QB is allowed to wear a bra. Lucy would be so jealous.

The attendant walks past our table, giving each of us a once-over. QB and I keep our hands where he can see them. I hold my spoon tightly, hoping that he won't notice that my hand is shaking.

"How do you keep it charged?" I whisper.

"One of the orderlies does it for me."

"Wow," I say, genuinely impressed. My heartbeat slows to normal.

QB grins. "You'd be surprised what you could get away with when you've been here as long as I have."

She actually sounds proud. Her teeth are stained; they let us brush our teeth here, but it doesn't look like she does that much. I run my tongue over my teeth.

I don't want to be here long enough to learn what this girl knows.

The girls across from us are getting up. Lunch is over. QB swings her leg over the bench. (The benches are attached to the tables, which are nailed to the floor, which means, unlike in a normal cafeteria, the end of lunch doesn't include the sound of chairs scraping against the floor, but dozens of slippered feet shuffling across the linoleum.)

My hands twitch. What was I thinking? I should've texted my parents. I should've begged them to come get me.

I could ask to use her phone again tomorrow.

No, not tomorrow. Tomorrow we're sneaking Lucy out.

Well, the day after that, maybe.

"Time to get up, Hannah." An attendant stands over me, someone whose name I don't know but who (obviously) knows mine. I nod and stand, almost tripping over the bench.

"Whoa there," he says, reaching out to catch me. I want to shrug off his touch, but I don't. He might report it to Dr. Lightfoot. I imagine her noting the incident in my file.

Hannah Gold doesn't like to be touched by nameless strangers.

Out in the real world, that's good common sense. In here, it's a symptom.

I look at the floor, though I know Lucy is probably trying to catch my eye from across the room. She wants to know if our plan worked. She wants to see me nod, or wink, or smile in her direction.

But I don't feel like nodding or winking or smiling.

Queen Bee's not going to let me use her phone again, not unless I can offer her something in exchange.

Only the first one's free.

I know enough about queen bees to know *that.*

twenty-two

Step One: Decide to break Lucy out.

Step Two: Figure out *how* to break her out.

Step Three: Assume Lucy's loyal boyfriend will be willing to risk it all to get Lucy to her audition on time.

Step Four: Trick Queen Bee into letting us use her phone to reach said boyfriend.

Step Five: Get Lucy the hell out of Dodge.

Today is September sixteenth.

Today is Step Five.

When lunch is over, the patients gather by the stairwell: Half of us go up, half of us go down. The stairwell is dimmer than the cafeteria. I'm so used to the bright fluorescents that it always takes my eyes a second to adjust. The attendants call out the names of the girls with grounds privileges.

But they don't call out the names of those of us who don't have privileges. They simply lead us up the stairs.

Lucy and I squeeze our way into the middle of the group of girls with grounds privileges. I count: There are seven of them.

"I'm nervous," Lucy whispers.

"Worst case scenario, they catch us and send us back to our room." I try to sound nonchalant, but my pulse quickens. We both know there are worse possibilities: They take away our lunch privileges. They take away our showers. They take away our books.

"That's not what I meant. I haven't danced since I came here. I'm so out of practice. I'll probably blow my audition."

"You won't."

I reach down and lace my fingers through hers. I haven't held hands with a best friend since sixth grade. Her palm is warm against mine. I squeeze.

At the bottom of the stairs, the group turns left. A door stands open at the end of a windowless hall. Outside, the sun is shining so brightly that I don't even notice the overhead lights for once.

We follow. Suddenly, Lucy tugs me back.

"Where are we going?" I whisper. This isn't part of the plan. We're supposed to follow the patients with grounds privileges outside.

"Look," Lucy points.

The girls file outside one by one. An orderly stands at the door and scans their plastic bracelets as they exit.

We can't get out that way.

And we have to move before the orderly sees us.

I curse under my breath.

"Next," the orderly says. Luckily, he keeps his gaze down on the bracelets in front of him. But there's only one girl left.

Without the group for cover, it's obvious that Lucy and I aren't where we're supposed to be.

Lucy pulls me in the opposite direction.

I want to ask her what she's planning, but I'm scared the orderly will hear me.

So I follow without a word.

Lucy leads me down another windowless hallway lined with doors. This one has an emergency exit at the end of it.

"You can't open that door," I whisper. "The alarm will go off." I stop walking and point at the sign that says so.

What if Lucy ignores my warning? She could make a run for it, be out of sight before they catch her, hide in the woods until it's safe for her to meet Joaquin. It would be me they'd find, still inside. It would be me they'd punish, revoking the few privileges I've earned.

I glance at my roommate. Would she leave me like that?

Lucy tightens her grip on my hand.

Suddenly, she pulls me back against the wall. Someone emerges from a doorway just ahead of us. We flatten ourselves against the wall like we could blend in somehow.

A woman in yellow scrubs—a nurse, I think—closes the door shut behind her and walks toward the emergency exit without glancing in our direction. She pushes it open.

No alarm sounds.

She reaches into the pocket of her scrubs and pulls out a cigarette and lighter. The scent of smoke fills the air.

It feels like it takes her an hour to finish that cigarette.

"When she comes back inside, she'll see us," I hiss desperately.

Lucy nods, then pulls me in the opposite direction, back toward the stairwell. For a second I think she's going to admit defeat and lead the way back up to our room, but instead, she crouches on the lower steps. The nurse would have to look closely to see us hiding here.

We peer down the hall. The nurse finishes her cigarette, drops it on the ground, and grinds it with the heel of her black clogs.

She blinks as she reenters the building. I swear she sees us. We both hold our breath. Lucy lets her dark hair fall in front of her face like it's a mask she can hide behind.

The nurse walks down the hall. I count her steps.

One, two, three, four.

She stops. For a split second, I think she's about to break into a run toward us.

Instead, the nurse goes back through the same door she came out of five minutes earlier.

"Let's go." Lucy grabs my arm and breaks into a run. Our slippers shuffle and slide against the linoleum.

Lucy pauses for a second when we reach the door, then shoves it open. She steps out and throws her arms overhead in triumph. I reach out and clap my hand over her mouth before she can let out a joyful shout.

The sun is warm. I look up.

The light is blinding. I blink, but my eyes won't adjust. I shift my gaze to the ground, wondering if I'll ever get used to sunlight again.

A breeze blows inside. *Real* air, not manufactured air-conditioned air.

I shiver pleasantly.

"You better get going." I hold the door open so I won't get locked out.

Lucy hesitates. "You could come with me. Moral support and all that."

It's tempting. I breathe in the smell of grass and leaves and trees. I slide one foot out the door. The ground is soft beneath my slippers. Dirt, not linoleum.

"You coming?" Lucy prompts.

I slide my foot back. "I better stay. I have Lightfoot this afternoon. We have to stick to the plan."

Me staying behind is a big part of the plan. Lightfoot probably won't notice that Lucy's not in the room when she comes for my afternoon session: Lucy usually has art therapy. And hopefully, the "teacher" who runs today's art therapy session won't think much of Lucy's absence. Lucy said girls miss class all the time—because they lost privileges for acting out or because they're in treatment. (Though she didn't know what it meant to be "in treatment.") It happens so often the teacher doesn't even keep track. Or so Lucy assured me.

But Lightfoot will definitely know something's up if *I'm* not in the room for our session.

"Go," I whisper.

Lucy doesn't hesitate.

I linger in the doorway to watch her, shading my eyes with

one hand. She sprints to the trees, her long, almost-black hair flying out behind her like a cape. She kicks off her slippers and runs barefoot. (Lucy said Joaquin would know enough to bring her spare toe shoes and an appropriate outfit in his car.)

Even the way Lucy runs looks like a dance. She lands on the balls of her feet, loping gracefully from one step to the next.

She doesn't have to worry about blowing her audition. She's ready.

I smile.

I take another small step outside. I can't help it.

I take another step, then another, until only the tips of my fingers are holding the door open.

I think I can smell the ocean on the other side of the building.

September in the Santa Cruz Mountains looks nothing like September back home in New York. The sun is bright overhead, and the air is crisp and thin, not thick with humidity like it might be in New York this time of year, where the warm weather lingers through most of September. There are no clouds overhead, no hint of rain on the horizon.

I don't recognize September here.

If I'm not there for our afternoon session, Lightfoot will raise the alarm. I might be able to hide somewhere in the woods, but Lucy's parents would know exactly where their daughter went.

The San Francisco Dance Academy at 4 p.m. They'd get to her before she could audition.

I slide one foot back, and then the other. I'm standing entirely inside again.

I take one more deep breath of fresh air and carefully, quietly, close the door. The hall behind me is still empty, and the stairwell is too. Everyone else is exactly where they're supposed to be.

It's enough that Lucy is out. Enough that Lucy gets to feel the sun on her face. Even though I'm still trapped in this place, I can't stop smiling. I haven't had this much fun since they brought me here.

If only Lightfoot could see me now, giving up my chance to get out to make sure that Lucy gets hers.

∴

Step Six. I completely forgot to plan for Step Six.

The door to the room is locked.

twenty-three

I sit on the floor with my back against the door. I run through possible explanations in my head so I'll be ready when Dr. Lightfoot and Stephen show up.

I went the wrong way after lunch.

I wasn't paying attention. My head was in the clouds.

By the time I got here, there was no attendant to let me in.

I thought someone would come get me, so I waited.

I close my eyes and picture Lucy jumping into Joaquin's car, whooping in triumph as he drives away. In my imagination, the car is a convertible and Lucy's hair lifts in the breeze. Joaquin steps so hard on the gas that they leave tire tracks on the asphalt.

Jonah didn't drive a convertible. Actually, Jonah didn't drive at all. He thought it was better to ride a bike or walk. He cared a lot about the environment. It was something we had in common. Not the environment part—I care about it as much as the next person, but it's not my focus like it was his. I mean, the not-driving part. I don't have a car either. I never really needed to drive in Manhattan.

So Jonah couldn't have come for me like Joaquin came for Lucy. Not because he doesn't care. Not because he wouldn't want to rescue me. Not because I wasn't technically his *girlfriend*. He literally wouldn't have the means to rescue me.

I finger the bracelet on my wrist. It's tight enough that I can't move it up or down my arm much. I guess they don't want to risk it being loose enough that patients could slide it over their hands. My skin itches beneath it.

Unlike Jonah and me, Agnes had her own car. This summer, if I had to go anywhere that wasn't within walking distance, Agnes would offer me a lift. She and her parents had driven her little hybrid from North Dakota to California at the beginning of the summer. Her parents had given her the car for her seventeenth birthday. It was so fuel efficient that even Jonah approved of it.

In June, Agnes drove us—just the two of us—into San Francisco, across the Golden Gate Bridge and up into Muir Woods for a girls' day out. With traffic, it took nearly two hours to get there, but we turned up the radio and rolled down the windows, and sang along at the top of our lungs. Driving over the bridge, the temperature must have dropped fifteen degrees, but as we headed into the forest, it got warm again. Between the trees, there were patches of sunlight bright on the ground. Agnes slathered on sunscreen that smelled like coconuts, but her shoulders were still sunburnt at the end of the day. I wondered if Jonah would rub aloe into the burns later. We hiked for an hour, stopping to take pictures. The woods didn't look all the different from the woods around this place. What little I saw of them, anyway.

Tap tap tap.

I look up and see Lightfoot headed down the hall toward me. I scramble to my feet and offer one of my prepared excuses.

The doctor uses her plastic key fob to open the magnetic lock on the door. She steps aside so I can go in first. I take a deep breath as if I'm diving underwater.

Once again, the room looks smaller. And emptier. Empty. For the first time, it occurs to me that Lucy might not come back after her audition. We never discussed that step.

Stephen takes his place at the door, but Lightfoot leaves her plastic chair out in the hall. Bad sign.

Maybe Lucy assumed I wouldn't expect her to come back. I mean, who would come back if they didn't have to? Then again, if she doesn't come back, she'll definitely be in trouble. It might not matter how well her audition goes. Lightfoot could track her down and force her to return. She could keep Lucy here for months as punishment—past when she'd get her acceptance to the dance academy, past when she'd show up for orientation or move into the dorms.

Lightfoot could keep Lucy here for years.

So Lucy *has* to come back, right?

Lightfoot stands in the center of the room and looks at me expectantly. My excuse—*My mind was in the clouds*— obviously wasn't enough to satisfy her. I shake my head. I shouldn't be worrying about Lucy, about whether she's coming back or how she's going to get back inside if she does. I should be worrying about *myself*. I can't get into trouble. I won't give Lightfoot an excuse to keep me here any longer than is absolutely necessary.

I sit cross-legged on the bed. (It's harder to think of it as *mine* now that I don't know whether Lucy's coming back). I try to look like a normal teenage girl.

"Why weren't you paying attention, Hannah?" Lightfoot shifts her weight from one foot to the next. "What had you so distracted that you lost your way?"

What would a normal teenage girl be distracted about?

A normal teenage girl would be sitting on a couch, not a bed, when she had therapy. Then again, maybe a normal teenage girl wouldn't need therapy. Though plenty of the girls in my school had therapists. Sometimes it was because their parents were getting divorced and were worried about *how the kids were adjusting.* Or because the pressure to get a perfect score on the SATs made them stop sleeping and they'd started to abuse their Ritalin (or Adderall, or Dexedrine, or Focalin…) prescription. Or maybe they were struggling with depression. Or an eating disorder—not like the E.D. girls here (no one at school was sick enough for inpatient treatment, as far as I know)—but plenty of girls obsessed over their bodies enough that their parents might gently suggest they needed therapy.

Were those girls *normal*?

"Hannah?" Lightfoot prompts. "Are you *still* distracted?"

If Lightfoot gets suspicious, she might figure out that Lucy's gone AWOL.

Stop. I should be worrying about myself, not about Lucy.

twenty-four

Quickly, I say, "I was thinking about the girls at school. My real school, I mean, not summer school. Back home. In the city."

Dr. Lightfoot nods. Her face softens a little. "What was your old school like?" Lightfoot jerks her chin in Stephen's direction. He brings in her folding chair. Dr. Lightfoot sits and crosses her legs. I'm not in trouble anymore. Or if I am, Lightfoot is more interested in what I might say than in punishing me.

I have to keep going. Keep her interested.

Lightfoot surely has notes about my school in her thick "Hannah Gold" file. Back in Manhattan, I go to a private all-girls' school on the Upper East Side. It's famous (supposedly the school in *Gossip Girl* was based on us back in the day) but small. There are no more than twenty girls in each classroom and no more than fifty girls in each grade. About half of the students have been there since kindergarten, like I have. Last year, 70 percent of the senior class went to Ivy League universities, and the other 30 percent went to equally prestigious places like Stanford and Duke and Vanderbilt and the University of Chicago.

The school paper printed a list of who was going where like it was big news. Copies of the list were sent home to parents with children in kindergarten through eleventh grade, so they'd have something to look forward to. The list was even sent to alumnae, so they'd know the school hadn't gone downhill since they graduated.

"I've gone to the same school since kindergarten," I answer finally.

"So it was like home to you?"

"Yeah," I say, but I'm shaking my head. "I mean, not as much as it was for some of the other girls."

"And why's that?"

"A bunch of them knew each other since *before* kindergarten. They were in the same preschool classes, the same Mommy and Me classes, or whatever."

"But not you?"

I shake my head again. "My parents didn't send me to preschool. They took me with them everywhere they went." By the time I was five, I'd been more places than most fifty-year-olds.

"That must have been nice, knowing your parents wanted you with them instead of leaving you with a babysitter."

I nod. "Of course it was." Maybe Dr. Lightfoot had parents who traveled a lot for work, or for pleasure, who had active social lives that didn't involve their children. (I'm assuming Dr. Lightfoot isn't an only child. Most people aren't.) Maybe she always wished her parents would let her be part of their big, exciting, grown-up lives. Maybe she's jealous of me because my parents did.

"On trips, I always had my own hotel room—"

"Always? Even at five years old?"

"Sure," I answer with a shrug. Maybe when I was a *baby*-baby, they had me sleep in a crib in their room. Or sometimes we'd have a two-bedroom suite, so I guess that's not technically my own room. A lot of the time we were in adjoining rooms, side by side with a door between us. But more than once, the hotel messed up our reservations so that I was down the hall rather than right next door.

"That's unusual," Lightfoot suggests.

"How much trouble can a kid get into in a hotel room?" I say it, but it's my mother's voice I hear. That's what she used to say when they left me alone.

"It's not always about getting into trouble," Lightfoot says. "Most little kids would be frightened."

"I wasn't."

"It'd be okay if you were. Being left alone would upset most children."

I shake my head. I wasn't like most children. "I ate in Michelin-starred restaurants all around the world. That's better than going to Mommy and Me class, right?"

A Michelin star is the reason I started kindergarten two weeks late. My parents had been on the wait-list for reservations at this new restaurant in Paris for months. When a September date opened up, they booked our trip immediately, even though the tickets and hotel were more expensive than usual because it was such short notice. They didn't worry that I might fall behind on any important lessons. After all, I was already reading and writing at a second-grade level. (I can practically hear my mother's voice: *Missing a couple weeks of kindergarten won't hurt.*)

"You can't exactly be upset with your parents for taking you to the nicest places on Earth," I say.

"Hannah," Dr. Lightfoot says gently. "It doesn't matter how nice the trips were. You are allowed to be angry at your parents."

I shake my head. "I knew I was lucky, even then. I knew that traveling would influence the person I'd turn out to be." My father's voice this time, all that emphasis on *broadening my horizons*.

That restaurant in Paris was where I first tasted truffles and Époisses cheese. (I pretended to love both because my parents did. Secretly, I thought they were stinky and gross.) I tasted sweetbreads that night too. No one bothered to tell me that they tasted a whole lot different than the name implied. (Sweetbreads are actually made from animals' pancreas and thymus glands.) When the waiter put a plate of sweetbreads in front of me, my parents laughed at the surprised look on my face.

By the time I got to school, most of the girls in my class had already made their best friends.

I didn't know then what I know now: kindergarten best-friendships are usually pretty fickle. Most girls have at least three best friends before winter break.

I only knew that I needed a best friend ASAP.

I had to pick from the girls no one liked: the smelly, strange, leftover girls. But I discovered I could make them less smelly, less strange. Soon my cast-off girls became the cool, pretty girls, and everyone else wanted to be friends with me and my projects.

"It sounds like your parents expected you to act like an adult even though you were still a little kid."

Agnes said, *I've been taking care of my little sisters for as long as I can remember. I never got to join clubs and teams at school because I had to be home to babysit.*

I guess that's something Agnes and I had in common. Both of us had parents who expected us to act like grown-ups from the very start.

I learned the word *precocious* when I was four years old.

We're so lucky to have such a precocious little girl.

Since I didn't go to day care or preschool, kindergarten was the first place I really interacted with kids my own age. I was already good at getting along with adults. I'd listen to their conversations and come up with clever rejoinders to my parents' friends' comments. And when I got tired of doing that, I'd pretend to sleep in the booths of five-star restaurants so the adults could talk. It got so I knew exactly when they'd had enough of oohing and ahhing over me and wanted to talk business, or gossip about who was sleeping with whom, that sort of thing. I knew exactly when to yawn and let my eyes flutter shut. But getting along with kids was new to me.

"I was born mature," I say with a smile. Of course, Lightfoot isn't in on the joke.

She shakes her head. "No one is born mature."

That night at the Michelin-starred restaurant in Paris, after my parents laughed, I ate every last bite of the sweetbreads. I ate the Époisses and the truffles even though I couldn't stand the smell. My parents were proud of me.

From his place in the doorway, Stephen clears his throat. Dr. Lightfoot doesn't wear a watch or carry a phone into our sessions. (*Patient may pose a danger to herself and others.*) She counts on Stephen to keep track of the time, so she never stays a minute longer than our allotted session. Not even when I'm having a breakthrough, like maybe she thinks I am today. In medical school, they probably taught her that it was important to maintain *proper boundaries* in a therapeutic relationship.

Lightfoot stands. "Our time is up." She smiles at me. She looks so pleased with all my sharing that I'm not sure she even remembers she found me sitting outside my room at the beginning of this session.

I smile back. A real smile.

twenty-five

Here's something this place has in common with the world's nicest hotels: Windows in hotel rooms usually don't open either. Of course, I was never locked in a hotel room like I am here, but when I was little, I wasn't allowed to leave by myself and I never broke the rules. I would wait for my parents to return from the places they said little girls—even *precocious* little girls like me—couldn't go: casinos, nightclubs, bars. They usually only left me at night, when they thought I'd sleep through their absence. And most of the time, I did. But some nights I stayed up waiting for the sound of the door opening in their adjoining room or for Mom to check on me, bringing with her the scent of perfume and alcohol and cigarette smoke. Sometimes she didn't come until the next morning, waking me to say it was time to get up, get dressed, we had so much more to explore.

Tonight, I'm waiting for Lucy.

At hotel after hotel, I never doubted that my parents were coming back. Some little kids panic when their parents leave them, like they believe there's a chance they might never see them again. And I read once that puppies can't tell the difference between being left alone for five minutes and being left alone for five hours. I wasn't like that. Part of being *born mature* was being born *practical*. When my parents said I'd see them again in the morning, that meant I would see them in the morning. It would have been impractical to believe otherwise.

Then again, there was always the possibility that something might have prevented them from getting back to me: a car accident or a run-in with a murderous cab driver or some other tragedy. But when I was little, I didn't know about dangers like that. At least, I didn't think about them.

So I waited for my parents patiently, confident in the fact that eventually I'd hear the sound of the door opening, smell the scents of the outside world.

Tonight, I'm waiting for Lucy—but can I really call it waiting when there's a chance she might not return? There should be another word for this sort of waiting that's both waiting and not waiting, both expecting the door to open and knowing that it might stay closed. It's the Schrödinger's cat of waiting.

We learned about Schrödinger's cat in physics class last year. It's a thought experiment that an Austrian physicist named Erwin Schrödinger came up with in the 1930s. It basically says that if you lock a cat in a box with a radioactive atom, the cat's survival depends on whether or not the atom decays and emits radiation. So until you open the box and see the state the cat is in, it's both alive and dead.

I didn't entirely understand what the cat had to do with

physics beyond the fact that Schrödinger was a physicist and the experiment involved atomic radiation, but I liked the sound of a *thought experiment*. So I try to convince myself that I'm currently engaged in a thought experiment: Until Lucy walks in that door, she is both on her way back and never returning.

It's comforting that I remembered Schrödinger's cat at all. My brain can't be turning to complete mush in here if I still remember a year-old physics lesson.

∴

It's dark when she gets back, long past lights-out. I'm in bed but I'm not sleeping. I hear the metallic click of the lock coming undone, the creak of the door opening.

Lucy brings the scent of the outdoors with her: fresh air and mud and grass. I let out a breath. The cat's alive after all.

Light spills in from the hallway before she gently closes the door. She's wearing the same papery clothes she was wearing when she left, the same slippers. *Click.* The door locks behind her. The room is dark again except for the sliver of light coming in from beneath the door. Only a little light comes through the window from outside. It must be cloudy tonight.

Maybe it's raining outside. Not so much that you'd be able to hear it tapping against the roof or window, but enough of a mist that Lucy's hair would be moist. I sniff, trying to detect whether Lucy smells like rain.

"How did you get back inside?"

Lucy gasps. "You scared me."

"It's not like you didn't know I was here."

"True. But I thought you were sleeping."

"What time is it?"

"Dunno. When Joaquin let me out of the car, it was midnight. But it took me a while to get in after that."

"Like Cinderella," I say.

Lucy laughs. "Yeah, I feel like a real princess."

I laugh too, but I'm careful to keep my voice down.

"How did the audition go?"

I can see the whites of Lucy's teeth when she grins. "Amazing. I was on point. No pun intended. Actually, all puns intended."

She sounds so happy that I decide not to tell her I got into trouble with Lightfoot this afternoon.

Anyway, I didn't really get into trouble. I managed to talk my way out of it. So there's really no reason to tell Lucy.

Instead, I say, "I'm so glad it went so well!"

"I know! I couldn't believe it. I mean, I thought I would suck after all this time without practice. I thought my body would be like, *Are you kidding me? You haven't warmed up for this.* But then the music started and it all just clicked."

"Muscle memory."

"I guess."

"How did you get in?" I ask again.

"Joaquin gave me cash. You'd be surprised what the orderlies will let slide for a hundred bucks. I even got a fresh pair of slippers to replace the ones I lost in the woods."

I nod, thinking about QB and her contraband phone. She must pay the orderly who charges it for her. I wonder where she gets the money. I wonder how much it costs.

I can make out the silhouette of Lucy running her hands through her hair. "Whoops," she says with a giggle. "Leftover bobby pin."

"Huh?" I ask dumbly.

"Joaquin and I had to stop at a pharmacy so I could get ponytail holders and bobby pins to pull my hair back into a bun. I thought I got all of them out on my way back." She sighs. "I can't get it out."

I sit up. "Come here."

The bed squeaks when Lucy sits on the edge of it. In the darkness, I run my fingers through her hair until I feel the snag. Patiently, careful not to pull her hair, I begin undoing the knot around the bobby pin. Lucy exhales.

"You must be tired," I say. I feel Lucy nod in agreement. Finally, I free the bobby pin from her tangles. I search for her hand in the darkness and place it in her palm.

"Contraband," I say, and Lucy giggles. The bed squeaks again as Lucy gets up. She pauses then heads for the window. She places the pin on the narrow windowsill.

I lie back and close my eyes. I hear Lucy get into her bed.

"I have to stay on my best behavior now. So they'll let me out in time to attend. If I get in."

I exhale with relief. Part of me had been wondering whether Lucy might try to leave again, now that she knows how to get out.

But if she's determined to stay on her best behavior, that means she's not going anywhere. At least, not until Lightfoot clears her to leave. And that could still be months from now.

"You'll get in," I say confidently.

"Do you really think so?"

"I do."

Agnes's voice: *When you say it, I actually believe it.*

"Do you think that girl would let you use her phone again?" Lucy asks.

"I'm not sure."

"Joaquin is going to check my email, to keep an eye out for the acceptance letter. He said he'd text that number to let me know."

"I'll ask her at lunch tomorrow."

"Thanks. Sucks to be stuck at the stupid E.D. table."

I open my eyes. "That's what you have me for, right?"

Lucy may be the one of us who got away from this place today, but now that we're both back inside, I'm the one with a link to the world outside. Or with access to the girl who has a link to the world outside.

I can't make out much more than a lump on Lucy's side of the room, but I imagine she's nodding in agreement.

I'm not ready to go to sleep yet, so I keep talking. "Joaquin must've been happy to see you, huh?"

"He hugged me so hard I thought it'd crack a rib." For once, I don't roll my eyes. I actually want to hear more. Or maybe I just don't want the room to go silent.

"How long have you guys been together?"

"Six months."

"How did you meet?"

"At school. He was in my history class."

"And he doesn't mind? You being in here, I mean. He doesn't mind waiting for you out there?"

I can hear Lucy's sheets rustle. "If he loves me, he'll wait. And if he doesn't, I'll find someone else who does." She says it simply, like finding a new person to love is as easy as replacing a pair of shoes after you've worn down the sole. She sounds happy. She's been outside, she nailed her audition, she has someone who will wait for her, someone she can reach out to from this miserable place, even if I'm the one doing the actual reaching.

I say, "Maybe I'll text someone too."

"Who? Your lawyer?"

I sigh. "Not my lawyer. He couldn't keep me out of this place, so what good is he?"

"You could text your parents that you want another lawyer."

"Sure," I agree. That's what I wanted, wasn't it? To text my parents before I handed the phone back to QB yesterday. "But maybe I'd text Jonah." I haven't said his name out loud since they brought me here. "Jonah Wyatt." I say it slowly, savoring each syllable. Lucy doesn't know that I don't have his number. For a few minutes, I allow myself to forget that I can't reach him, with or without a phone.

"Who's Jonah Wyatt? Your boyfriend?"

"Don't you think if I had a boyfriend, I'd have told you about him by now?"

"Not necessarily."

"You told me about Joaquin within seconds of meeting me."

"Yeah, but you're not like me."

"What's that mean?"

Lucy's bed creaks as she sits up. "It's not a bad thing. It's just—I've always had a boyfriend. Before Joaquin there was Mikey, and before Mikey there was Pedro, and before Pedro—"

I sit up too. "Okay, I get it. You're the type of girl who always has a boyfriend." We had a few of those at school, girls who managed to meet boys despite our single-sex education. The guys would wait for them on the corner outside school, hands stuffed in their pockets, all bad posture and hunched shoulders, victims of growth spurts they hadn't gotten used to yet. Those boys didn't interest me. Sure, I'd gone to parties and dances, I'd flirted and been kissed, but until Jonah, I'd spent more time with adult men like my dad and his friends than I had with guys my own age.

"So who's Jonah?" Lucy asks again.

"He's this boy I was hooking up with over the summer." I've never said that out loud either. I couldn't, of course. What happened between us was a secret.

"But he wasn't your boyfriend?"

After a moment, I answer, "It was complicated." I like how mysterious it sounds.

"But you liked him?"

"Of course." I wouldn't have gone to all that trouble—keeping our relationship a secret, lying to my best friend—if I hadn't cared about him, right?

"Did you looooove him?" Lucy sounds like the boy-crazy girl in an eighties' movie.

"Shut up," I say, though I like how it feels to let Lucy think I (sort of) have a boy on the outside too. I throw my pillow at her bed. It's so light and thin it doesn't even make it all the way across the room. At home, I have four pillows on my bed. All filled with (humanely sourced) goose down. Lucy leans over the edge of her bed and tosses the scrawny pillow back to me.

"I'll take that as a yes."

"Take it as whatever you want it to be."

"Hannah and Jonah, sittin' in a tree. K-I-S-S-I-N-G. First comes love. Then comes marriage—"

Now I lie back and cover my face with the pillow. "Make it stop!" I beg, my voice coming out all muffled. "This isn't a slumber party, and we're not in eighth grade!"

We're too old for these games.

"Okay, okay, I'll stop," Lucy promises, laughing. I put my pillow beneath my head.

Then she says, "But you wanted him to be your boyfriend, right?"

I roll over so my back is to her, folding the pillow in half so it fits in the crook of my neck.

"I never thought about it," I say quietly. It's not a lie. Jonah had a girlfriend. He wasn't going to break up with her, so what would have been the point of thinking about whether or not I wanted him to be *my* boyfriend? That would have been completely impractical and like I said, I'm very practical. "Go to sleep," I add.

Lucy giggles, then sighs, but I listen as she adjusts her pillow and blanket. I hear her breathing slow.

"Lucy?"

"Hmm?" she murmurs sleepily.

"Why did you come back? I mean, you could've stayed out there."

Her voice is muffled. "It seemed like it'd be too risky to stay away."

"Oh," I answer. Lucy must have had the same thought I had: If she got into enough trouble, Lightfoot could keep her here so long that it wouldn't matter how well the audition went. She'd never get to attend the dance academy.

Coming back was the practical decision. It would have been incredibly impractical to stay away. And it would have been equally as impractical to come back for any reason other than staying out of trouble. Like because she didn't want to leave me alone.

Lucy's breathing is shallow and steady; she's asleep. The room feels so much warmer with her here.

twenty-six

The next day, no one comes to get me for lunch. In our after-noon session, Dr. Lightfoot tells me I lost my cafeteria privileges.

"Why?"

"Because you weren't in your room after lunch yesterday."

"But that wasn't my fault! By the time I got back up here, there was no one to let me in." Even though I'm lying, I feel like a victim. Lucy went all the way to San Francisco, and she still got to go to the cafeteria today.

I should've found an orderly to bribe like Lucy and QB. Or how my parents tipped busboys at hotels, slipping cash into a handshake, just enough to get a free upgrade to a room with a nicer view, free breakfast, free Wi-Fi.

I bet even this place has Wi-Fi.

Not that it's a hotel.

But I don't have any money for tipping. And you probably can't really call it *tipping* in circumstances like these.

But if Lightfoot won't let me go to the cafeteria, I can't convince QB to let me use her phone again. If I can't use her phone again, I won't be able to find out whether Lucy got into the dance academy. I won't be able to text my parents to demand a better attorney. (Demand, like an adult. Not beg, like a baby.)

"I told you I was distracted." It comes out sounding like a whine. Like a plea. I hate my voice.

"Nevertheless—"

"I didn't do it on purpose."

"That may be true, but you still broke a rule."

The words *that may be true* are infuriating. Despite the manufactured cool air, I'm sweating.

Funny thing about lies. When someone doesn't believe you, you feel like you have the moral high ground. How dare they accuse you of lying?

"I told you, I was thinking about my old school. I was thinking about my parents. I was thinking about Jonah."

If I had his phone number (and cafeteria privileges), I would demand that QB let me text him. No. I want to *call* him. (How could I possibly do that? In the middle of the cafeteria? Everyone would notice if I had a phone to my ear. Even if I tried to hide it, they'd see it. Crouching under the table wouldn't work. You can only pretend you dropped your plastic spoon for so long.)

But if I could call him, then I could hear his voice. Deep and gravelly and calm.

Maybe I do know his phone number. I mean, maybe I used to know it. Maybe if I wrack my brain long enough, I can remember it. Human beings only use 10 percent of their brains, right?

Maybe his number is hiding somewhere in the other 90 percent. Maybe I could find it if I tried hard enough.

I shake my head. I'm only thinking about Jonah because of Lucy. She got to be rescued by her knight in shining armor (more like skinny, acne-marked boy in a beat-up old car, I bet) for a few hours yesterday, so now I want to be rescued too. Even though I'm not that kind of girl, and a brief escapade with Jonah won't bring me any closer to *really* getting out of here.

It's a completely impractical thing to wish for.

"Who's Jonah?" the doctor asks. I have to stop myself from raising my eyebrows. Obviously, she's pretending not to know. No doubt Agnes's parents told Lightfoot about Jonah weeks ago. Lightfoot probably interviewed him when she was trying to get info about me.

He wouldn't have told her about *us* of course. But if Agnes and I were joined at the hip this summer, then Jonah was joined to her other hip.

"Hannah, who's Jonah?" Lightfoot repeats. She crosses and uncrosses her legs. I hate when she does that. She looks like a praying mantis.

"Nobody."

"He must be somebody if he distracted you enough that you missed getting back to your room after lunch."

"He was a boy I liked before." Inwardly, I curse. I shouldn't have referred to him as a boy I *liked* before. I should've said he was a boy I *knew* before.

"Before what?"

"Before I came here." Before Agnes's fall.

Dr. Lightfoot cocks her head to the side, considering.

"Jonah Wyatt. He was in the summer program with… Agnes and me." The two syllables of Agnes's name feel heavy in my mouth.

"Did he know Agnes?"

When will Lightfoot stop pretending she doesn't know exactly who Jonah is? I sigh, looking at the ceiling. "Yeah, he knew her."

In the biblical sense, probably. Though I never knew for sure. I didn't ask, because it wouldn't have mattered either way. What mattered was how he held her hand. How he slept in her bed most nights, resting his fingers on her hip bone. The stuff he did with her that he couldn't do with me.

I imagine Dr. Lightfoot's brain working out the details. The *wrong* details, by the way. She probably thinks I only wanted Jonah because Agnes had him.

"Just so you know, I liked him before he got involved with Agnes. I liked him as soon as we met." I hate the way my voice sounds more childish with every word. I sound like a little girl protesting, rambling, trying to cover her tracks. "I met him before Agnes met him."

She *can't* take the cafeteria away from me. Next thing I know, it'll be no showers. And definitely not the grounds privileges Lightfoot teased me with days ago.

"Hannah, I'm afraid I'm not quite following."

I take my eyes off the ceiling and look at Lightfoot's face. My psychiatrist looks genuinely confused.

Maybe she really doesn't know about Jonah.

Come to think of it, I don't remember Agnes telling her parents about him in all the phone calls I overheard. Maybe they wouldn't have approved of her having a boyfriend. Maybe they were the kind of parents who didn't let their daughter date, who wanted her to focus on her responsibilities at home and at school. Maybe they thought Agnes was still their sweet, little girl who'd never been kissed.

No wonder they didn't like me. The girl from the big city. The bad influence.

Well, it's time they knew the truth about Agnes. She fell for Jonah all on her own. I had nothing to do with it. It was the last thing I wanted.

"Jonah was Agnes's boyfriend. They were together all summer."

Lightfoot blinks, crossing and uncrossing her legs again. (Female praying mantises eat their mates. Just saying.) "I thought Agnes's boyfriend's name was Matt."

I shake my head. "No, *Jonah*." I try to imagine someone mistaking Jonah's name for Matt. *Matt* sounds like a boy with blond hair and blue eyes, the sort who plays football and wears and letterman jacket. Nothing like Jonah with his tawny hair and hazel fox-eyes, who spends his weekends hiking in the woods and shuns team sports.

"But," Lightfoot continues, "how could you have met him? Matt lived back in North Dakota. He didn't come out west to visit until Agnes was in the hospital."

Agnes had a boyfriend back home? *Another* boyfriend?

I can't let Lightfoot see that I didn't know about Matt. Can't let her see there were secrets Agnes didn't tell me. Lightfoot will use it against me: She'll think Agnes and I weren't as close as I said we were. That weren't really best friends. That Agnes didn't trust me with her deepest, darkest secrets, like the fact that she was cheating on her boyfriend with Jonah.

Lightfoot will think I've been lying.

My whole defense rests on the fact that Agnes and I were best friends. That Agnes loved me.

Trusted me.

Wasn't at all frightened of me.

Lightfoot adds, "Apparently, Matt and Agnes were inseparable back home. They'd been together since seventh grade."

Were they *joined at the hip* too?

Actually, this is all starting to make sense. I just need to put the pieces together:

Obviously, Matt was the guy she'd started dating prepuberty. The guy who'd never leave North Dakota, the guy her parents wanted her to marry, the guy who would knock her up and lock her down.

You can't imagine how trapped you feel. Your whole life is waiting to get out. Not knowing if you ever will.

I told Agnes she'd get out. *Girls like you don't stay in one place for the rest of their lives.*

When you say it, I actually believe it.

She'd probably wanted to end it with Matt for years. She

166

just didn't have the courage to acknowledge it until she met me.

Then she cheated on him with Jonah, who was nothing like Matt. And of course, she couldn't tell her parents. They never would have approved.

And all this time I thought Jonah and I were the cheaters, the liars, the ones who were sneaking around.

I look squarely at Lightfoot. "Jonah was in the summer program with us. His room was down the hall from ours. Jonah Wyatt."

The doctor nods. She doesn't say so, but I know she's planning to look into it. She'll look Jonah up. Call him. Call his parents. Get to the bottom of this.

That may be true, she said, like the truth was beside the point. Well, who's the liar now?

Stephen clears his throat from his position in the doorway.

"Time's up." I nod at Lightfoot's bodyguard. I wonder whose idea it was that he accompany her from one patient's room to the next. Does the hospital insist on his presence, insurance after some kind of incident? Or maybe Lightfoot asked for him because she's scared of her patients. Maybe when she went to medical school, she thought she'd end up working with patients whose parents and teachers sent them to therapy for issues like their parents' divorce or the stress of getting into an Ivy League college—nice, smart girls, easy cases. Maybe Lightfoot thought she'd have an office with wood paneling and built-in bookshelves and that her patients would be the kind of girls who didn't require security guards. Good troubled girls, not bad troubled girls.

Now it turns out Agnes wasn't so good after all.

Agnes can't play the innocent victim with two boyfriends. The whole Matt-Agnes-Jonah love triangle could help my case. Judges and juries are easily swayed by this sort of thing, especially when it comes to teenage girls. (Double standard and all that, but at least it might play in my favor.)

Not that any of this will ever go to trial. But it's good to have some new ammunition, just in case.

twenty-seven

I can't sleep. If I complain, they'll probably give me sleeping pills. I'm surprised they haven't already. In the movies, patients in places like this always take pills. Pills in the morning, pills at night, pills at random hours in between. Blue pills, yellow pills, white pills. Chalky pills and long slim capsules. Pills to take on an empty stomach. Pills to take with food.

In the cafeteria at lunchtime (back when I still had cafeteria privileges), I watched orderlies distribute pills in little, white paper cups to some of the patients. Some girls had to open their mouths and stick out their tongues to prove they swallowed.

If someone refused to take her pills, the orderly stood over her with his hands on his hips.

If she still refused, the orderly reminded her that they could give her an injectable dose of the drug instead.

If she continued to refuse—the orderlies would sigh as if to say, *Why can't these girls see reason? A pill is so much less invasive than a shot*—then the girl was led away, sometimes peacefully, sometimes kicking and screaming.

The orderlies don't understand that a pill can be more invasive than a shot. Taking the pill implies that it's your *choice*. Willingness to swallow what they hand you suggests that you agree with them: there's something wrong with you; you need to take your medicine.

If they force a shot on you, at least you're taking a stand. At least they haven't made you believe there's something wrong with you.

"What's the matter?" Lucy mutters from her side of the room.

"I thought you were sleeping."

"With all that tossing and turning over there?"

"I can't sleep."

"No kidding." Lucy rolls over to face me, the rise of her hip silhouetted in the darkness. "Why not?"

Agnes and I used to do this. I mean, not *this*, not being locked in a room unable to control whether the lights were on and off. But we'd stay up nights, talking in the dark when everyone else was asleep.

What's it like to be an only child?

Dunno. I've never been anything else.

Me either. I mean, I've never been an only child.

That's not true. You were an only child for four years before your little sister was born.

Agnes has two little sisters, Cara (four years younger than Agnes and I) and Lizzy (seven years younger than Agnes and I).

Wait, proper grammar. Cara is four years younger than Agnes and *me*.

I don't remember what it felt like to be the only kid in the house.

C'mon, you must remember something.

Agnes closed her eyes. It was too dark for me to see the patch of freckles behind her ear, but I imagined her hair falling across it. *I remember climbing into my parents' bed after I had a bad dream. Right in between them.*

You never did that after your sister was born?

She slept in their room at first. I couldn't risk waking the baby.

Her voice sounded different. She'd had to become so selfless at four years old, had to train herself not to cry if she had a bad dream because it might disturb her baby sister.

Agnes loved her sisters. But I was the only person who knew she also resented them sometimes.

I couldn't join the soccer team because practice was after school, and after school I had to take care of Cara and Lizzy until my mom got home from work.

I couldn't make weekend plans without making sure my mom didn't need a babysitter.

Once when I was babysitting, I heard a loud thump from upstairs, and Cara started wailing. I counted to sixty before I went to her room just to see if she'd stop crying on her own. Agnes's voice dropped to a whisper. *When I finally went upstairs, I saw that she'd fallen out of bed. Her arm was twisted in this wacky direction. She'd broken it.* Agnes bit her lip, tears brimming in her clear blue eyes. *I never told anyone that. That I waited sixty seconds.*

How could she tell me so much while never once mentioning Matt, the boyfriend back home everyone else seemed to know about?

Lucy sighs. "If you're going to keep me awake with all that noise, the least you can do is answer my question."

"What was your question?" I already forgot. Or maybe I wasn't listening to her to begin with.

"Why can't you sleep?"

"I'm thinking about my friend."

"Which friend?"

I haven't told Lucy about Agnes. She doesn't know why I'm here. My reasons aren't as self-evident as hers.

"I made this new friend over the summer. Agnes Smith. From North Dakota." Now I've told Lucy about Jonah and Agnes. Not everything about them, but at least Lucy can say she knows they exist. That's more than Agnes did for me where Matt was concerned.

"Why are you thinking about her?"

I don't answer right away. Agnes *must* have told me about Matt. Maybe I forgot after everything that happened with Jonah.

No. I wouldn't have forgotten. I would have remembered how greedy she was, taking Jonah when she had Matt back at home.

Selfish. Nothing like the girl who kept quiet so her baby sister could sleep.

Maybe Agnes enjoyed being someone else for the summer. Someone who didn't have to babysit (she convinced her parents to let her go away for the summer because Cara was finally old enough to watch Lizzy), someone who hadn't only kissed one boy (Lightfoot said Agnes and Matt had been together since seventh grade, surely Agnes hadn't kissed anyone before that), someone whose best friend lived in New York City, whose boyfriend lived in Washington State, someone who was going to live someplace else someday.

I'd feel sorry for her if I wasn't so angry at her.

"Why are you thinking about Agnes?" Lucy asks again.

"I think she might have kept a secret from me."

"Everyone has secrets," Lucy says, as though it's no big deal. I picture her shrugging in the darkness.

"I thought she told me everything."

I hear Lucy shift in her bed. The sheets in this place are so thin and cheap they crinkle when we move.

"Did you tell her everything?" Lucy asks. I don't answer.

"I guess nobody tells anyone everything," Lucy says finally. She makes it sound perfectly normal, as though the things we don't tell each other aren't actually *secrets*; they're simply pieces of information we happen to leave out. Like accidents.

"I guess not," I agree.

twenty-eight

Dr. Lightfoot makes a big deal of sitting down for our next session. I don't mean she sits with a flourish, I mean she takes her time: unfolding the chair, lowering herself into it, crossing her legs at the ankles and then tucking them up beneath the chair, arranging her clipboard on her lap and reaching up to adjust her glasses. Then she must remember she's not wearing glasses (*patient may pose a danger to herself and others*), she's wearing contacts, so she blinks. She licks her lips and swallows.

Apparently my doctor has something to say that she suspects I'm not going to like. I can't tell whether she's taking her time telling me whatever it is because she's dreading my reaction or because she's savoring the moment, enjoying the fact that she knows something I don't. I glance at Lucy, who's watching all this from behind Lightfoot's back. She winks at me as if to say, *Who cares what Lightfoot says anyway?*

I hate to admit it, but I care. I care because I need Lightfoot on my side whenever we finally meet with the judge.

The doctor begins. "The boy you mentioned yesterday—Jonah Wyatt?"

"What about him?"

"I reached out to Agnes's parents last night, and they said they'd never heard of him."

Jeez, that's what all her fanfare was about? I mean, how stupid can Lightfoot be? Of *course* Agnes hid her relationship with Jonah from her parents. She was cheating on her all-American, parent-approved boyfriend back home. Who wouldn't?

I shrug. "She's keeping the relationship a secret."

"Agnes is hardly in a position to keep secrets anymore," Lightfoot points out. She reaches up to adjust her phantom glasses again.

I bite my lip. Actually, Agnes is in a perfect position to keep secrets now. If she never wakes up (has she woken up?), she'll be able to keep all her secrets forever. Instead, I say, "I guess Agnes never told her parents about him."

"That's what I thought at first too, but then I reached out to a few other students who lived in the dorm with you both. None of them knew Jonah either. In fact, they all agreed that Agnes didn't have a boyfriend here in California."

"They're protecting her. You know, because of her boyfriend back home. Matt." Wait, but I didn't know about Matt. (Did I? No. Right?) What are the odds that Agnes told the other kids in our dorm if she didn't tell me?

"That would make sense," Dr. Lightfoot says slowly, softly. Like she feels sorry for me. Like she's building up to sharing something else she suspects I won't want to hear. "Hannah, I requested the records from your summer program, and there was no Jonah Wyatt listed as living in your dormitory."

"Maybe he lived in another dorm," I suggest, even though I know perfectly well he didn't. He lived right down the hall, on the boys' side of the floor. That's how they divided us: girls on one side, boys on the other. Someone told me that during the school year when the real college students live there, the dorm rooms alternate—boy, girl, boy, girl—but since we were all still in high school, they thought it'd be better to space us out more. Not that it kept anyone from bed-hopping.

"I thought the same thing, but then I searched further and discovered that there was no Jonah Wyatt registered for classes at the university this summer."

"Maybe he was…" Maybe he was what? Auditing classes? Squatting?

Lightfoot nods sympathetically. (They probably taught her that in med school too.) "If Jonah was who you say he was, wouldn't he have visited Agnes in the hospital by now?"

I shake my head. "Like you said, Agnes's parents didn't know about him. So they couldn't have called to tell him what happened. And I didn't have a chance to tell him myself before I was brought here either."

"But wouldn't Jonah have heard what happened from your classmates in the dormitory? The summer program lasted another week or two after you came here."

"You just said he didn't live in the dormitory."

"Right." Lightfoot gives me another med-school nod. "But *you* said he did." Her face twists with pity. No; it's more than pity. She thinks she knows more than I do, and she's waiting for me to understand it too.

Well, I understand everything. I understand that Dr. Lightfoot is lying to me, playing some kind of game, enjoying a sick power trip. Maybe she's still mad at me for getting locked out of my room the other day. Maybe she wants to remind me that *she's* the one in control, that as long as I'm in this room, the truth is whatever she decides it is. If *she* says Jonah didn't live in our dorm or attend classes, I'm powerless to prove otherwise because *she* makes the rules, *she's* the one calling my classmates and the school for evidence, not me.

Well, screw that. I mean, seriously, she can take away showers and cafeteria lunches and keep me in this room, but now she's trying to take *Jonah* away? Lightfoot may be in charge of my life inside this place, but she doesn't get to take away the life I had before I came here.

I'll throw more than a chair this time. I grip the edge of the bed, then remember it's nailed to the floor. I glance at the window. I'm so angry that I actually believe I could smash it with my bare hands, climb the eff out of here, and go home. I'd find Jonah myself and bring him back here just long enough to prove Lightfoot wrong, then run away and never come back. I ball my hands into fists in front of me like I'm ready to fight my way out of here.

The instant I stand, Stephen's arms are wrapped around me.

When did he get so close? I can't move. There's nothing nice about being held like this, nothing that remotely resembles a hug, an embrace, an act of affection. My arms are pinned to my sides. Despite my very limited mobility I'm completely out of breath, sweating as though I sprinted here all the way from San Francisco.

"It's all right." Lightfoot stands, kicking her chair toward the door. "I'll give you a sedative to help you calm down."

I try to shake my head, but I can't even move that much. I want to scream, shout, but I can't catch my breath. Am I crying? Why can't I get the words out?

There's a prick in my arm. (Where did that come from? Does Lightfoot always keep a needle in her pocket just in case?) Almost immediately, I slump in Stephen's arms.

"You can loosen your hold, Stephen." Lightfoot's still speaking in that pitying voice that's probably supposed to be soothing but it only makes me angrier. Or, it would be making me angrier if she hadn't just shot me up with whatever medication she shot me up with.

I don't like how it feels to be sedated. I know I'm angry, but I can't quite *feel* it, like there's a barrier between me and my emotions.

Stephen lowers me onto the bed. The sheets wrinkle beneath me. The springs dig into my back. I want to roll over but I can't. Lightfoot stands over me.

"I've suspected this for some time," she begins gently. "Hannah, I know this is hard to hear, but I believe Jonah was a hallucination."

How can she have suspected this for some time? She didn't even know about Jonah until yesterday.

Liar, liar, pants on fire.

My mouth feels sticky. I can't speak. Lightfoot reaches out and brushes tears off my cheeks.

I'm not crying anymore. I'm not *anything* anymore.

"Your brain invented Jonah," Lightfoot explains, as though I might not know the definition of the word hallucination. She sits on the edge of the bed. I feel her hip against my arm, limp at my side.

If my muscles didn't feel like soup, I'd shake my head. If my brain were going to invent a boy, why would it invent Jonah, a boy I had to share? A boy who picked someone else.

Not that my brain would invent anyone. I mean, I'm not naive—I know some people have diseases and imbalances that make their brains do that. People who hear voices and see things that aren't there. But I'm not one of *those* people.

"I'd like to try putting you on a course of antipsychotics."

Antipsychotic sounds like *antibiotic*. Like Jonah is a virus we need to eliminate.

Psychotic. How is it that I never realized the word *psycho* must have originated with *psychotic*? I imagine someone in a place like this a couple hundred years ago—an orderly or a nurse—randomly abbreviating the word to refer to one of her patients. I bet she had no idea it would catch on the way it did.

*Anti*psychotic. Anti means one that is opposed. I studied word origins for the SATs.

Lightfoot wants to use pills to oppose the psycho.

"I'd like you to take the medication willingly," Lightfoot continues, "so I'll give you some time to think about it."

The words she doesn't say are clear: It doesn't matter what I decide. She'll force me to take the medication if she has to. I'm under eighteen; if my parents consent, I'm taking it. And even if they don't consent, Lightfoot could probably get the judge to agree to it. I think of the girls in the cafeteria, the ones who take their medication obediently, and the ones who kick and scream. Which will I be?

"I'll come back to check on you later." The bed squeaks as Lightfoot stands. She nods at Stephen. I can't turn my neck, but I imagine he's holding the door open for her. (Such a gentleman, the man who practically assaulted me moments ago.) I hear the magnetic click as the door locks behind them, leaving me alone in this tiny room.

No. Not alone. Lucy is here. I manage to flop my neck to the side so I can see my roommate sitting on her own bed. She's holding a book—a romance novel we've both read three times each—and looking at me.

Does Lucy believe Dr. Lightfoot? Does she think that Jonah was nothing more than a hallucination?

"I'm sorry," Lucy says "I thought if I tried to stop them, it would've made things worse."

She's right. They might have sedated her too. Maybe they would've separated us.

At least the look on Lucy's face is nothing like the look on

Lightfoot's. She doesn't pity me. She hates this place as much as I do.

Lucy doesn't believe Dr. Lightfoot. She believes *me*.

twenty-nine

Hours later, after lights-out, the sedative is still coursing through my veins, but my muscles feel less like soup and more like Jell-O. I imagine them jiggling all on their own, my organs like pieces of fruit suspended in the gelatin. My tongue feels sticky, one size too large for my mouth.

My limbs might be rubber, but my brain is still my own. *I* control my brain. I *am* my brain. My brain is *me*. That's all we are, right? Everything we think and feel, every habit and movement, every personality trait and quirk: It's all a result of our brains. Maybe it's nature, maybe it's nurture—but whoever we are, we are because our brains are what they are. People talk about their hearts (*my heart broke, my heart sank, my heart healed*), but our brains are in control. When we fall in love, it's a chemical reaction in our brains, not our hearts. The heart's just a muscle. Even when our hearts pound because we're scared or nervous or excited— that's our *brains* telling our hearts to do that. If a heart stops working, doctors can even replace it with another one, a trans- plant from a stranger's dead body. When a heart won't beat, EMTs can perform compressions or shock it back to life with electricity. But once a person's brain-dead, there's no coming back.

I *know* my brain. My brain wouldn't *invent* a person.

Jonah was real. I felt the callus on his right thumb from his guitar-playing. ("It's only a phase," he promised me. "I'm not going to be one of those guitar-playing douchebags in college.") I ran my fingers through his tawny hair, felt the crunch of too much hair gel, and convinced him to use less. I felt the weight of his body on mine, the press of his lips against mine, the stubble on his cheeks against my skin. I even fought with him.

Admit it. You care about Agnes more than you care about me. We were walking back from class together, careful to keep our voices down so passersby wouldn't overhear.

Come on, Hannah. You know *I care about her.*

That infuriated me. He admitted to caring but wouldn't say how much.

You care about her too, he added. *If you didn't care, you'd have told her about us. But you do, so you haven't, just like I haven't.*

That's some pretty serious sentence construction you've got there, I said. The sun was so bright I had to squint to look up at him. My mother would have scolded me for not wearing sunglasses; squinting was a surefire way to develop wrinkles. Jonah stopped walking, so I did too.

He smiled. *You said that the day we met.*

I smiled back. *I know.* We walked the rest of the way to the dorm in silence, the backs of our hands brushing against each other.

If Dr. Lightfoot thinks that was all a hallucination, then *she's* the crazy one.

There's got to be an explanation for everything Lightfoot said today. Maybe Jonah registered for the summer program under a different name—maybe Jonah is actually his middle name, so he was registered under his legal first name but never mentioned it because he's always gone by Jonah. Or maybe after Agnes's accident, he never went back to the dorms, and since he didn't technically finish the program, they took his name off the registry.

Or maybe I had it right the first time: Lightfoot is lying just to mess with me.

My heartbeat is steady and slow, but my palms are sweaty and my hair sticks to the back of my neck. I've never wanted to pull my hair into a ponytail so badly. Not that I could, even if I had an elastic, with the sedative still in effect.

The bed squeaks. I exhale as the mattress dips under Lucy's weight. She reaches up and brushes my hair off my face with her fingers, twists it into a bun on top of my head. She adjusts my pillow. I feel a breeze from the AC vent above on the back of my neck.

"I'm not crazy," I manage to say. Thanks to the sedative, the words come slowly.

"I know that," Lucy says.

"Jonah wasn't a hallucination."

It's dark, but I can see Lucy nod. I exhale. Lucy understands. She's locked up in this place too. "Maybe you should take the antipsychotics," Lucy suggests gently, lying down beside me.

"What?" I can't make my voice sound as angry as I want it to. I'm hot again. I hate being hot. I hate being so sedated that I can't kick off the covers Lightfoot pulled over me before she left. I hate that a lump is rising in my throat, and I can't swallow it away no matter how hard I try.

I've never felt so powerless.

"It's not that I don't believe you, but we both know she's going to make you take them whether you want to or not. They make me take antidepressants even though I'm not depressed."

"They do?" I've never seen her take a pill.

Lucy nods. "Every day at lunch. They make all the E.D. girls take them."

"Why?"

We're lying so close that I can feel Lucy's shoulders rise and fall when she shrugs.

"They think everyone with an eating disorder is depressed. Like the E.D. is a symptom of a larger problem. They never believe me when I tell them I just want to be skinny enough to dance."

"They don't understand anything."

"No," Lucy agrees. "They don't."

"And they don't listen to us." Vaguely, I remember reading about a study where a group of perfectly sane physicians had themselves committed so they could better understand what their patients went through. The doctors and nurses and orderlies didn't believe the physicians when they claimed to be sane; they were treated just as badly as the real patients.

I sigh heavily. "Like you said, she's going to force the medication on me no matter what I say."

"But if you take the pills voluntarily," Lucy counters firmly, "it will show Lightfoot that you're not afraid of her and her theories about you. It will show her that you're confident. That you know your own mind better than she ever could."

I hadn't thought of it that way. But I don't want them to change my brain. I think of the girls in the cafeteria, silently nodding along to Queen Bee's decrees. "I don't want to become one of those zombie-girls."

Lucy puts her arm around me. "I'm willing to bet there's not a pill in the world strong enough to turn you into one of them."

I try to smile, but I can't—and not because of the sedative. It's because I know Lucy's lying and she does too. She squeezes me tighter.

"Anyway, that's not the kind of pill they're going to give you, right?"

"Right." I close my eyes and try to imagine it: a nurse handing me a paper cup filled with pills. (How many? Two? Three? One jagged half? I have no idea what my dose would be.) What color are the pills? What shape will they be? I gulp and imagine a pill sliding down my throat. Will they be easy to swallow or will I almost choke? Will they feel like the lump I get in my throat when I'm trying not to cry?

"Go on the antipsychotics," Lucy urges. "Prove Lightfoot wrong."

thirty

When I agree to take the antipsychotics, Lightfoot looks pleased, like I'm a puppy who learned to go to the bathroom outside after months of accidents on the living room carpet.

She hands me two pills and explains that she's starting me on a low dose. She had the medication with her, so clearly she was planning on giving it to me whether I offered to take it or not.

I want to ask her if the low dose means she thinks I'm only mildly psychotic, but I don't. I go on being a good puppy, put the pills in my mouth, and swallow them with the water she hands me. (She brought that along with her too. I wonder what else she keeps in her pockets. Probably a syringe filled with more sedatives and another with the antipsychotics in case I put up a fight over taking them orally. Isn't it foolish to keep stuff like that in your pockets when you're in a room with a girl you think may be *a danger to herself and others*?)

"These will take a few days—even a few weeks—to kick in. It might take some time to feel the full effect." Lightfoot smiles at me, that same pitying smile from yesterday. If I still had water in my mouth, I'd spit it right in her face to get that stupid look off it.

After Lightfoot leaves, I stare out the window. Lucy isn't here. She's at art therapy. That means it's a Monday. Or a Wednesday. Or a Friday. It doesn't matter. For thousands of years, human beings lived without keeping track of the days of the week. In fact, when they did introduce days of the week, it was probably for religious purposes, so they'd know when Sunday was to take a day of rest. Or Saturday, if you're Jewish, which I am, though my family isn't very religious, so we never observed the Sabbath from sunset on Friday until sunset on Saturday.

Anyway, the point is, for hundreds of years, human beings would have tracked the passage of time by the change in the weather, the summer fading into fall, into winter, into spring. They knew when one day ended and another began because of the sunrise and sunset, not because they were charting dates on a calendar.

Of course, years ago, people also didn't know that it wasn't the sun rising and setting that caused daylight and darkness, but the Earth spinning on its axis. They probably thought that people who saw things that weren't really there were witches and wizards. Instead of medicating them, maybe they venerated them. Or maybe they shunned them.

I rest my chin on the windowsill. It's not really a sill, just a frame around the square-shaped window that's only about twice the size of my head. Lucy's bobby pin is still here, so small and plain that you'd never notice it unless you knew it was there. I gaze outside and wonder what the hell is going on inside my head.

At least for a few more days—*even a few weeks*—my brain will stay the same.

The leaves are changing color. Unlike back home, the leaves here turn brown instead of bursting into color. It looks like everything is dying.

Dr. Lightfoot didn't say how we'd know when the meds kick in. Jonah isn't here, so it's not like he could—*poof!*—vanish into thin air.

And just because Lightfoot couldn't find him, doesn't mean Jonah isn't real.

I mean, if Jonah were a hallucination, wouldn't my brain have brought him here with me to keep me company? Wouldn't my brain have made him the perfect boyfriend, like Lucy and Joaquin?

But if he were real, wouldn't Lightfoot have found him? Wouldn't the Smiths? Wouldn't the *police* have found him? He should have been called as a witness in the case, interviewed, his statement taken. His name would be all over Lightfoot's files.

When Lucy comes back to the room, I'm lying in bed pretending they sedated me again. I don't feel like talking. I don't feel like thinking, either. Thinking means doubting, and doubting means Lightfoot has gotten under my skin like a rash that won't stop spreading. Doubt means I'm beginning to believe what she says about me. I wish there were an antidoubt drug I could take instead of whatever Lightfoot gave me.

A nurse shows up the next morning, along with our break-fast. She hands me a little paper cup with my pills—turns out they're blue and chalky, but small so they're easy to swallow. Other than their voices trilling, *Room check*, I haven't interacted much with the nurses here. This woman has long, black hair plaited neatly down her back, and she's wearing papery scrubs like Lightfoot's, though hers are peach. The color flatters her. I think April Lu (Rebekah-with-a-K's former best friend) would probably look good in that color, too. But April has hated me since eighth grade, so she'd surely ignore my advice, however helpful it might be.

At lunchtime, they open the door and lead Lucy and me to the cafeteria.

I don't plan to sit next to QB, I just do.

I don't plan to beg to use her phone, I just do.

I'm going to text my mom. I'm going to tell her that they're putting me on medication, and she has to find a way to get me out of here. I'll tell her that I've been kept in near-solitary confinement since they brought me here. It's not entirely true—not anymore—but surely that will be enough to get her atten-tion, to make her come rescue me.

"No way," QB says.

"Why not?"

"The last time you used it, we almost got caught."

"No, we didn't." I would stomp my foot, but it wouldn't do

much to emphasize the point when I'm wearing slippers. "I promise to make it worth your while."

QB folds her arms across her chest. "How?"

"When I get out of here, I'll—"

QB starts laughing before I can offer anything.

"Do you really think I'm such a sucker that I'd say yes any time someone promised to do something for me *when I get out of here*?" She shakes her head. I hate the way she's talking to me like she's so much older and wiser than I am, but all QBs do that. "Believe me, sweetheart, once you get out of here, you're not gonna look back. No one does. At least, not until they get sent back here, and then they don't have a choice." She cocks her head to the side. "Besides, from what I heard, you're not getting out any time soon."

My hands are cold. "What are you talking about?"

"Word is, they put you on antipsychotics." She holds her pointer finger level to her ear and twirls it, a kindergartner's taunt.

"How do you know that?"

She shrugs. "How do I have a phone?"

Jeez, haven't they heard of doctor-patient confidentiality even in a place like this? Then I remember: Of course not. I literally have therapy in front of another patient half the time. I shake my head, then realize it's not only my head that's shaking. I'm trembling. Not with fear. Not with cold. I'm angry.

I don't plan to do it; I just do.

I reach for QB's shirt and try to grab her phone. She's quiet at first. She doesn't want to draw attention to what's happening.

Her phone would get confiscated if the wrong person saw. But when she tries to tug her shirt out of my grip, I pull so hard that it rips right up the middle—and it's not a papery shirt like the one I'm wearing. QB wears her own pajamas. She starts to scream.

The attendants move so fast I don't see them coming. They pull us apart, and a needle jabs into my upper arm.

The familiar sensation of the sedative takes hold.

thirty-one

When Lightfoot comes for our afternoon session, I'm lying in bed. I feel like I weigh two hundred pounds.

The doctor stands over me. "I hear you had a run-in with Cassidy."

Cassidy? I think. *That's Queen Bee's name?* That's the kind of name they gave queen bees in the eighties and nineties. Watch any old movie, and you'll see.

"We confiscated her phone," Lightfoot adds. Apparently even the orderlies she had wrapped around her finger weren't willing to risk their jobs for her, so they turned her in. I don't feel bad. If QB isn't willing to share her toys, she shouldn't get to keep them.

Eventually, some new orderly will start working here, and Cassidy will work her QB magic on him. She'll get another phone. Girls like her always do.

"How did you know she had a phone?"

I shrug. The sedative hasn't worn off, but it's been long enough (or maybe it was a lower dose) that I'm able to move a little. I'm able to speak.

"Annie told me, I think. I don't remember for sure." I'm not lying.

"Cassidy says you used it before."

"She's lying." Good thing I deleted the text I sent to Joaquin.

"Somebody's lying," Lightfoot replies. I bet they taught her that in medical school too. Don't outright accuse your patient of lying. But let her know when you think she might be. *That may be true.*

"Well, it's her word against mine then, isn't it?"

Lightfoot nods. "I guess it is." She tucks her dark hair behind her ears, adjusts the invisible glasses over her brown eyes. "She was very upset."

Of course she was, I think with sarcasm. QBs are usually good at getting authority figures to feel sorry for them.

"You're not the only one who was impacted by your actions. An incident like this could influence Cassidy's recovery as well." Lightfoot sits on her chair beside the bed. I turn my head so I can see her.

"Cassidy doesn't care about recovering."

"What do you mean?" she asks.

"She doesn't want to go home." She likes it better here.

Lightfoot shakes her head. "I can't go into details, but let me assure you that Cassidy and I have been working very hard together so that she can go home."

I shrug. "That's just what she wants you to think."

Lightfoot pauses. "Perhaps," she concedes. "Or it could be the exact opposite."

Now it's my turn to ask, "What do you mean?"

"Perhaps she wants *you* to think she doesn't care about her recovery, that she doesn't care about going home."

"Why would she care what I think of her?"

"Do you care what she thinks of you?"

I shrug again, though the answer is yes.

"Maybe she doesn't want you to see her vulnerabilities any more than you would want her to see yours."

Lightfoot's plastic chair sways a little when she stands, but it doesn't topple over. I turn to face the ceiling instead of my doctor.

"I know this is an enormous adjustment for you." Lightfoot's voice is gentle, like I'm a wild animal she doesn't want to startle. "I want you to know that I haven't lost faith in you because of this incident."

I didn't know she had faith in me to begin with. She's the one who thinks I'm crazy.

"You'll still be permitted to shower this afternoon, though not with the other girls."

I never got to shower with the other girls, but Lightfoot says it like it's a privilege I lost.

"And, if you keep up the good work," (*Good?* I got into a fight this afternoon. I guess taking the pills willingly overrides that. And apparently sitting around waiting for the antipsychotics to take effect qualifies as *work*), "I'll grant you walks on the grounds," she says. "Won't that be nice?" she adds when I don't respond.

I think Lightfoot and I have different definitions of the word *nice*.

This place is a prison no matter how many privileges you earn. It gets bigger when you're allowed to leave the room, leave the building—but a cage is a cage is a cage. Anyway, if I'm as sick as Lightfoot thinks I am, maybe the grounds will look different once the antipsychotics take effect. Maybe the leaves on the trees aren't turning brown after all. Maybe there aren't any leaves at all. Maybe it's not even September. Maybe it's the dead of winter. December, January, February.

If I could hallucinate a person like Dr. Lightfoot says, then surely I could hallucinate the season.

"What's today's date?" I ask, feeling desperate.

"September nineteenth." The last time I asked Lightfoot to tell me the date, she refused. I guess that's another privilege taking the meds earned me.

September nineteenth. I knew that. September fifteenth was Lucy's audition. That was four days ago.

After dinner but before lights out, the nurse with the long braid comes back with another pill. This one is yellow, even smaller than the antipsychotics.

"What's this?"

"It'll help you sleep."

A sleeping pill shouldn't be yellow. It should be blue or green or purple. Yellow is the color of the daytime. "They never gave me anything to help me sleep before."

"The medication you're taking can affect your sleeping patterns."

"I've been sleeping fine."

The nurse's expression shifts. She narrows her eyes. "Are we going to have a problem here?"

"Because I'm asking questions?"

"It seems to me you're trying to avoid taking your medication."

"I just don't think I need *this* medication."

"Having a consistent sleep schedule is important for someone with your condition."

What *condition* does she think I have exactly? I don't ask because apparently this woman considers questions problems, and Nurse Ratched looks like she's one problem away from calling someone like Stephen to force the medicine down my throat.

Nurse Ratched is a character in a movie from the seventies that my dad loves called *One Flew Over the Cuckoo's Nest*. It was a book too. I never saw the movie or read the book, but my dad used to refer to someone as a Nurse Ratched whenever he thought that someone was being needlessly rude—when a chef refused his request for a substitution at a nice restaurant, when a concierge wouldn't grant him an upgrade from a deluxe-suite to a supreme. The movie was about being trapped in a mental institution; I wonder if my dad has rewatched it since I got sent here. I wonder if he still loves it. I wonder if he'll still refer to it the next time a chef refuses to substitute brussels sprouts for broccoli.

When the nurse holds out the pill again, I take it. It gets caught in my throat, and I cough so much that my eyes fill with tears.

She slides a latex glove on one of her hands. "Open your mouth," the nurse says when I finally catch my breath.

"Huh?"

"Open your mouth." I do. "Now stick out your tongue." I do. She takes my tongue between her fingers, pulling it from one side of my mouth to the other, then lifting it so she can see what's beneath it. "Good," she says finally. Her glove snaps when she takes it off.

I slide my tongue back in my mouth where it belongs.

"You didn't do that this morning," I point out.

"You didn't give me any problems this morning," she counters. Then she adds, "Sleep well," with false cheer, as if she didn't just stick her fingers in my mouth.

The lights go off a few seconds after she closes the door behind her. I get into bed.

From her side of the room, Lucy calls the nurse a name my mother would hate. Mom doesn't like insults that have a gendered connotation. If she were here, my mother would tell Lucy, *Just call a woman a jerk. That's what you'd call a man.*

But my mother isn't here, so I repeat Lucy's insult out loud before the yellow pill puts me to sleep.

thirty-two

I should be counting: How many days I've been taking the medication. How many blue pills I've swallowed, and how many yellow (though I've since decided they look more beige than yellow). But I don't count. I don't know the exact dosage, so what difference does it make?

There are two nurses who bring me pills. One is the horrible woman with the long black hair and the peach scrubs who tells me to stick out my tongue so she knows I've really taken the pills. (She makes me do that every time now, whether I ask questions or not.) The other is a seemingly always-smiling woman with an enormous Afro. Her scrubs are yellow—real yellow, not like the beige-yellow of the sleeping pills—and she always wears red lipstick. She calls me honey, and she never asks me to stick out my tongue. She's younger than the other nurse, so I guess she's not as jaded. Not yet, anyway.

Tonight, Lucy tells me not to swallow the sleeping pill. She has something she wants to tell me.

"I don't have a choice if it's Nurse Ratched," I point out.

Lucy shakes her head. "It won't be."

"How do you know?"

"It's not her night."

At least one of us has been keeping track of the days.

∴

"So, what did you want to tell me?" I ask after lights-out. I spat out the yellow pill and left it to dissolve in my bedpan.

I hear Lucy's papery clothes rustle as she leaves her bed and crosses the room to sit on the edge of mine. My thin mattress dips beneath her weight. "Don't you ever wonder what I did to get sent here?"

"You're bulimic."

"Also anorexic sometimes," Lucy counters defensively. "I hardly ate breakfast today."

"You're right. Sorry." I had to put her leftovers on my tray, so the attendants wouldn't give her a hard time.

"But come on, you know they don't send us to a place like this just for an eating disorder."

I squint in the darkness, trying to see my friend in the moonlight, but it's so dark tonight that I can't even make out her silhouette. Eating disorders are serious. I've read about girls with such severe anorexia that their parents went before judges to have their rights taken away. Girls who are dangerously malnourished might be declared mentally incompetent and sent to places like this by court order. "You're depressed too. At least, they think you are."

"I'm not depressed. And I wasn't depressed before I came here and they pumped me full of antidepressants. I was *angry*."

"I don't think they make pills for that."

Lucy laughs her hoarse laugh. It's not a happy sound. "There was this girl in my ballet company. Rhiannon. Just her name was enough to make her think she was better than everyone else." Lucy shudders with disgust. "She was so skinny. It's not that she didn't have to diet. I mean, she didn't, but that wasn't the worst part."

"What was the worst part?"

"She didn't even *care* about food. She didn't worry about deciding what to eat, whether to have a piece of cake, a sip of a soda, a bowl of pasta. While the rest of us complained about having to give up all the 'bad' food we loved so we could be dancers, Rhiannon shrugged like it was no big deal. To her, it *wasn't* a big deal. She didn't even *want* to eat that stuff." Lucy shifts on the bed, twisting her limbs so she's sitting cross-legged. Her right knee digs into my side, but I don't complain. "It was so easy for this girl. And I hated her."

Lucy stops talking abruptly, like she forgot I was here listening. "What happened?" I prompt.

I pushed her. Not a push, not really. A little tap. Just to see what would happen.

I sit up. Did Lucy say that?

Those are *my* thoughts, *my* memories from the night Agnes fell.

We're getting too old for these games.

Agnes was right. Not that we were too old to play Light

as a Feather, Stiff as a Board. But she also said that you can't really play with only two people. We tried Never Have I Ever, but that was boring because we'd already told each other all of our secrets. (Except for the fact that I was hooking up with Jonah, and Agnes didn't even suspect enough to trick me into admitting it, like, *Never have I ever hooked up with my best friend's boyfriend*.) (And except for the fact that Agnes had a boyfriend back home, and I didn't know enough to trick her into admitting that either.)

When the doctors asked me what happened that night, I told them.

When Agnes's parents asked, I told them too.

I wasn't lying. Really, I wasn't. But I wasn't telling the whole truth either.

I didn't *remember* the whole truth.

We started playing Truth or Dare. We already knew (we thought) each other's truths, so we must have agreed to do mostly dares.

I remember running up and down the hall in my underwear—Agnes must have dared me to do that. It wouldn't have been much of a dare because the hallway was empty, and I'm not shy anyway.

I remember saying, "Dare or dare," to Agnes when it was her turn.

I imagine that she grinned, but maybe she rolled her eyes. Maybe she was bored. She would have answered, "Dare."

Maybe I asked her to do something smaller at first. Maybe the game had been going on for hours by the time I offered her one final dare: "Stand on the window ledge."

I know this much for sure: Our room was on the second floor of the dorm, and our windows looked out over a terra-cotta courtyard. The sills were over a foot wide both inside and out, wide enough that we sometimes sat with our legs hanging out on warm days and never felt the least bit unsafe.

Maybe Agnes didn't want to do it. Maybe she thought I was kidding. Maybe I reminded her that I'd just streaked through a public hallway, and maybe she reminded me it wasn't really streaking because I hadn't been completely naked.

Or maybe Agnes simply shrugged and agreed to do it, because it was easier than arguing with me. Maybe she wanted to get the game over with.

She would have taken off her socks—bare feet are less slippery—and I would have opened the window wide. She'd have had to crouch to get outside. I can picture her standing, pressing her back against the top half of the window, which was closed. Some parts I remember clearly: She held her arms almost perfectly straight. She pressed her hands back so far they were almost reaching back into the room through the open bottom window. Her fingers were balled into fists. There wasn't anything for her to hold on to.

Her knees were almost at my eye level. The outer windowsill was wider than her feet. I don't remember being scared. It didn't look precarious. It was late, but there were lights on in the courtyard.

I can still see the moment she opened her fists and moved her arms out, feeling brave. Her blond hair caught the light. It looked like it was glowing.

Other details I remember distinctly: Agnes losing her balance. My arms reaching out. Her blond hair rising around her head like a golden crown as she falls. The little yelp she made as she hit the ground.

There was nothing light as a feather or stiff as a board about Agnes's descent. She landed feetfirst, but her ankles buckled uselessly beneath her, not strong enough to sustain her weight. She fell forward and her skull hit the courtyard with a crack.

I turned and ran out of the room, dialing 9-1-1 as I rushed down the hallway. I think I almost fell as I ran down the stairs. How ironic that would have been, if both of us fell, one right after the other.

I heard the sirens before I saw the ambulance.

I was crouched beside her in the courtyard. Agnes was crumpled on her side, her cheek pressed against ground. There was blood in her blond hair. I didn't try to move her. I knew you weren't supposed to do that.

By the time the EMTs rushed toward us, a small crowd had gathered, but everyone else hung back.

I rode with her in the ambulance.

I answered their questions as best as I could.

We were playing Truth or Dare.

She fell.

No one had to tell me that Agnes had suffered a brain injury, lapsed into a coma. No one had to tell me that she'd never be the same. No one had to point out that Jonah wouldn't want her like this. I'd known it, felt it in my belly the instant I heard that sound—*crack*.

It wasn't until Agnes's parents showed up and the police came that they asked whether I'd pushed her. I said no. Of *course* I said no. I said I wouldn't have, couldn't have done that.

Agnes's parents didn't believe me.

They didn't ask whether I *wondered* about pushing her.

Not a push, not really. Just a little tap.

The answer would have been no, I didn't wonder. I heard a voice whisper in my ear.

Just to see what would happen.

It sounds like Lucy's voice: deep and hoarse from years of vomiting.

But I didn't know Lucy then.

The voice I heard that night *can't* have been Lucy's.

I open my eyes. "What happened to the girl, Lucy? Rhiannon, the one you pushed?"

Lucy doesn't answer. Her knee isn't jutting into my side anymore. Was I so lost in my own thoughts that I didn't feel her get up and go back to her own bed? I reach my arms out, trying to find her.

"Lucy?" I say again, louder this time, even though there's no need to raise my voice in this tiny room. We can hear each other's whispers even when we're in our own beds.

I get up and cross the room. It's so dark that I can't see Lucy's bed. I hold my hands out in front of me like I'm Frankenstein's monster. I shout Lucy's name. I run my hands along the wall, my fingertips sliding over the nooks and divots of the cheap brick. I lean my head against the window's cold glass to make sure it hasn't opened, that Lucy couldn't have slipped outside. I drop to my knees and crawl on the floor, knock over the pile of romance novels, hit my head on the side of my bed, and then crawl beneath it, groping in the darkness, trying to find where my roommate is hiding. I scream for someone to turn on the lights.

"Lucy!" I shout. Now my voice is hoarse. "Lucy!"

thirty-three

When the lights come on, I'm still screaming.

Lucy!

Lucy!

Lucy!

I'm crying like a little kid, with my face screwed up and my eyes shut tight, but I can tell the lights are on because I see color through my eyelids: red and orange and yellow.

I don't want to open my eyes.

I'm scared of what I'll see.

Actually, I'm scared of what I *won't* see.

Who I won't see.

I feel hands on me. I hear Dr. Lightfoot's voice say, "Put her on the bed, Stephen."

I didn't know Lightfoot and Stephen worked this late. Maybe they stayed late tonight because they knew what was going to happen. Or maybe it's not actually that late. How would I know?

Stephen lifts me up—I was still crouching on the floor—and puts me on the bed. I stay curled in the same position, awkward as a rat on its back. I'm still repeating Lucy's name but more softly now. My throat is so raw that even whispering hurts.

"Should I get a sedative?" It's the first time I've heard Stephen's voice. It's higher pitched than I expected from such a big man. I brace myself for the prick of a needle, the manufactured sense of calm stilling my muscles, if not entirely my brain. Much to my surprise, I *want* it.

"No, I don't think so," Lightfoot answers. "We should let her feel this. This could be a breakthrough for her."

I don't want to feel this. I don't know what *this* is, but I know I don't like it. Numbness has never been so appealing. For the first time in my sober life—never a drink when the other kids were partying, never so much as a puff off a joint or a cigarette—I want drugs. I want something, *anything*, to dull what I'm feeling.

"Hannah," Lightfoot says, sitting on the edge of my bed (where Lucy sat). "Hannah, can you hear me?"

Of course I can hear her. "What did you do with her?" I whimper.

"With who?"

"With whom," I correct irritably. My throat hurts. "Jesus Christ, *with whom*. Didn't they teach you anything in medical school?"

"Not grammar," Lightfoot answers, and even with my eyes closed, I know she's smiling. When I first got here, she'd have marked my grammatical correctness in her notes as a symptom. But now—now that she feels sorry for me, feels superior to me, feels like she understands me better than I understand myself— it's nothing more than a cute affectation.

I hate Dr. Lightfoot. I open my eyes and spring to my feet.

"With Lucy!" I search the room once more, practically climbing the wall to look out the window, as though Lucy might have made herself small enough to squeeze her way out. "What did you do with *Lucy*?"

Stephen moves to grab me, but Lightfoot holds up her hand, stopping him.

"Who's Lucy?" Lightfoot asks. Her voice is annoyingly calm, like she's trying to soothe a mad dog.

"My roommate," I answer hoarsely.

"Your roommate's name was Agnes."

"Not that roommate. *This* roommate." I hold out my arms, gesturing to the room around me. "Lucy Quintana. Ballet dancer and bulimic."

"Hannah, you haven't had a roommate here." She cocks her head to the side like she thinks I'm dumb: *Why would we have given you a roommate when we said you were a danger to yourself and others?*

I shake my head. Lucy was *here*. I felt her weight on my bed. Smelled her hair when she sat close.

"Hannah." Lightfoot holds her hands out in front of her as she walks toward me, guarding herself against me. "You've been on the antipsychotics for several days. They've had time to take effect."

"What are you saying?" I can barely get the words out.

"I think you know what I'm saying."

I shake my head again, but this time I can't stop. I can't stop shaking. My hands, my teeth, my chin: everything trembles, everything chatters. Why do they make it so cold in this godforsaken place?

Lucy was *here*. Lucy was *real*. This is all some kind of trick.

But then I see something I didn't notice before. Lucy's bed, the bed across from mine, the bed I had to step around on my daily walks about the room.

It's gone.

thirty-four

They're trying to make me believe I'm crazy. There's a word for it: they're *gaslighting* me. We watched a movie called *Gaslight* in my women's lit class, even though it didn't really qualify as women's lit being neither a book nor written by a woman. (We also watched *Fatal Attraction* and *Heavenly Creatures*. My high school is very progressive.) In *Gaslight*, a husband conspires to make his wife (Paula, played by Ingrid Bergman) believe she's losing her mind so he can take her money. He makes her stop her studies. He moves her away from her friends. He steals a brooch so she thinks she lost it; he hides a picture and tells her she moved it. He controls the lights and tells her she's imagining that they dim and brighten.

He wants more than her money. After all, there are other, easier ways to take your wife's money than to make her think she's insane. No, he's after her sense of reality. Her sense of self. He's shaking her to her very core. She gets him back in the end, though.

How is that different from what they're doing to me here?

Keeping me from school. Isolating me from the familiar. They even control the lights, just like Paula's murderous husband.

How can I be crazy when I'm able to remember so many details about a movie made so long ago that they had to film it in black and white?

How can I be crazy if I got an A in that class for writing a paper comparing the movie *Gaslight* with the Charlotte Perkins Gilman short story "The Yellow Wallpaper" that was so good my teacher asked to keep a copy of it on file for when she next taught the class?

Lucy was *here*. Her hair brushed against my arm; I felt the warmth of another body in the room. Lucy sometimes mumbled to herself in Spanish; she told me she'd grown up in a bilingual home. I don't even *know* Spanish.

Maybe Dr. Lightfoot stays in business by making her patients believe they're crazy. Can't make money if you can't keep the beds full, that kind of thing. Gaslighting to pay the bills.

Lucy is the one who told me to go on the antipsychotics. She wouldn't have done that if she'd known they'd make her disappear.

But then, how would Lucy have known, if she only existed inside my brain? *I* didn't know.

I didn't know Spanish either.

But…where did her bed go? It was here before the lights went out. It was *nailed to the floor* like my own. They couldn't have moved it while I was sleeping. The noise would've woken me up. And anyway, I haven't slept at all tonight.

Does that mean I didn't just hallucinate a person, I hallucinated *furniture*?

But Lucy was a *patient* here. She went to *therapy*. She sat in the *cafeteria*.

And yet…I can't remember if Dr. Lightfoot or Stephen ever actually talked to her or acknowledged her presence. When I helped her sneak out for her audition, how did Lucy get back in without being caught?

She said she paid off an orderly.

Okay, but why didn't the attendant/orderly/nurse ask where Lucy was during that evening's room check?

Well, she had privileges I didn't. She might have been at group therapy, at dinner, weaving a stupid basket.

But why did she come back here at all that night?

She said it would have been too much trouble to stay away.

I close my eyes again, remember walking down the stairs. Lucy held my hand. I felt her palm against mine. She tugged me in the opposite direction when she saw how the orderly was scanning patients' bracelets. I almost tripped and fell. We were nearly caught.

I was so happy when she made it outside, when she ran through the woods toward her boyfriend's waiting car.

Her boyfriend. I texted Joaquin! Lucy told me his phone number.

Does that mean I texted some stranger? I invented all of it?

Impossible.

I shake my head, my eyes still closed.

Everyone hears voices sometimes. I mean, not *voices* neces-sarily, but *memories* of voices. My dad telling me to *broaden my horizons*, Agnes saying *we're too old for these games.*

They're just doing this to keep me here. My plan to get out by showing them what a good friend I could be was working, and they don't want to let me win.

So, they're saying that Lucy wasn't real because no one would expect them to release me for being a good friend to a *hallucination.*

I'm trapped. I'm trapped, I'm trapped, I'm *trapped.* In this seven-by-eight room with disappearing furniture and a disap-pearing girl. I open my eyes, wide, like maybe I'll see something I missed before—some giveaway, some proof that they're lying.

"Doctor." It's Stephen's too-high voice. "Are you sure you don't want to give her a sedative?"

I'm still screaming. Or I'm screaming again. I'm running from one end of the room to the other (when did I get out of bed?) knocking into the walls, still searching for Lucy's mattress, Lucy's slippers, a stray strand of Lucy's almost-black hair.

Dr. Lightfoot sighs heavily, standing up. "All right, let's move her. I don't want her to hurt herself."

PART TWO

in between

thirty-five

They bring me to another room. A room on a different floor.

(What floor? I can't keep track. I try to remember what I knew before:

First floor: admitting, offices, emergencies.

Second floor: cafeteria, classrooms (?).

Third floor: a long hallway of closed doors, the shower, the room Lucy and I shared.

But what does it matter, what I knew before? I *knew* I had a roommate then too. I knew *nothing*.)

This room doesn't have walls. No, there are walls, but they're padded. I'm in a padded room. They put me in an *actual padded room*. I can't keep track of how many steps it is from one side of the room to the other because the floor curves up into the sides into the ceiling. There's no sharp angle where floor becomes wall.

They're still trying to take my sanity. This room without walls or windows would be enough to drive anyone over the edge.

That's not true. Not the part about how this room could drive anyone insane, but the part about the window. There is a window. But not one to the outside. The window is in the door, which is every bit as padded as the rest of the place except for a small circle of glass, like a porthole on a boat. Through the glass, Dr. Lightfoot looks at me. Nurses look in on me—both the not-so-nice one and the nice one. I guess she didn't get fired for not double-checking whether I took my sleeping pills. Stephen looks in on me, and I want to ask if he spells his name with a *V* or a *PH*, but I don't think he can hear me and even if he could, the words I say don't always sound like the words I'm thinking. They open the door to give me food and medicine. Dr. Lightfoot tries to continue our therapy, but I'm incoherent.

I only know that what I'm experiencing is incoherence because Lightfoot tells me so. She says I'll be in this room for just a little while—just until I calm down, just until I adjust.

"This is temporary," Lightfoot assures me. "We'll have you out of here and back in your own room in no time."

Your own room. My room is in Manhattan, three thousand miles away from here on East 78th Street, one of three bedrooms in our classic Upper East Side apartment with views of Park Avenue. My room is two, three, four times the size of my room on the third floor of this place. I don't know exactly because I never bothered counting my steps back home.

"I'm not crazy," I tell Lightfoot when I'm finally able to make my words match my thoughts. She stands right inside the door. Stephen stands behind her.

Lightfoot shakes her head. "I don't use that word. But you are sick. Your brain works differently than other people's."

I shake my head, pressing my palms into my temples. Sick is her euphemism for *crazy*; she practically admitted it. They probably taught her to say that in medical school. "Stop trying to trick me."

"I'm not tricking you," Lightfoot says, her voice saccharine-calm. "Think about it."

"Think about what?"

Lightfoot pauses. "Tell me about Jonah. Did Agnes ever talk to you about him?"

"Of course she did," I answer irritably. "I've told you a thousand times, we were *best friends*. Best friends tell each other about their boyfriends."

"Yes, they do," Lightfoot agrees, and I hate how calm and steady she keeps her voice. "I'll be back later."

When she's gone, I try to remember if I ever heard Agnes actually talk about Jonah. I remember him sleeping in her bed, his hand on her hip while she whispered to me. I remember seeing them holding hands, but did Agnes ever actually speak to him, ever actually reach out and touch him?

No. My brain wouldn't invent a pseudo-boyfriend who didn't put me first any more than it would've invented a roommate who irritated me at times.

If I was going to invent someone, I'd make them perfect.

I tell Lightfoot as much when she comes to talk to me again later. I fold my arms across my chest. How can she argue with logic like that?

How can she call me sick (which really means *crazy*) when I'm so logical?

"The human brain is very complicated," she says. "I don't know why yours didn't give you the perfect boyfriend. And as for your imperfect roommate..." She pauses. "Hannah, I've never lied to you. The day we met, you asked to see your file, and I showed it to you. Do you remember what it said?"

I shrug. "That I was here for observation."

"What else? Do you remember?"

I shake my head and turn away so she won't see the tears forming in my eyes.

Of course I remember. I never forgot. I thought of it the minute Lucy showed up.

Patient may pose a danger to herself and others.

"Maybe you made that up to trick me." I don't sound desperate anymore. I sound weak. I sound sad.

Lightfoot shakes her head. "I'm not trying to trick you," she promises. "I can show you the court order. I can put you on the phone with the judge." She pauses and smiles one of her medical-school smiles. "I assure you, I'm not powerful enough to make a judge forge a court order."

I don't smile back.

"So, Hannah, knowing what you know is true—do you really think we would've given you a roommate when the court order that brought you here specifically told us not to?"

I bite my lip, but I can't stop the tears from overflowing. I turn all the way around so Lightfoot won't see, but my shoulders are shaking. She can tell I'm crying.

I should've figured this out sooner.

They never would've given me a roommate. They wouldn't have let me spend unsupervised time with another girl.

Lightfoot said: *I've suspected this for some time.*

I should have asked, *How long?* Did she guess before she even met me, when she was reading over the police file, reviewing my answers about what happened that night?

There's one more piece of evidence, something even Lightfoot doesn't know: It was Lucy's voice I heard the night Agnes fell, Lucy's voice saying, *just a little tap,* before we ever met.

Not that we ever really *met.*

thirty-six

I don't know how long they keep me in the room without walls. It feels like it's been days, weeks, months, *hours*.

I don't know how long it takes for Lightfoot to find the right combination of medication, the right dose so the madness wanes and sanity takes hold.

But can you really call it *sanity* when it isn't real, it isn't natural, it's chemically induced? When it doesn't technically belong to me because I wouldn't have it without the pills they keep giving me?

Maybe I'll never know for certain what's real, what's madness, what's the medication.

I ask Lightfoot for a sedative.

"Why?" she asks.

I want my muscles to go heavy. I want to fall into a dreamless sleep. I want to be numb.

After a moment, I answer, "Because I can't stop crying."

Lightfoot nods sympathetically, but refuses to sedate me. "The antipsychotics are doing their job," she says. "We're only keeping you in this room so that you're safe while we adjust your medication. I don't want a sedative to interfere with our work."

Our work. Doing their job. When I take the blue pills, I imagine businessmen dressed in suits, carrying briefcases as they make their way down my throat and into my belly and from there up into my brain. Then I picture them dressed like construction workers, doing heavy lifting and rewiring to get my brain cells into proper working order. I imagine a sedative as a traffic jam keeping the workers from getting to all the right places, from making it to their corner offices in time for their all-important meetings.

How will Lightfoot know when *things normalize*? What does *normalize* even mean? How can there be a *normal* when—left to its own devices—my brain invented people and furniture and scents and language? Is *normal* for me different than it is for other people?

I can't remember having doubted myself like this before. My mother used to say I had a healthy ego. She sounded pleased about it, proud that she'd raised a daughter who was so sure of herself in a world where society tells little girls to question themselves, to think before speaking, to let the boys speak first. Not me. My mother thought it was proof she and my father had done such a good job raising me.

Now all I have is doubt.

∴

They bring me back to the room. *My* room. On the third floor. (The padded room is on the first floor.) Someone has made my bed. *The* bed. The only bed in the otherwise empty space.

The pile of romance novels on the floor is gone. "Where are our books?" I ask. "*My* books," I correct.

"I'll bring you some new ones from the library," the nurse promises. It's the kind nurse in the yellow scrubs. Though she makes me stick out my tongue after I take my pills now too.

She leaves me alone in the room. In my room.

It looks exactly like it did my first day here. Except for the absence of a second bed. (Was my brain planning to create Lucy from the day I arrived, or did I hallucinate the bed later without realizing it?) Did the room feel this empty on day one? I mean, it's not as though I wasn't alone in here plenty of the time, even after Lucy came. Every time Lucy had group therapy, art therapy. Or when she had shower privileges that I hadn't yet been granted. And of course, when Lucy went on her audition.

I walk to the window, stand on my tiptoes. If they were trying to gaslight me, they'd have known to take Lucy, to take the extra bed, even to dust the floor for any remnants of her long hair. But they wouldn't have known about the hairpin on the windowsill.

It's gone.

I should've known she wasn't real the instant she came back after her audition. Nobody would've come back here if they didn't have to.

Stupid, broken brain.

I should've known that Jonah wasn't real the instant I realized he never gave me his phone number. Agnes and I exchanged numbers almost as soon as we met. I wouldn't have spent a month hooking up with Jonah without sending and receiving a few text messages.

Stupid, broken girl.

I kissed him for the first time behind the athletic center. Did I stand there all alone kissing the air, or did I hallucinate the entire exchange alone in my dorm room, while Agnes was in class?

Dr. Lightfoot comes to see me after lunch.

"Where's Stephen?" I ask. He isn't guarding the door. Lightfoot doesn't try to stop me when I step into the hallway to see if he's waiting outside.

Lightfoot smiles. "I don't think we need Stephen here anymore."

I wonder if she remembers that she told me Stephen was a student, here observing her work. Does she assume I knew she was lying?

"I asked them to bring me some books."

Lightfoot nods. "I'll make sure you get some after I leave." She doesn't say that reading might distract me from the work we're doing. Apparently, she's not worried about my getting distracted anymore. She smiles again. This smile doesn't look like the kind they taught her in medical school. In fact, this smile is probably the type they tried to train her *not* to use. This is a *real* smile, a human reflex, an involuntary reaction. It's full of pity and sadness. It's sticky with sweetness. The doctor feels sorry for me. She doesn't think I'm a danger to myself and others anymore, not now that I'm medicated. She sees me not as a threat, but as a sad, sick girl who's confronting an illness she can no longer deny.

Lightfoot gestures to my uneaten lunch, the tray on the floor beside my bed. "You can have lunch in the cafeteria from now on."

"Okay."

"I know this is an enormous adjustment for you."

Getting to have lunch in the cafeteria after the padded room?

Oh, she means my new status as a capital-C Crazy Person. Though she would probably say capital-S Sick Person.

"I have some good news for you," the doctor continues, still smiling.

I wonder what she thinks qualifies as good news. Shower privileges? Grounds privileges? The word *privileges* has lost all meaning.

The word *good* has lost all meaning.

"Your hearing has been set for next week."

I blink dumbly. "What?"

"I know you've been frustrated with the wait, but I really do think it's for the best. The time we've had allowed us to really dig into your troubles."

My *troubles*. Isn't that what the Irish call their problems with the United Kingdom? The Troubles. How strange that the same word can be used to describe my brain as well as a conflict between two major European counties. The country of Shakespeare and the Beatles goes up against the country of Yeats and Joyce, and my brain goes up against itself, and we all call it trouble.

Ashes, ashes, we all fall down.

Did you know "Ring Around the Rosy" is about the plague? At least, that's what I told my classmates in kindergarten because that's what my mother told me. I found out later it was just an urban legend, but by then it didn't make much difference. It had already been etched into my brain as a song about life and death.

Dr. Lightfoot mistakes my silence for concern. "I don't want you to worry about the hearing. I've already sent an updated report to the judge, and I'm sure my findings will be taken into account."

Her *findings*. My *troubles*. So many euphemisms. Call it what it is: the judge will have to consider my apparent insanity when he rules on the case.

Dr. Lightfoot will tell him that I hallucinated Agnes's boyfriend.

She'll say that I made up a new roommate when they brought me here. A new best friend. Maybe she'll even tell him that we had an imaginary book club, an imaginary adventure, imaginary late-night heart-to-hearts that my addled brain thought were every bit as real as the heart-to-hearts Agnes and I shared.

Dr. Lightfoot won't use the word *imaginary*, though. She'll say *hallucination* and *psychosis*. After all, even people with normal (Lightfoot would say *healthy*, not *normal*) brains have imaginary friends.

Maybe the judge will think I made up Lucy to fill the void Agnes left behind after she fell. Maybe he'll think: *My goodness, Hannah must have really loved Agnes if her brain had to invent a person to make up for her loss.*

(Dr. Lightfoot says hallucinations are rarely so straightforward, though they can be manifestations of our deepest anxieties and fears. She said she once had a patient whose Mom had left her with a relative for a year when she was three, and that girl's hallucinations took the form of a voice telling her to kill her mother. But the truth was, she was terrified of losing her mother again.

"Well, that's kind of backward," I said. "Why wouldn't the voices tell her to kidnap her mother, so she could have her all to herself and keep her from leaving again?"

Lightfoot nodded. "Why wasn't Jonah the perfect boyfriend?"

Touché, Dr. Lightfoot.)

The judge will probably feel sorry for me. I'll probably stand before the bench exactly as I'm sitting in front of my therapist right now, and the judge will stare at me with a similar pity-filled smile on his face. Except, unlike Lightfoot, the judge will be wearing a long black robe instead of blue scrubs. He'll have gray hair and a white moustache that's yellow at the edge of his lips because moustaches are impossible to keep clean, an extension of all the bacteria in your mouth. Unlike Lightfoot's light-brown skin and dark-brown eyes, the judge will have pale skin dotted with age spots, and he'll wear bifocals when he reads over my file.

I wonder: Does that count as a hallucination, my imagining

a judge I've never met? I don't think so because he is an actual person, and I am going to actually meet him.

It will take me some time to figure out the rules regarding what's real, what's imaginary, what's hallucinatory.

If I ever figure them out at all.

I imagine the judge looking down at me, taking off his glasses, and slowly shaking his head. His voice will be scratchy, his decision dotted with words like:

Poor girl.

Didn't know what she was doing.

Wouldn't hurt a fly.

My brilliant plan to show them what I'm really like by being a good friend to Lucy might still work out in the end. They may still send me home because of her.

Even if I didn't show them what I thought I was showing them: what a good friend I could be.

Even if it turns out they're the ones who showed me: I was being a good friend to someone who didn't exist.

That's almost funny, isn't it? I consider saying as much to Lightfoot, but she still has that sad, sympathetic look on her face. I don't think she'll see the humor in it. I look past Lightfoot to the empty space across the room where Lucy's bed used to be.

If Lucy were still here, she'd make a silly face behind Lightfoot's back.

∴

They bring me two books before lights-out. One is a romance novel that's missing its cover. I wonder whether it was ripped off by an angry patient or just fell off from having been read over and over again. The second book is so ironic I almost laugh out loud. It's a *real* book, a *good* book, the sort I would have begged Lightfoot for weeks ago, even though I read it in eighth grade, so reading it now wouldn't have gotten me any extra credit at school.

It's *Jane Eyre.*

"I'm surprised they allow this in here," I say, though (I know) there's no one else in the room to hear me.

If Lucy were still here, this novel would give us so much to talk about.

"This must be a mistake," I add, shaking my head. "A book where the villain is the crazy lady locked in the attic? Total contraband."

I wonder if Lucy ever read *Jane Eyre.* If not, I just gave away the ending: Mr. Rochester was married before Jane, but he keeps his first wife locked in the attic of Thornfield because she's insane.

Does Lucy know there are feminist scholars who argue that the first Mrs. Rochester might not have been crazy at all, that Mr. Rochester locked her in the attic to get rid of her after she behaved in ways he considered unbecoming to a Victorian Englishwoman? Or maybe because he simply didn't want her.

Lucy definitely wouldn't read it that way. She's too much of a romantic. She'd root for Rochester and Jane to end up together.

If Lucy were still here, we'd argue for hours. Lucy would insist that Mrs. R had to have been nuts—she burned the house down, didn't she (among other things)? And I'd answer that after years of being locked up in the attic, who could blame the poor woman for trying to burn her way out?

Except of course, we wouldn't really argue at all. Not for hours and not for one second.

Lucy wouldn't have read *Jane Eyre*. She'll never read *Jane Eyre*. She'll never have an opinion about gothic romance or feminist scholars, and she wouldn't have made a face at me behind Lightfoot's back this afternoon.

There was never a Lucy to argue with.

To read a single word with.

To make funny faces behind Lightfoot's back.

Lucy can't *still* be here.

Lucy never was here to begin with.

thirty-seven

They give me real clothes. Underwear and a bra. Ballet flats with a decorative bow on the side. They're not the clothes I was wearing when I got here. They're not even any of the clothes that were left in my dorm room after Agnes fell and they brought me here, clothes I assume someone packed up and shipped home to my parents.

These clothes are new. The tags have been cut off, but they have that never-been-worn smell. Except for the bra. I recognize it from my drawers at home. I didn't bring it with me to California because it's a touch too small, back from when I used to be an A-cup, before I blossomed into an A/B-cup, which isn't much of a blossoming when you think about it.

My mother must have sent these clothes. I imagine her going into my room, surveying the clothes in my closet, deciding that none of them would do for this particular occasion, and resolving to go out and find the perfect outfit. My mother loves to shop, and finding the right clothes for the right occasion feels like a true accomplishment for her. I don't mean that she's shallow or

superficial; I honestly think that finding the right outfit probably felt like something she could do to help me. She must have
gone shopping in the city—Bloomingdale's or Saks or even
Bergdorf—then realized when she got back to our apartment
that she forgot to pick out a new bra, so selected one from the
top drawer of my dresser.

I picture her walking through a department store. (This is *not*
a hallucination, imagining one scenario or another is something
normal people do.) (Isn't it?) Mom would have carefully judged
which items would look good on me, trying to guess which
would fit best, since I wasn't there to try anything on. We always
went shopping together, even when I was very young. Mom
asked my opinion on everything she bought. I knew all about
Oscar de la Renta and Dolce & Gabbana at an age when most
kids are still wearing clothes featuring pictures of their favorite
cartoon characters.

Mom would've considered more than just the way these
clothes would fit. She'd have wanted an outfit that was dressy
enough to show respect for the court, but not so dressy that it
looked like I was showing off. I would need to look serious, but
not so somber that it could look like I was headed to a funeral.
That might remind the judge that except for a twist of fate—a
strong gust of wind as she fell, a slightly different angle of
descent—Agnes's injuries could have been fatal.

I imagine my mother wandering through one store after
another, discarding some clothes for being black or gray, dismiss-
ing others for being too bright. Finally she would've landed on

a crisp, white blouse. Then, a navy skirt. No, make that pants. No, again—a skirt with an elastic waist so she wouldn't have to worry about whether it will fit perfectly.

I wonder if she cut the tags off before she sent them here (perhaps someone told her to), or whether Lightfoot snipped the tags before she brought me the clothes this morning.

The skirt stops just below my knees. Beneath it, my legs are bright white—pale from so much time inside. They're also fuzzy. You can't call it stubble because it's long past the stubble phase. If my mother had asked me, I would've told her I'd prefer pants.

Lightfoot helps me dress, as though I might have forgotten how to put on real clothes. Stephen is here again, but he turns his back when I change, so I know he's not here to protect Lightfoot from me. The clothes feel heavy compared to the paper I've been wearing. The wool skirt itches and I want to rip it off, but I don't because it's not *normal* to prefer paper clothes to real clothes. I tell myself I just need time to get used to them. I wish I could see how my new outfit looks, but there's no mirror in this place, not even in the bathroom or shower room.

"Stephen will be coming with us," Lightfoot explains, as she leads me out the door and down the hall. "He's spent almost as much time with you over the past few months as I have, so the judge may want to ask him some questions."

She smiles, that same pitying smile. *The past few months.* She makes the length of my stay here sound so vague. As though she hasn't been keeping track of each passing day.

Lightfoot is also wearing real clothes instead of her usual blue scrubs: gray pants and a matching jacket, the kind of suit eager college graduates wear for job interviews. I wonder if she keeps this outfit in her office, whips it out for occasions like this, and then shoves it back out of sight. She's wearing makeup—eyeliner around her brown eyes and peach blush on her cheeks. Only now do I realize I've never seen her wear makeup before. Her long, wavy, dark hair is twisted into a neat bun at the nape of her neck, but it's not her hair and makeup that make her look so different. Today, she's wearing glasses instead of contacts.

Stephen is wearing black jeans a black T-shirt and the same heavy boots he always wears. They're surprisingly quiet on the linoleum floors.

Not like Lightfoot's shoes. She's wearing high heels, what my mother would call pumps. She *click-clack-clips* with every step. Without her slippers, Lightfoot's steps are anything but light.

She holds my arm as we descend the stairs, Stephen a few steps behind. The doctor's grip is firm; not so tight that I feel like a prisoner, but tight enough that I know she's not about to let go. I think she's trying to be comforting, not restrictive.

I squint in the sunlight. I'm suddenly very aware that I'm not wearing a stitch of makeup, not even moisturizer or sunscreen. My hair is loose around my shoulders, and when the wind blows, it whips across my face.

"Warm out today," Lightfoot says, and I nod in agreement despite the distinct chill I feel in the air.

Warmth in California is very different from warmth in New

York. In California, because it's a *dry heat* (as they say), the air feels thinner. It feels like the sunlight is the only source of heat such that every time a cloud rolls overhead or you step into a shady spot, the temperature drops. On a hot day in New York, the *air* feels warm. Shade offers next to no relief.

I'm sure this isn't a scientific assessment of the differences between the climates of these two states. There are probably important factors a meteorologist would tell me I'm disregarding, like heat indexes and humidity levels and the like. Surely there are days in New York when the air feels thin and days in California when the air feels thick.

Lightfoot directs me to a car. I don't know what I was expecting. Maybe a van with the name of the institute painted on the side, as if to say *Caution: Contents Are Dangerous (To Themselves and Others)*.

But the car is a normal, brown sedan. I wonder if it's Lightfoot's personal car. She leads me to the back seat and puts my seatbelt on for me like I'm a child. She gets into the passenger seat directly in front of me, and Stephen gets into the driver's seat. (Maybe it's his car?) I try to roll down the window on my side, but when I press the button, nothing happens.

"Child safety locks," Lightfoot explains, craning her neck so she's almost facing me. She tries to say it casually, as if the person who really owns this car actually has kids, has the locks in place for their benefit. But it's obvious the locks are for patients like me. If I tried to open the door, I wouldn't be able to do that either. "I'll turn the AC on to cool it off in here."

I wasn't treated this much like a child when I actually *was* a child.

I lean my forehead against the window and look outside. I thought the world might look different—because of the pills, because I've been in a cage for so long, because I've never really seen autumn in California—but everything looks the same as it did in August, just a little deader now that it's October. (Lightfoot told me the date of the hearing.)

Stephen winds us down a long driveway, toward a big metal gate. He stops the car and leans his muscular arm out the window (his window opens without a problem), and punches some numbers into a keypad mounted on the side of the road. There was a time when I would've watched him, memorized the numbers he pressed. Just in case I needed them someday. But now I can't imagine leaving this place unsupervised.

After punching in three numbers, Stephen looks back at Lightfoot helplessly.

"What's the code again?" he asks.

Lightfoot glances back at me, then leans over to whisper the correct numbers in Stephen's ear. She may have diagnosed me, and she may feel sorry for me, but she still doesn't completely trust me.

The gate swings open and Stephen takes his foot off the brake. I wait to feel something like a surge of excitement at leaving the property after so much time.

But all I feel as Stephen accelerates out of the driveway and onto Highway 1 is a twinge of nausea from riding in the back seat. All I felt when Lightfoot led me out the front door was that my eyes hurt in the sunlight.

My itchy new skirt rubs against my hairy legs, and I'm sweating despite the AC. Cars whizz past us in the opposite direction. I wonder if those drivers catch of glimpse of me and assume I'm a kid going on an outing with my parents. If traffic slowed enough that they could look closely, they'd see that I don't resemble Stephen or Lightfoot, and Lightfoot's probably too young to have a daughter my age. I don't even know how to spell Stephen's name, though, of course, an outside observer wouldn't know that. But the cars are going fast, and no one's paying attention to us. You'd have to be pretty clever (and a little bit psychic) to put the pieces of the real story together.

The signs say we're headed north, toward Silicon Valley and the peninsula. The Pacific Ocean is on the left, but I don't turn to look at it. I'm on the right side of the car, still leaning my forehead against the window. All I see are the brown hills and mountains and cliffs. Cows graze on the hills above us. I can't imagine what they're eating. The ground beneath their feet looks dry and dead.

You'd never know the biggest ocean in the world is just a stone's throw away.

thirty-eight

Stephen parks the car in a lot across the street from the courthouse. Dr. Lightfoot has to put her purse through an X-ray machine, and we all have to walk through a metal detector to get inside. Lightfoot goes through twice because first her jewelry and then her glasses set off the machine. Stephen has to take off his boots because they have steel toes. She and Stephen both show their photo IDs to the security guard. Meanwhile, I glide right through: no purse, no jewelry, insubstantial shoes that barely fit because I wasn't there to try them on when my mother bought them.

Everyone in this building is fully clothed: The security guards wear uniforms and most everyone else is in a suit. There's not a pair of paper scrubs or a set of pajamas in sight.

Stephen leads the way down a hall toward a set of double doors. I brace myself for what I'm going to see on the other side: a courtroom with a judge in a black robe perched on his bench above the rest of us. One table on either side of the room: one for the defendant and one for the plaintiff. Rows of seats full of spectators as though this is a sporting event.

But instead of a courtroom, we walk into a conference room with linoleum floors (beige, not gray) and stucco walls.

I see Agnes's parents first. They're standing at one end of the long table which sits in the center of the room. Agnes's mother looks paler than she did when I met her in the hospital, as if she's been trapped indoors just like I have. (I suppose spending all this time at her daughter's bedside is a kind of imprisonment.) Agnes's father is taller than I remembered, well over six feet. He has Agnes's blond hair and blue eyes. I remember Agnes calling her parents *Mama* and *Daddy* when they spoke on the phone.

My own parents are sitting on the other end of the table, their backs to the door. For as long as I can remember, I've called them *Mom* and *Dad*. Surely there must've been some *Mommy*-ing and *Daddy*-ing when I first learned to talk, but I don't remember it. Lightfoot walks ahead of me, and my parents swivel in their chairs. The doctor shakes their hands, says something about how nice it is to see them again after months of talking on the phone.

I realize that my parents have already heard my diagnosis. That probably everyone in this room—both sets of parents, Stephen and Lightfoot, my parents' lawyer, another man I assume is Agnes's parents' attorney, and someone else who's maybe Agnes's doctor—thinks I'm crazy. *Knows* I'm crazy. They know my brain works differently from however their brains work. They know I hear disembodied voices and see people who don't actually exist.

Unlike Agnes's parents, my parents aren't pale. They still have a touch of a tan left from their summer vacation. My mother stands and hugs me, but the hug feels formal, the kind of hug you'd give to a cousin whom you only see every few years at occasions like weddings and funerals, someone you're related to but who's essentially a stranger. I can feel Mom stiffen at the scent of the generic shampoo I was given to wash my hair. She avoids looking directly at my makeup-free face. When she steps away, I can still smell her perfume, the same scent she's worn my whole life. It's always been too heavy and floral for my taste. I used to beg her to try something new, something a little more subtle, but she refused. *Scent is the sense most related to memory,* she'd say. *If I changed scents after all these years, I wouldn't be the same person I used to be.*

Maybe she sprayed a little extra perfume on her wrists today, to make sure she'd smell like the mother I remembered, just in case I was so crazy I might have forgotten her.

My father doesn't hug me at all. He rests his hand on my shoulder and gives it a squeeze. He makes a big show of clearing his throat, and I wonder if he's trying not to cry or if he simply doesn't want to talk to me.

I don't know what I was expecting: a tearful embrace, a loving reunion? I've never gone this long without seeing them.

Maybe my parents have concluded that I'm not the same girl I used to be. Maybe this isn't a loving reunion because I've become a stranger to them: a problematic daughter, a crazy girl. A girl they've heard stories about—courtesy of Dr. Lightfoot—but don't really *know.*

"Why don't we sit down?" Lightfoot suggests brightly. She's

an expert at this. She probably goes to a half dozen of these hearings each month. She pulls out a chair and gestures for me to sit. My parents don't sit next to me. There are at least three chairs between us. Lightfoot sits on one side of me and gestures for Stephen to sit on the other. Agnes's parents are across from us, and I wonder if they're relieved that there's a doctor on one side of me and a security guard on the other.

The door opens and closes. Around me, everyone stands, so I stand too. (At least I'm still able to read social cues.)

The judge isn't wearing a black robe. She's wearing a Hillary Clinton–esque pantsuit and has a no-nonsense look about her. (My mother would say I was a bad feminist because until this moment, it never occurred to me that the judge might be a woman. All this time I'd been picturing an old man.) If the judge were a teacher, she'd be the type most students were frightened of. I always liked those teachers. I was always their favorite. Now, I keep my eyes trained on the table in front of me when she speaks.

"We're here to determine whether Hannah Elizabeth Gold did unlawfully and with harmful intent contribute to Agnes Smith's severe injuries."

I look up, expecting the judge to make eye contact, to ask me to enter a plea, for anything that resembles what I've seen in movies and TV shows. Instead, she sits, and then everyone else sits, and the judge directs her gaze at the other side of the table, waiting for someone else to speak.

The Smiths' attorney opens his mouth.

"Agnes Smith's life will never be the same," he begins.

thirty-nine

My attention span isn't what it used to be. I've spent most of the past two months rereading the same books over and over, books that weren't all that challenging to begin with. Lightfoot's visits were never more than an hour, and when she talked, it was never for more than a few minutes at a time. I haven't watched a TV show or a movie or attended a class since August. I haven't had to actually *pay attention* in a long time.

This is what I'm able to absorb when Mr. Clark speaks:

First, he introduces himself as Agnes's attorney. Technically I guess he's her parents' attorney, but it's hard to remember that because he begins by saying he's here to speak for Agnes since she cannot yet speak for herself. He describes Agnes's life before the accident.

Straight-A student.

Dutiful daughter.

Loving big sister.

Faithful girlfriend.

He shows us the *Get Well Soon* cards her sisters made. "Her sisters are back in North Dakota," he says, "and this has been an enormous hardship on Agnes's parents. They've gone into debt flying back and forth between California and home, dividing their time between their three daughters. It's not yet clear how much care Agnes will need going forward, what level of brain function she will retain."

He continues, "Even after Agnes is well enough to leave the hospital, she will have years of physical therapy, speech therapy, and occupational therapy ahead of her. And even if Agnes is able to walk and speak as she did before the fall, she may still be different in ways the doctors can't predict. A brain injury may affect countless aspects of a patient's life."

Mr. Clark lists possible long-term consequences: memory loss, trouble with concentration, loss of stamina, chronic pain, blurred vision, seizures, trouble sleeping, increased or decreased appetite, mood swings.

"To name only a few possible side effects of her injuries," he says.

Then he adds, "But let's reflect on what Agnes Smith has already been through: After the incident, Agnes was in a coma for two weeks. The doctors didn't know if she would ever wake up."

Then,

"A neurosurgeon had to drill burr holes in her skull to relieve the pressure on her brain."

Then,

"When she finally woke, she appeared to have lost all verbal function."

Then,

"Eventually, she was able to communicate through blinks and grunts."

Then,

"She needs assistance to leave the bed to perform her bodily functions."

And finally,

"Two weeks ago, after vigorous therapy, Agnes finally said the first word she's managed since the accident." He pauses. "Mama."

A choked sob escapes Mrs. Smith. Mr. Smith stares at me.

I look at my hands. No one told me Agnes woke up before.

Maybe Agnes's father sees the differences between his daughter and me: I'm able to walk and talk and use the bathroom.

But I can't help seeing all that Agnes and I have in common: we've both been trapped in a hospital since August.

Maybe they moved her to a room in the hospital that's green, just like mine.

Like me, surely any hint of her summer tan has long since disappeared. Then again, Agnes had one of those complexions that never got much color, skin that burned even when she covered herself with sunscreen. I wonder if it's possible for her to be even paler than she was when I knew her. Do the freckles behind her right ear and on the back of her right hand stand out more, or have they faded? Has her white-blond hair turned yellow, or is it even whiter after all this time indoors?

I reach up and twist a few strands of my hair through my fingers, wondering whether it's changed color too.

Like me, Agnes can't get up and go to the bathroom when she wants.

Neither of us can pick up the phone to call our parents or our friends or even our attorneys when we want to call them.

Neither of us can send text messages and emails.

Neither of us started our senior year of high school on time.

Both of us have brains that work differently than other people's.

Both of our brains have been diagnosed by the doctors in charge of our care. Agnes's diagnosis (a traumatic brain injury) has an abbreviation: TBI.

I think we might have more in common now than we did the day we met.

Mr. Clark says that weeks before the incident—I notice he never refers to it as an *accident*, he says *incident, fall, event, injury*—Agnes called her parents and expressed concern about her roommate's state of mind.

Mr. Clark holds out his hand, and Mrs. Smith drops a cell phone into it.

"I'd like to play this message that Agnes left on her mother's voicemail, dated July fourteenth."

Agnes's voice fills the room. Beneath the table I cross and uncross my legs. This room is every bit as air conditioned as the rooms in the institute, but I'm warm. I press my thighs together and feel the sweat on my legs.

Please tell Matt I said hi and that I miss him. I started to tell Hannah about him the other day, but she doesn't like to talk about boys. I think she's self-conscious because she's never had a boyfriend. She seemed angry that I even mentioned my boyfriend.

I cross my legs again, hooking my right foot behind my left ankle. I wasn't angry about Matt. I didn't *know* about Matt. When Agnes mentioned her boyfriend, I didn't want to hear it because I thought she was talking about Jonah.

Mr. Clark taps the phone. "And another message Agnes left for Mrs. Smith, this one dated July thirty-first."

Hi, Mama, it's me. It happened again today. Hannah was talking to herself, and this time she was talking about me. It's nothing, right? Lots of people talk to themselves. Don't worry about me. The girls down the hall say she's just strange.

I remember that day. I wasn't talking to myself. I was talking to *Jonah*, telling him all the reasons he should choose me. So yes, Agnes's name came up. And yes, I might have been listing her shortcomings. But I wasn't talking to *myself*.

Jonah said, *I know it's hard on you. It's hard on me too.*

We were sitting close, our foreheads nearly touching, so it took us a second to realize that Agnes was standing in the doorway. Jonah jumped up, made an excuse about having to study and left the room so quickly that Agnes never even had a chance to acknowledge him.

Not that she would have acknowledged him, even if he'd stuck around.

Like Lucy, he wasn't there to begin with.

Mr. Clark puts the phone down. They could've played some other message. One of the many messages I heard her leave—the one about going to Barnard with me, maybe. Or about how sleepy she was because we stayed up late talking again. But I guess those messages wouldn't help their case.

Mr. Clark holds up a medical file. "The night Agnes arrived at the hospital, Hannah Gold caused a disruption that nearly interfered with Agnes's care, further endangering her."

I open my mouth to contradict him—I would never have done that!—but Lightfoot places her hand on my wrist. "We'll have our turn soon," she whispers.

"Hannah insisted on being allowed into the ICU even though she's not family. She caused a scene that disturbed other patients and their visitors. Finally, the staff relented. At the time, they assumed she was simply a good friend—but they kept a close watch on her nonetheless."

Lightfoot keeps her hand on my wrist. Apparently, *she* isn't surprised by what Mr. Clark is saying. She would have seen a copy of the file Mr. Clark is holding. I glance at my parents. They don't look surprised either. Unlike me, they've heard this story before.

Did I really cause a disruption? Mr. Clark makes it sound like they have plenty of witnesses—doctors, nurses, other patients and their loved ones. But I don't remember any of that. And even if I did what he's describing, wasn't it the right thing to do? Shouldn't I have stayed with Agnes instead of leaving her alone? It's exactly what my father would have done, insisting on special treatment, to be permitted to go where others can't.

"When Agnes's parents arrived at the hospital, they insisted that Hannah be moved. Security was assigned to watch over

Agnes's bed to make sure Hannah couldn't get close to her again. You can imagine how relieved the Smiths were when the court ordered Hannah be placed under psychological observation. They wanted to focus all their energy on Agnes's recovery, not on keeping her safe from the girl who'd endangered her."

Lightfoot gives my wrist a squeeze, then lets go. Had she been trying to comfort me or to restrain me while Mr. Clark spoke?

When it's our side's turn to speak, my attorney makes a brief statement, then Lightfoot stands. "When Hannah came under my care, she couldn't distinguish reality from hallucination," she explains. I stare at my hands, folded neatly in my lap as though I'm waiting for a waiter to serve my meal at a fancy restaurant. (My father trained me never to put my elbows on the table.) I don't want to know if the people in this room—the judge, the lawyers, the Smiths, my parents, Stephen—are looking at the doctor or at me while Lightfoot speaks.

She continues, "Hannah doesn't remember these events the way they really happened. She *can't*. She was in the throes of a psychotic episode."

I realize that I'm not going to do any of the talking today. The judge isn't going to ask for my version of the story: not what led up to Agnes's fall and not the night of the fall itself. It doesn't matter if I insist that Agnes slipped and fell. It wouldn't even matter if I said I pushed her. The judge wouldn't believe me.

Lightfoot describes the psychosis that I couldn't control. Lightfoot explains that symptoms of my disease normally begin between ages sixteen and thirty, though signs have appeared in younger patients. "Men tend to experience symptoms a little earlier than women."

I risk a quick glance at my mother. Will there be a tiny hint of pride on her face because I'm keeping up with the boys, because I'm ahead of the average girl? But my mother is stone-faced, her gaze trained directly at the doctor. She's not looking at me, and she certainly doesn't look proud.

"No one is to blame for not having noticed Hannah's symptoms sooner. Without a family history, she had a mere one percent chance of having this disease." She makes the disease sound contagious, as if I could have caught it from my father or my grandfather. "One percent," Lightfoot repeats for emphasis.

Lucky me. I beat the odds.

"At the institute, we had a chance to observe Hannah carefully, and—despite the odds—we suspected her diagnosis early on. Interestingly, Hannah's disease manifested in a very functional form. Unlike some patients, Hannah wasn't experiencing an entirely alternate reality. Rather, she integrated characters into her *actual* reality."

Characters. I don't think that's a medical term. That makes them sound like people from a book, a movie, a play. A private performance for my personal entertainment. I suppose Lightfoot is trying to explain what happened in words that normal people can understand.

I don't mean *normal* as in people who aren't sick like I am. I mean *normal* as in people without medical or psychological expertise, *normal* as in laypeople, *normal* as in attorneys and parents.

"Most patients experience only visual and auditory hallucinations, but Hannah is part of the twenty percent who experience tactile hallucinations as well."

I don't suppose my *characters* would have integrated so well into my *reality* without the added bonus of *tactile hallucinations*. A roommate whose weight I could feel on the edge of my bed. A boy whose arms I could feel around me, whose kisses I could feel on my mouth. I brush my fingers against my lips while Lightfoot speaks.

Maybe if I hadn't experienced tactile hallucinations, I'd have figured out that Jonah wasn't real before Lightfoot did. Then again, maybe my brain would have adjusted Jonah's storyline to accommodate the lack of touching. I could have made him the sort of boy who wouldn't cheat on his girlfriend, who wouldn't have touched me, even if he wanted to.

"We're lucky to have caught Hannah's disease this early." Lightfoot sounds positively impressed by the clever way my disease manifested, and not a little bit pleased with herself for having diagnosed it. "We'll never know how her hallucinations might have developed if left unchecked." She pauses, then adds, "Some patients go years without a diagnosis, but Hannah's already getting the help she needs. Hannah is ahead of the curve in this respect—she'll be able to avoid the confusion and secrecy that many patients struggle with for years."

How many times has she said my name? Maybe they taught her that in medical school: *Use your patient's name when arguing her innocence. It humanizes her.* Or maybe she taught herself after years on the job. She continues, "Hannah will need treatment for the rest of her life, but with the right therapy and medication, she has a chance to live a healthy life. She may attend college, hold down a job, be a successful member of society."

For the rest of my life sounds like a very long time.

Lightfoot adds, "People with this disease are more likely to hurt themselves than others." She pauses to let her words sink in. "I've been working with Hannah for months now, and I believe that it's very unlikely she meant to hurt Agnes."

She makes me sound so passive, as though my brain was functioning without my consent. My disease was at fault, and I was an innocent bystander. Apparently I was wrong: My defense doesn't have anything to do with how close Agnes and I were. It's almost entirely based in biology.

Lightfoot's laying it on pretty thick. After all, if she guessed my diagnosis months ago and people with that condition are most likely to hurt themselves, then why did my file say that I was a danger to myself *and others*?

Then again, Lightfoot said it was the judge's decision that I be held for observation, not hers.

For the first time, I wonder if Dr. Lightfoot actually *likes* me. I mean, she definitely believes she understands me better than I understand myself. But I think there might be a hint of affection in her voice, like she's impressed by my illness and pleased that I have a chance to live a healthy life. She seems determined to make the judge understand, to make Agnes's parents understand that whatever happened wasn't my fault, and I deserve to go home.

Does Dr. Lightfoot actually *care* about her patients? All this time, I assumed she was working at that place because she was too incompetent to secure employment elsewhere, but maybe she's an idealist. Maybe she works at the institute because she truly wants to help girls whom others see as lost causes.

Like the person who goes to the animal shelter and says, *Give me the dog you're most likely to euthanize.*

I sit up a little straighter and look at the doctor instead of at my lap. I swallow hard.

"I assure you," Lightfoot continues, "Hannah's symptoms are being managed properly now."

Finally, she compares my disease to a broken bone: like a badly broken leg, my brain needed to be reset.

Agnes broke her ankle when she fell. Or more accurately, when she landed. The doctors set and wrapped it while she was unconscious.

Lightfoot finishes, "At the institute, by diagnosing Hannah, we set the bone and wrapped it in plaster. Now, it will require medication and therapy to function correctly in the years to come."

My doctor sits. She looks at me and smiles, reaching out to squeeze my hand.

forty

I win.

It doesn't feel like winning. No one throws their hands overhead and cheers, no one heaves an enormous sigh of relief. No one even smiles.

Instead, this is what happens:

The judge concludes there isn't enough evidence to prove Agnes's fall *wasn't* an accident. Not when the only witness (me) was psychotic at the time.

Even if Agnes were able to testify, she couldn't prove that I intended to push her. In fact, I might have been reaching out to catch her.

And if I did push her, it wasn't my fault because I was unstable as the result of an undiagnosed mental illness at the time. (Of course, our attorney doesn't mention that. He doesn't want to admit that I might have pushed her at all.)

Agnes's father shoves his seat out from under him so hard that it teeters, but doesn't fall over. "This girl is dangerous." His voice is angry and low. He'd probably hate that my file said: *Patient* may *pose a danger to herself and others*. He'd have preferred: *Patient* does *pose a danger to herself and others*.

The judge nods sympathetically, but says, "I know this is difficult for your family. You and your wife can discuss your options with your attorney. But when the Golds' attorney suggested a psychiatric evaluation rather than pressing charges, you agreed—"

They did? I guess my parents' lawyer was more effective than I gave him credit for.

"And the evaluation showed that Hannah Gold is crazy!" Mr. Smith interjects.

The judge continues, "The evaluation revealed that she needs treatment. But her diagnosis doesn't prove she's at fault for what happened to your daughter."

"There's no excuse for what happened to my daughter."

"That may be true, but there's simply no evidence that Hannah coerced your daughter onto that window ledge or pushed her while she stood there."

If we were in a courtroom, the judge might bang her gavel and order Mr. Smith to sit down. I wonder how many other cases she has to get through today, how many people she has to set free or imprison before she can go home tonight.

I wonder if Mr. Smith is as infuriated by the judge's use of *that may be true* as I was when Lightfoot said it to me.

"I've made my decision," the judge reiterates.

Agnes's mother doesn't say anything, but tears stream down her face. She reaches for her husband's hand, and he sits back down. The lawyer leans over and whispers something—words of comfort, maybe, a promise to appeal, perhaps explaining the differences between civil and criminal cases—but they don't react. Eventually, he stops talking and leans back in his chair.

I'm not supposed to say anything. It's been made abundantly clear that my memory of what happened this summer doesn't matter. It's October second; summer is over. My parents' lawyer says something about the paperwork that will need to be filed before I can be released from Lightfoot's care.

No one asked me for my version of events.

If they asked, would I tell them about the voice I heard?

Just a little tap.

Would it matter if I told? Just because I heard a voice doesn't mean I pushed her. *Did* I push her? I wish my brain could remember exactly what happened that night.

It wasn't like the movies. Agnes didn't sway gently before she lost her balance. Time didn't magically slow down, giving me a few extra seconds to consider what to do next.

It happened fast. It wasn't graceful. It didn't look pretty.

If they asked, would I tell them that?

I remember the voice, and I remember reaching out. I don't remember making contact with her skin, but if my brain could hallucinate touch, then surely it could hallucinate *not* touching too, right?

Lightfoot said it was *unlikely* I wanted to hurt Agnes.

Unlikely isn't impossible.

This girl is dangerous.

Hannah Gold is crazy.

A danger to herself and others.

I know I'm not supposed to speak, but the words come out of my mouth all on their own: "I'm sorry about Agnes."

Everyone in the room looks at me. If I weren't so heavily medicated, I might think the involuntary apology was a symptom of my disease. So crazy I can't stop myself from speaking when I'm supposed to keep quiet.

"I'm sorry about Agnes," I repeat, a little louder. I look at Mrs. Smith and choose my words carefully. "She was a good friend. We used to stay up all night talking. I miss her."

My parents' lawyer puts his hand on my shoulder tentatively, as if he's not sure what might set me off. "Hannah, there's no need for you to say anything at this point."

He speaks slowly, like he doesn't think I can understand him. Like my diagnosis means I'm hard of hearing on top of everything else. Will people talk to me this way for the rest of my life? Like I'm a wild animal they don't want to startle?

"But I *am* sorry." I stand, shrugging off the attorney's hand. He backs away from me. "I wish it hadn't happened."

"Hannah, what happened wasn't your fault." Lightfoot's voice is clear as a bell, full of authority. I shake my head. It *is* my fault. It wasn't just a terrible accident—or anyway, it wasn't *entirely* an accident. I'm the one who wanted to play games that night. I'm the reason Agnes got up on that windowsill. Whether or not I pushed her, she fell because of me.

"I'm sorry," I repeat. "*Please* let me be sorry."

Our brains make us who we are. Isn't that exactly what Mr.

Clark meant when he said *a brain injury may affect countless aspects of a patient's life*? So then if we alter our brain—through drugs, alcohol, injury (Agnes), or antipsychotics (me)—are we *less* our true selves than we were before? Because that means I was myself this summer:

Myself when I hooked up with Jonah,

Myself when I befriended Agnes,

Myself when I heard the voice telling me to give her a little tap.

The person I am now is different. Strangers pity her, her parents can't even look at her. The person I am now won her case, but I've never felt more defeated. Lightfoot thinks I want to hear that what happened isn't my fault. She doesn't understand that it's my brain, my *self*, that she's releasing from responsibility.

If I'm not responsible for my words and actions, then I'm nothing. No free will, no self.

Even toddlers are taught to say they're sorry when they've done something wrong. Do the people in this room expect less of me than they would of a three-year-old?

Agnes's mother finally speaks. "We don't want your apologies." She stands. "You have no right to miss our daughter. You have no right to say her name."

She and her husband don't take their eyes off me as they leave the room, like how you're not supposed to look away from an animal about to attack. But at least in their anger, in their blame, they treat me like a real person.

My parents thank the judge, shake our attorney's hand, and let him lead them from the room. When I don't immediately move to follow, Lightfoot takes hold of my elbow. She and Stephen escort me into the hallway where my parents are waiting.

Mom turns to the doctor. "Do you know where the restroom is?"

Lightfoot shakes her head. Mom looks disappointed, like she thinks an expert like Lightfoot ought to know the exact location of the bathroom.

Lightfoot asks a security guard, who points down the hall and to the left. Mom takes off in that direction.

"Hannah, why don't you go with your mother?" Lightfoot suggests. "We've got a long drive ahead of us."

Mom stops abruptly. She turns, and I can tell from the look on her face that escorting her crazy daughter to the bathroom is not what she had in mind. I glance back at Lightfoot. It feels like this is some kind of test, though I'm not sure whom she's testing: me (out in the world without institute supervision for the first time in months), or my mom (alone with her daughter for the first time since her diagnosis).

forty-one

My mother and I used to walk side by side: down Madison Avenue in Manhattan, on the Boulevard Saint-Germain in Paris, along the beach in Cannes. Today, in the courthouse in Silicon Valley, I walk a step behind.

Mom's wearing a fitted, cream-colored skirt and a navy-blue blazer with the sleeves pushed up to her elbows. Her legs are smooth and toned, blending seamlessly with her nude Louboutin pumps, the telltale red soles clicking against the linoleum floor. Her highlighted hair is styled neatly, and she's wearing a pair of oversized black sunglasses like a headband. She's chic and stylish without looking like she's trying too hard, though I know she tries very hard. I've sat on the bed in my parents' room while she spent hours deciding what to wear, even for the most casual affair.

She holds open the door to the bathroom for me, then ducks into one of the six stalls. We're the only ones in the restroom, but I don't choose the stall next to hers. I don't actually need to use the bathroom, but I close the door behind me and sit down all the same, papering the seat the way she taught me. (*Never touch anything in a public restroom*, she'd said when I was small.)

I wait for her to flush and then I do too. There are only two sinks, so I can't help but stand next to her when I wash my hands. (*Wash your hands for as long as it takes to sing "Happy Birthday" twice*, she'd taught me. I'm tempted to hum so she'll know I remember, but I'm worried she'll take the sound as a symptom.)

She hands me a paper towel and I dry my hands, then she leans forward over the sink to examine her face. I've seen her do this a thousand times; she always tucks her hair behind her ears, smoothes her eyebrows, touches up her lipstick. It's so comfortingly familiar that it takes effort for me to look away (will she think staring is a symptom?) and face my own reflection instead.

I look at my hair first. It's clean (relatively; my last shower was the day before yesterday) but stringy from months with no conditioner, no blow-dryer, no brush except the comb they let me use immediately after a shower. I think it does look darker than usual, but that could be an optical illusion as I've never been as pale as I am now. My lips are dry and flaky. I lick them, but that doesn't look any better.

I step back a little, trying to see more of myself. The white blouse is wrinkled and slightly too big. The navy skirt sits loosely on my hips.

Mom's highlighted hair falls just above her shoulders with layers framing her face. Mom washes and blow-dries her hair every day, and I imagine her in a nearby hotel room earlier today, a round brush in one hand and her blow-dryer in the other. Mom always packs her own hair dryer when she travels. She doesn't like to use the ones the hotels provide. She also brings her own soap, her own shampoo, her own conditioner, and her own body lotion. She says she doesn't feel clean otherwise. She opens her purse, and I watch as she takes out a tube of lipstick. It's light pink, the kind of color you wish your lips were naturally. That's all Mom ever wears. She thinks anything darker looks garish.

"Can I use that?" I ask.

Mom looks from me to the tube in her hands, to her reflection in the mirror, then back at me. She always said we shouldn't share makeup because it would spread germs. She wouldn't even let me use her blush brush when I forgot to pack my own on a trip. She had the hotel's concierge bring me a new one.

"Never mind." I shake my head, wishing I could un-ask the question. "I don't need it."

"No, of course," Mom says, holding out the lipstick. We both know I *do* need it. We both know that's why I asked for it even though she doesn't like to share. We both know I look terrible. I look nothing like the girl she sent to California back in June.

We also both know that pretty pink lipstick isn't going to be enough to help.

I bring the tube to my lips and press. My hands are shaking. The color is so light and my lips so wet from when I licked them that it doesn't make much difference.

"Why don't you keep it?" Mom says.

I shake my head, handing the tube back. "They won't let me." They'd confiscate it as soon as we got back to the institute.

"Of course." Mom doesn't look at me as she clicks the lipstick closed and drops the tube into her purse. I know she's going to throw it away and buy a new one as soon as she can.

I follow her out the door and back toward the lobby.

"I cried all night in Monte Carlo," I say suddenly. Mom stops walking and turns around.

"What are you talking about?" she asks patiently. "You loved Monte Carlo."

I shake my head. "No four-year-old loves Monte Carlo." Not even your precocious little pet. "It's a playground for adults, not kids."

I continue, "You left me alone in the hotel room, and I didn't know when you'd be back. I was frightened." My lip trembles.

"That's not how I remember it."

"It wasn't how I remembered it either. I didn't let myself remember what really happened."

"I think your doctor established that your memories are hardly reliable."

I nod slowly. "I guess I can't argue with that." I resume walking toward the lobby, but Mom takes hold of my arm before I pass her.

"Are you suggesting that you have this…" Mom pauses, as though she's searching for a word that doesn't sound too distasteful. "*Problem* because your father and I left you in hotel rooms when you were little?"

"I'm not suggesting anything. Except that maybe four years old is too young to be left alone in a strange place."

I expect Mom to argue, to remind me how lucky I was. Other kids went to amusement parks—Disney World, Universal Studios, Sea World (the last of which we boycotted for imprisoning whales and dolphins, not that my parents ever would have taken me there anyway), while my parents and I visited centuries-old castles in the Black Forest, saw wild sharks off the coast of South Africa, watched free whales breech in the Atlantic Ocean off the coast of Massachusetts.

But instead of arguing, Mom drops my arm and leads the way to the lobby where Lightfoot, Stephen, Dad, and our attorney are waiting for us. The six of us walk out of the courthouse (no metal detectors, no removal of shoes or jewelry on the way out) and into the parking lot. My parents and the lawyer trail behind. We're the world's most pathetic parade.

We stop beside Stephen's car.

"You'll be home soon," Dad says. He doesn't add, *and everything will go back to normal.* In fact, he sounds exhausted, like the prospect of taking me home is far more work than he's interested in doing.

I try to imagine what it was like for my parents when they brought me home from the hospital as an infant. Were they waiting until I was old enough to sleep through the night and hold my own fork? Did they count the days until I was old enough that they could treat me like a tiny grown-up, able to fit into their lifestyle, nothing like the parents who savored their children's babyhoods?

"Yes," Mom agrees. "At least this is over." I wonder whether she means the hearing or my outburst. She brushes one hand against the other. Literally wiping her hands of this whole affair.

Dr. Lightfoot opens the car door. Stephen is not so subtly poised to spring to action if I try anything. It's after 4 p.m. and the October sunlight is yellow and short. Sunset isn't that far off. The wind blows, making my skirt swish between my legs.

"Thanks for the clothes, Mom." I pull my sleeves down over my wrists.

"They're a little big," Mom says, as though I might not have noticed. "I didn't know whether you'd changed sizes while you were gone. I went up a size just in case."

I shake my head. "Nope. Still the same."

"It'll be a few more days while we process the paperwork, Hannah," the doctor promises. "Like your dad said, you'll be home soon."

I half expect my father to ask why I can't go back to the hotel with them now that the judge has made her ruling and I've been cleared of any wrongdoing. He's always doing things like that, requesting special treatment—cutting the line at customs, requesting an upgrade at a fancy hotel—as though the rules that apply to the rest of the world don't apply to him.

But my father stays quiet. A daughter with mental illness doesn't exactly fit into my parents' lifestyle. Maybe they think it's even worse than having an infant because unlike infancy, there's no end in sight. Perhaps they want the next few days to themselves, a few more days without their damaged daughter in tow.

My parents are the kind of parents who called their child extraordinary (*born mature*), and told her (*me*) not to strive to be normal. Dad said, *What's so great about being normal?* almost as often as he said I should broaden my horizons.

I don't think *this* is the sort of abnormal he had in mind.

I can still hear Agnes's voice: *The girls down the hall say she's just strange.*

My parents wanted me to be *special*, not *strange*.

Lightfoot would say I'm not *strange*, I'm *sick*. She'd say that no two people on the planet are alike; therefore, technically speaking, we're all at least a little bit strange to each other, because we're all at least a little bit different from one another.

Or maybe that's not something Lightfoot would say. Maybe that's the sort of thing some other mother or father would say to comfort a son or daughter who'd recently been diagnosed with a mental illness.

I'm tired. I want to go home. Not back to New York, but back to the institution, back to my room with the magnetic lock on the door.

As soon as Mom turns her back, I wipe my mouth with the back of my hand, removing the last traces of her lipstick. Lightfoot says my name again, gesturing to the sedan. "I know this has been an overwhelming day for you." There's a slight edge to her voice, a warning that if I stand out here much longer, Stephen will force me into the back seat and a syringe filled with sedative will miraculously appear from the pockets of the coat she had to remove to go through the metal detector earlier.

They think I might make a run for it. They think now that I've had a taste of freedom, I won't go back to the institute without a fight.

Don't they understand that this—standing in this parking lot—isn't *freedom*? With Lightfoot and Stephen at my side, with this medication coursing through my body, I may as well still be locked up.

Maybe I'll be in some kind of cage forever.

forty-two

The room—our room, *my* room—feels empty without Lucy in it. Without her stray hairs gathering dust on the floor, without her second tray of food waiting to be picked up, without her bed, her pillow, her wrinkled sheets. It feels bigger now that there's only one bed in here. (There was always only one bed in here.) I pace, trying to make myself believe the room is the same size it's always been: Seven steps. Eight steps. Seven steps. Eight steps.

I'm back in my paper clothes. I kick off my slippers and my bare feet slap against the linoleum. It's the only sound without Lucy's footsteps echoing my own—without her laughing, whispering, complaining. I wonder if she got into the San Francisco Dance Academy, but then I remember she never really auditioned.

She never really danced.

She never really breathed.

It's like she died, except she was never actually alive. I shouldn't miss her. The only thing crazier than imagining a person who isn't real is mourning that person once reality kicks in.

It's different with Jonah. He didn't break up with Agnes for me, he never came here to rescue me, he never called or wrote. (Of course, he *couldn't* have done any of those things because he wasn't real, but that seems beside the point.) I only missed him when Lucy brought up Joaquin, reminding me that she had a boyfriend waiting for her and I didn't.

Unlike Lucy, Jonah was already gone by the time I learned he was a hallucination.

The overhead lights flicker, then go out entirely. Lightfoot said I didn't need to take a sleeping pill tonight. She said I must be exhausted from my ordeal today. But I can't sleep. If Lucy were here, my tossing and turning would keep her awake.

But then again, if Lucy were here, I probably wouldn't have trouble sleeping.

Second grade. I was in second grade the first time I played Light as a Feather, Stiff as a Board. At Mary Masters's eighth birthday party. Alexandra—Alex—was my best friend then. I'd picked her out on the first day of school, the smallest girl in the class, her glasses so thick you could hardly make out her brown eyes behind them. Another friend I could mother and mentor. She wouldn't have been invited to Mary Masters's party if she hadn't been friends with me.

It was Alex's first night away from home and she was frightened, nothing like the other girls who were so excited for their first sleepover party. She stayed glued to my side the whole night: When Mary's parents served us pizza and cake. When they put on a movie for us to watch. When they pushed the coffee table to the side so all nine girls could unroll our sleeping bags in the living room one right next to another.

Alex's bag was next to mine, and I could hear her whimpering when Mary's parents turned off the lights and left us alone.

Mary Masters suggested we play Light as a Feather, Stiff as a Board.

"What's that?" Alex asked dumbly. I didn't know what the game was either, but I knew better than to admit it.

Mary explained the rules: one girl would lie down on her back in the center of the group, and the rest of us would put our fingers beneath her. We'd chant *light as a feather, stiff as a board* over and over until the girl in the middle started to rise.

"My big sister taught me how to play," Mary added. Mary's sister was fourteen, and we were young enough that we thought having "teen" as part of your age meant you knew what you were talking about. For the first time ever, I truly wished I had a sibling. But I wanted an older sister, not a baby.

"But what's the point?" Alex asked. "We just pick one of us up?"

Mary shook her head. "It's more magical than that."

"I think we should play," I said. I turned to Alex. "It'll take your mind off your homesickness." I could tell Alex was embarrassed I'd said that in front of everyone, but we both knew she couldn't be mad at me because I was trying to help her.

Since she was the smallest, Alex was selected to lie in the center of the room. Mary showed us how to slide our fingers under Alex, who giggled when my fingers slipped beneath her arm. Her glasses were inside her sleeping bag, but I told her she didn't need them because her eyes were supposed to be closed anyway.

Even without a big sister, I'd learn about all the other games eventually: Truth or Dare, Never Have I Ever, Spin the Bottle, Seven Minutes in Heaven. I played them all. But none of those games involved magic the way Light as a Feather did. (Unless you considered that fate played a hand in whom the bottle landed on in Spin the Bottle, and I always gave more credit to momentum and gravity.) And sure, it wasn't *really* magic when we lifted Alex off the floor that first time, any more than it was magic when we lifted Rebekah years later. But somehow, with the lights out and our voices chorusing *light as a feather, stiff as a board*, it *felt* like magic.

When Alex fell, we thought it was because the magic stopped working. Now I wonder: Did I let go on purpose?

Dr. Lightfoot's voice runs through my mind: *Symptoms usually start between ages sixteen and thirty*. But she also said my symptoms were subtle, functional. Maybe my brain has been working differently for years, in second grade with Alex, in eighth grade with Rebekah.

Maybe I heard a voice at Mary Masters's sleepover party. Maybe it was Alex's stuffed rabbit, hidden deep inside her sleeping bag. No one else knew that Alex brought her toy that night. She didn't want the other girls to think she was a big baby.

I close my eyes and concentrate until I remember it: the little rabbit told me to let go. I thought it was magic, the same magic that lifted Alex.

I open my eyes. Maybe I never heard a voice at all. Maybe my special/strange brain is trying to trick me all over again, to make me think I've been sick my whole life.

I roll onto my back and straighten my sheets. I'm sweating despite the artificially cool air.

That night with Rebekah, was there a voice then? Did it tell me to let go? Did I listen?

But that was an accident. Like Gavin Baker said: *Accidents happen*. It didn't occur to him—or anyone else—that it was anything other than an accident. Two weeks later, Gavin kissed me at some other girl's party. Rebekah didn't get her first kiss until tenth grade, and then it was with some guy she barely liked, because she wanted to get it over with. Did I drop Rebekah because I wanted Gavin for myself? But I didn't even like Gavin.

Symptoms usually start between ages sixteen and thirty. Thirteen isn't that far from sixteen, and I did so many other things ahead of schedule: long division, reading chapter books on my own, saying *please* and *thank you* without prompting. Maybe I got sick ahead of schedule too.

At the courthouse today, Dr. Lightfoot explained my disease carefully, as though she didn't think the judge or Agnes's parents would understand it otherwise. She said that she'd worked with patients whose hallucinations were much more elaborate than mine; patients who had crowned themselves queens of their own kingdoms, who'd gone on adventures to foreign lands. I only created a best friend and a bad pseudo-boyfriend.

Lightfoot made it sound as if I had an advantage over those

patients because my hallucinations didn't entirely remove me from the real world. My hallucinations were subtle enough to allow me to continue functioning in the real world. It should make me feel like my illness is less serious than those other patients, the ones whose brains took them to their own private Middle Earth or Narnia or Hogwarts. But instead, I feel inadequate, like those other patients are *better* at this disease than I am. Like they had more fun with it.

I wonder where my disease might have taken me if I hadn't been diagnosed so early, if I'd gone years without therapy and medication. Lightfoot's voice: *We're lucky to have caught Hannah's disease this early.*

(*Caught* it. As though it were running and hiding.)

That night with Agnes was different from the nights with Alex and Rebekah. It was just the two of us. Light as a Feather doesn't work with two people.

Truth or Dare was so much easier to play than Light as a Feather, Stiff as a Board. It was Jonah who gave me the idea.

Truth or dare, he asked me once, in between kisses. We were in the room that Agnes and I shared, but Agnes was in class and we (obviously) weren't. We'd both memorized her schedule by then.

Truth, I said.

What's your favorite body part?

On me or on you?

Jonah laughed.

Truth or dare, I challenged him back.

Dare.

I dare you to kiss me outside, where anyone might see us. Before Jonah could argue, I added, *You can't say no. That'd be breaking the rules.*

So Jonah led the way outside, through the dorm lobby and out into the sunlight. It wasn't actually all that much of a dare, when you think about it. The first time he'd kissed me had been outside.

Afterward, Jonah leaned in and whispered, *Truth or dare.* His breath was hot on my neck.

Dare, I answered, my heart pounding.

I dare you to play this game with Agnes later.

I press the heels of my hands to my temples, then my eyes, until I see spots in the darkness. Or do I? Will I ever know the difference between hallucination and reality? Will I spend the rest of my life questioning every new acquaintance, every overheard whisper? Who's to say whether Jonah and Lucy were the first people my brain invented? Maybe there were others who came before: a man smiling at me on the street, the checkout girl at the deli around the corner from school, a teacher calling me in for a private meeting. I'll never know for sure.

Maybe I'll never be certain of anything ever again.

No. There are some things I'm certain of:

I'm certain that I didn't like it out there in the world today. I didn't like sitting in the back seat of Stephen's car on the winding and twisting roads from here to the courthouse. And I didn't like the look on my parents' faces in the conference room or the parking lot. None of it felt good or safe.

This room is safe. It's not even that small, now that I have it to myself. I could stay here forever.

But they're sending me home. Because I have a diagnosis, and the judge said what happened to Agnes wasn't my fault. Soon, I'll be flying back across the country, sleeping in my own bed, walking through Manhattan with my mother. My mother, who hated being alone with me for just five minutes this afternoon. My mother, who was careful so her fingers wouldn't brush against mine when she handed me her lipstick. I get out of bed and pace in the darkness.

When they brought me here, they said I might pose *a danger to herself and others*. I can still picture the words written on the first page of my file.

At the courthouse today, Lightfoot said, *People with this disease are more likely to hurt themselves than others.*

Her voice practically sounded like a prescription. I stop walking and slide my pants down my legs. Tie them around my neck even though it means being naked from the waist down. I pull as hard as I can, willing the world to go dark, but the pants rip. I let them drop to the floor.

I cross the room and stand on my tiptoes beneath the window. There are no bars on the other side of it, but in the moonlight I can see that the glass is laced with safety wire. The wire will make it hurt more when the glass shatters.

Hurt themselves.

Hurt yourself.

I don't hear anyone's voice but my own.

I use my elbow. It hurts, but not enough.

Enough will be when the glass breaks.

Enough will be when I hear it shatter.

Enough will be when I'm bleeding, and the wire is wrapped around my wrist like a bracelet.

And maybe then it still won't be enough.

forty-three

It hurts.

Bang.

Could I break my own elbow?

Bang.

Hurt themselves.

Bang.

Hurt yourself.

Bang.

I'm out of breath, sweating. My hair sticks to my forehead.

Bang.

Why am I doing this? I wanted to go home, and now they're sending me home.

Bang.

I wanted to get my life back on track.

Bang.

My life will never be on the same track it was on before.

Bang.

Louder this time.

Bang.

I'm standing on my tiptoes. Half the time I hit the wall beneath the window instead of the glass because I can barely reach it and my aim isn't that accurate. It doesn't matter. It hurts either way.

Bang.

An orderly bursts through the door. I shout for him to wait.

Bang.

He can drag me back to the padded room, just let me break the glass first.

Bang.

Or my elbow. Whichever breaks first. As long as something breaks.

Bang.

Shoot me up with sedatives, just wait long enough for me finish what I started.

Bang.

He doesn't wait.

The last time someone burst into my room after lights-out, it was Lightfoot and Stephen when my meds kicked in and Lucy disappeared. Tonight, it's an orderly I've never seen before. Lightfoot and Stephen must have gone home for the day. Maybe it's later than it was that night. Or maybe Lightfoot didn't stay tonight because she thought she didn't have to worry that I might act up.

I don't fight when the orderly puts his arms around me. I go limp as he drags me from the room, into an elevator and down to the first floor. (I didn't even know this place had an elevator. Did they use it when they carried me to the padded room? I don't remember.) He brings me to a room I've never seen before. Two rows of beds are lined up along the walls. The beds are separated by curtains, like the beds in the ICU where they put Agnes, but this room doesn't have nearly as many tubes and machines.

The orderly puts me on a bed and holds me down. (He doesn't seem to notice that I'm not struggling.) A nurse comes over and tucks a blanket around me, covering my bottom half. She lifts my elbow to examine it.

"What did you do to yourself, sweetheart?" she murmurs. I've never met this nurse before. I used to hate when strangers used terms of endearment to address me.

"Is it broken?" the orderly asks.

The nurse holds up my left arm. Gently, she straightens and bends the joint. She looks at my face, trying to gauge how much pain she's causing me. "Doesn't seem to be," she says. "But she's going to have a hell of a bruise in the morning."

She wraps my elbow with an Ace bandage. I wonder if she knows that I've never broken a bone, never so much as sprained an ankle.

The orderly is standing over me with tan leather straps. For a half a second, I think he's going to beat me with them, to punish me for acting out.

"Is that really necessary?" the nurse asks. "If she struggles, it could aggravate her injury."

"It's protocol after an event like this," the orderly says. "The doc can remove them in the morning."

He leans over and buckles the strap to the metal bar on the right side of the bed, my uninjured side. He sticks my hand through a loop on the other side of the strap, then tightens the loop around my wrist. It's soft on the inside, not leather but something fuzzy and soft. Like the world's strangest part of shearling gloves.

He moves to the other side of the bed, forcing the nurse to step out of the way. He's careful as he slides my battered arm into the restraint. "She's not struggling," he adds. "Guess she wore herself out."

"I'm going to administer a sedative nonetheless. I don't want to risk her flailing about and doing more damage to that elbow."

I've never actually minded when people talked about me like I wasn't there. My parents used to do it at restaurants: to waiters, maître d's, to their friends sitting across the hall. Sometimes, I'd pretend to nap just to hear them praising my good behavior, how precocious I was, how sophisticated.

I feel the prick of a needle, and the sedative enters my veins. The familiar heaviness settles over me.

"At least we can keep an eye on her down here," the nurse says, clucking her tongue. *Click.* She tosses the needle into the designated medical-waste trash can.

The first time they sedated me, I felt so powerless that I worried they'd used too much, that my heart would beat too slowly and my lungs would stop absorbing oxygen.

I certainly never thought that being tied up would feel as secure and cozy as being wrapped in my favorite blanket back home. But right now, I like how it feels to be sedated and restrained.

The nurse reaches out and brushes my hair off my forehead with her fingers.

"You're safe here."

They can't possibly send me home now.

I'm *a danger* to myself.

I *hurt* myself.

Maybe they'll keep me here forever.

Maybe they should.

Maybe this is the only place where I can be safe.

Where people like her can keep an eye on me.

forty-four

Something cold wakes me.

The nurse must notice my eyes fluttering because she says, "I'm sorry, sweetie."

I shake my head, still not fully awake. I don't remember where I am at first. I'm used to sleeping alone in my room in the dark, not with a nurse hovering above me in a room with the lights on. I usually sleep lying on my left side, but now I'm flat on my back. I try to roll over, but a tug on my wrist stops me.

Oh, I remember. They tied me up.

I blink and turn my head. There are empty beds on either side of me. Apparently I'm the only patient who had an incident overnight.

"I hate to wake you, but I didn't think we should put off icing this elbow any longer."

This elbow. My elbow. My left elbow.

In the old days, people thought being left-handed was a curse. My mother's mother's mother was left-handed back in Poland before Word War II, and they tied her left hand behind her back, forcing her to use her right hand instead.

Of course, in the old days, people believed that seeing things that weren't there was a sign of possession, rather than a symptom of a medical condition.

I look down at my elbow. It's twice the size it used to be. When the nurse adjusts my bandage, I see that my elbow is pink, and I imagine the blood pooling beneath the surface of the skin, waiting to turn into a dark-purple bruise. I lift my arm (the little I can with the restraints around my wrist), but the nurse stops me.

"Best not to move it," she says, placing it back on the ice pack lying at my side. I shiver when my skin comes in contact with the cold. The nurse puts another ice pack over my elbow. "We'll see if we can't get the swelling down."

Fat chance, I think but do not say.

"The doctor will be here soon." She pats my shoulder gently before walking away. She isn't the same nurse who was here last night, but she might as well be. She has the same sympathetic look on her face that the other nurse did.

I'm surprised when Dr. Lightfoot shows up a few minutes later. When the nurse said *the doctor will be here soon*, I thought she meant a medical doctor, someone to examine my arm, wrap it in a bandage, prescribe painkillers. Instead, Lightfoot stands at the foot of my bed, her dark hair pulled into a messy ponytail at the nape of her neck.

"Do you want to tell me what happened?" she asks unnecessarily. Of course, the nurse already told her what I did. Maybe they called her in the middle of the night, woke her up. Maybe

Lightfoot had to get out of bed so she could answer the phone without waking the man (woman?) sleeping beside her. It occurs to me that I don't know if she's married (she doesn't wear a ring), and I don't know whether she has children. I don't know where she grew up or where she lives now.

They're definitely going to put me back in the padded room so I can't hurt myself again. Stephen is probably waiting beyond the curtain to escort me. Maybe they'll even cover the window in the door. Lightfoot will explain that after what happened last night, I can hardly be trusted around windows.

"Let me know how many days go by," I say finally. I hated how confusing it was last time.

"How many days go by?" Lightfoot echoes.

"Before you let me go back to my room." *My* room. *My* elbow. *My* diagnosis.

Will they let me have ice in the padded room? My elbow is so swollen I can't bend or straighten it; it's trapped somewhere in between.

"Hannah, we're sending you back up to your room this afternoon. You haven't broken any bones, so there's no reason for you to stay down here."

No reason?

"Aren't you worried I'll hurt myself again?" I press my elbow into the ice pack beneath it. The pressure hurts.

Lightfoot sits on the edge of the bed. "Are you planning to hurt yourself again?"

I shake my head. Not because I don't think I might hurt

myself again, but because I don't have any actual *plans*. I didn't *plan* any of this.

I've never had fewer plans in my whole life.

"We'll adjust your meds," Lightfoot continues. I wait for her to tell me about the mood stabilizer they're adding to my regime, that she'll never let me skip a sleeping pill again, or their plans to keep me at least mildly sedated from now on, but instead she says: "I'm going to add an antidepressant to the mix."

"Depression wasn't part of my diagnosis."

Lucy complained when they put her on antidepressants even though she wasn't depressed.

Wait. Lucy wasn't real.

I wonder how long it will take before I don't have to remind myself.

I take a deep breath, blow it out slowly.

"Trying to hurt yourself can be linked to depression." Lightfoot smiles. A real smile, not a medical-school smile. "Don't worry, you'll still be able to go home soon."

I try to sit up, but the restraints keep me lying prone. The ice pack on top of my elbow slides off, and Lightfoot leans forward to put it back in place. I can feel the warmth of her body near mine.

"You're still sending me home?" I ask incredulously.

"Of course."

"But I tried to hurt myself. I'm depressed. You said so."

Lightfoot smiles again and leans in close like we're old friends sharing secrets. She's wearing her glasses again, not her contacts. "Believe it or not, this isn't all that unusual; plenty of patients with diseases like yours experience periods of depression. And let's not forget, your entire world has been rocked by this diagnosis. It's normal to feel sadness or anger before finding acceptance."

Doesn't Lightfoot understand that nothing about my situation is *usual* or *normal*?

Lightfoot pats my leg and stands.

"Even though you're getting better, you lost a friend."

"It's been months since I lost Agnes." I've had plenty of time to get used to being without her.

Lightfoot shakes her head. "Not Agnes," she says. "You lost *Lucy.*"

I look at Lightfoot in surprise. "But Lucy wasn't real. *You're* the one who made sure I knew that."

"She was real to you."

Lightfoot makes it sound simple, as though it's perfectly reasonable to miss a hallucination.

I hate that she understands me. I hate how she seems to know that I can't stop thinking about Lucy. Every time I think of her, I have to remind myself she isn't real. I'm like an elderly person with Alzheimer's who keeps forgetting her husband died, who has to mourn all over again each time someone reminds her.

I never missed any of my other friends, those real girls. When those friendships ended, I was always ready to move on to someone new.

I wasn't ready with Lucy.

"Don't worry," Lightfoot repeats. "I'll make sure your doctor back home is aware of what happened last night."

"I don't have a doctor back home. Not a psychiatrist, I mean."

I have a general practitioner—the same one my mom goes to. (My parents stopped sending me to a pediatrician as soon as I turned fourteen.) I have a dentist, and I once saw a neurologist when I had a headache that lasted three days. He prescribed some codeine and it was gone like that.

"Your parents and I have already found someone to take you on," Lightfoot explains. It's strange to think of her having conversations with my parents that I'm not a part of. "Everything's all set."

All set.

Game. Set. Match.

I can't believe my plan to *stay* failed, and my plan to *leave* succeeded.

forty-five

They escort me back to my room. There's no sign of last night's temper tantrum (my first). I never succeeded in breaking the glass, so the window looks exactly the same. I guess it's a good thing I didn't crack it after all. If I had, they might have brought me to some other room, at least until the window in this room was repaired.

I'm not, obviously, in restraints anymore, but my left arm is in a sling and bandaged so tightly I can feel the blood throbbing underneath. I can see the bruise, already shifting from pink to purple, peeking out from either end of the bandage. I didn't complain when the nurse—the one from last night—wrapped the arm, but the pain must've been written on my face because she murmured, "I'm sorry, honey, but we need to keep it tight so you can't move it enough to do any more damage."

So, in a way, I'm still being restrained.

An attendant comes later to take me to shower. She unwraps then rewraps my arm so the bandage won't get wet. I shower alone with the attendant watching me, but this time it doesn't feel like group showers are a privilege I haven't yet earned. She's watching to make sure I don't hurt my arm any more.

At dinnertime, instead of bringing me food on a tray, I'm led down to the cafeteria with the other girls. Cassidy—QB— waves when she sees me coming, gesturing at the bench across from her. No hard feelings, I guess. Maybe Lightfoot told her I was working hard to go home too. I could sit with her, become the newest member of her clique, even if only for a day or two.

Maybe she's already smuggled in another phone. Maybe I could finally text Jonah—no, I can't text Jonah. Jonah doesn't have a phone. Jonah doesn't have a pocket or a hand or fingers.

I look across the room at the E.D. girls: three tables, no more than four girls per table, and each table has its own attendant keeping watch. It all looks exactly like it did when Lucy sat there. Except, of course, Lucy never sat there.

Eventually I sit next to Annie. Her hair is greasy again—she lost shower privileges, she says, though she doesn't say why and I don't ask. She sinks into her usual chatter. I wonder if the drugs they give her make her more energetic.

Dinner tonight is lukewarm chicken stew, but it's too hard to hold the spoon with my right hand so after a few clumsy tries, I push the tray away. At least when I get home, the food will be hot. Maybe Mom and Dad will take me out to dinner to celebrate my homecoming. Sushi, maybe. Or oysters. (Neither of which are hot, but both of which they'd never give us here.) My dad was so proud of me the first time I ate oysters. Maybe we'll go downtown to that restaurant in Soho with the amazing raw bar.

After I took my SATs this spring, Dad and I celebrated by eating oysters there. It didn't even matter that we didn't have my scores yet—Dad said he was already proud of me.

He said he'd always been proud of me. I can still see the look on his face, like he couldn't believe his luck, having fathered a daughter who filled him with such pride. (I guess most fathers feel that way at some point or another.)

I wonder if he'll ever look at me with so much pride again.

Maybe he won't ever want to take me for a special meal.

Maybe he won't want to celebrate anything about me.

Annie keeps talking. I stare at the stew that I can't eat and wait for an attendant to tell us it's time to go back upstairs.

∴

The next day after lunch, I line up with the girls who have grounds privileges. (Despite my episode, Lightfoot said I could go outside, though she reminded me that—like all the girls with grounds privileges—I would be supervised.) I follow a handful of other patients to the door where Lucy and I—no, just I—saw the other patients exit the building on September sixteenth. An orderly scans our bracelets and hands each of us a drab, gray sweatshirt before we step outside. A few other orderlies are already outside, ready to keep an eye on us, make sure we don't stray too far. It's colder today than it was in September. The name of the institute is ironed on to the front of the sweatshirt in faded white letters, and it smells like someone else was wearing it yesterday. I barely manage to get my bandaged arm through the sleeve.

The other girls run up ahead, staring into the sun and running their hands along the bark of the redwood trees that line the path ahead of us. They look like a group of second graders who've been let outside for recess.

I tilt my head to the sky and squint in the sunlight. The warmth feels like it did before they medicated me. I step on a pinecone, and my flimsy slippers aren't enough to protect my foot from its sharp edges. I bite my lip to keep from crying, folding my good arm over my bandaged one across my chest.

Maybe when I get home, I'll retrace every step I ever took. Go back to every store I ever shopped in, reread every book I ever read, re-eat every meal I ever loved, re-watch every movie I ever saw. How else will I know if I imagined anything else along the way? Lightfoot says she believes my symptoms began recently, but she doesn't know for sure.

I'll keep a list of the things that are the same.

1. *Warmth of sunlight.*
2. *Pain of stepping on something sharp.*

Distinguishing what *is* real from what *was* fake could take the rest of my life.

The idea makes me so tired I sit down right then and there in the dirt. I close my eyes and wait for an attendant to help me up and lead me inside.

They take the sweatshirt back before escorting me to my room, so some other girl can use it tomorrow.

forty-six

Lightfoot gives me my pills and sends me on my way. Or more accurately, she gives my mother my pills—one bottle of the blue antipsychotics, another of the yellow sedatives, and last but not least, a bottle of the chalky pink ones that are my antidepressants—and sits down with us in her office for one final conversation. There are enough pills, she says, to last until the end of the month. After that, we'll refill the prescriptions at our pharmacy in New York.

She says it like that—*we, our*—but of course, Lightfoot won't be there, and they're *my* prescriptions. Not hers, and not my parents' either. (Even if my parents are the ones who'll pick up and pay for the medication each month.)

I've never been inside Lightfoot's office, and it surprises me how different it is from the rest of this place.

My mother and I sit in heavy chairs made of wood and uphol-stered with leather, nothing like the plastic chair Lightfoot brought to my room for our sessions. Lightfoot sits in a high-backed chair on the other side of her desk, facing us. Her office is on the first floor. My father stands behind us, and I imagine his hand hovering above my shoulder, not quite sure whether it's safe to touch me.

That's just my imagination, not a hallucination.

That's okay.

The walls are lined with wooden shelves full of textbooks and manuals.

"I didn't know you had so many books in here," I interrupt. My elbow is still bandaged, my arm still in a sling. I press my hand against my chest like I'm giving the pledge of allegiance, though it's the wrong hand. I spot a row of classic novels tucked between the textbooks. "I would've loved to be reading *Anna Karenina* instead of the nurses' cast-off romance novels all this time."

Anna Karenina would've made for an excellent book club discussion. "Lucy and I could've gone round and round on the first line for hours."

Are all happy families really alike?

Are unhappy families actually that different?

Discuss.

Beside me, my mother swallows audibly. I shift my gaze from the books. Mom's face is flushed.

And I lose Lucy once more.

Maybe it was Lightfoot who sent me *Jane Eyre* a few days ago. I scan her shelves for an open space where the book might have been. Maybe reading a classic novel was a privilege I earned without realizing it. Maybe Lightfoot wanted me to recognize how lucky I am: *See what they used to do to people with mental illness—lock them up and throw away the key?* Or maybe she thought I'd identify with the first Mrs. Rochester, a woman who was considered a villain for more than a hundred years after the novel was published until some readers considered there might have been more to her story.

"How long until she forgets about these imaginary friends?" Dad asks.

Lightfoot shifts in her seat. Her clothes—she's wearing her usual papery blue scrubs; she'll be seeing other patients when this meeting is over—rustle when she moves. Yesterday she told me I could wear real pajamas, but it didn't seem worth the bother to ask my mother to bring me more clothes when I'd be leaving so soon. *Anyway, I said, imagine the damage I could have done if I'd had real clothes the night I hurt myself.* I remembered how the green pants had ripped when I wrapped them around my neck. *There's a reason this place makes wearing real pajamas a privilege.*

Lightfoot smiled then, a real smile. She said she trusted me not to hurt myself again.

Why? I asked.

Because if you were going to hurt yourself again, you wouldn't have told me you understand that real clothes could be dangerous.

Now, Lightfoot turns to my father and says, "They weren't 'imaginary friends.'"

"But she's still talking about having a conversation with someone who was never there!" Dad sounds frustrated, like the service in this place is below par.

He did that at hotels and restaurants all the time.

A place this expensive ought to include free drinks from the minibar.

We've been sitting here for twenty minutes, and the waiter still hasn't taken our order.

They have the gall to call this mush *flourless chocolate cake?*

For the first time, it occurs to me that my dad is actually kind of rude.

"Lucy was there," Lightfoot explains calmly. "Just not in a way that you and I can experience. *Hannah's* brain works differently." I hate the way she emphasizes my name. It underlines how different I am from my parents, separating me from them even further. "Hallucinations are when the brain experiences a sensation without corresponding external stimuli. In fact, Hannah may remember Lucy and Jonah *better* than she remembers other friends because she herself generated them. It's called the generation effect. Hallucinatory memories can be particularly powerful."

"But with the medication—" Mom begins and then stops. "She'll be normal again, right?"

"I prefer not to use words like *normal.* Or *crazy* for that matter," Lightfoot adds. She smiles one of her medical-school smiles, the *I-know-how-hard-this-must-be-for-you-to-understand* smile. "As I said, Hannah's brain works differently. Remember, this is a disease, a medical condition."

At my hearing, Lightfoot compared my disease to a broken bone. She said that she'd set the bone and wrapped it in plaster. But broken bones aren't diseases, and people who break their arms and legs don't usually have to worry about them all that much once the cast comes off. Then again, perhaps a bone that's been broken is more likely to break again.

"Medication and therapy aren't a cure," Lightfoot continues, which is just a fancy way of saying: *Hannah won't ever be like you again. In fact, she was probably never like you to begin with.* "They're part of her treatment plan."

"You said her symptoms were under control," Dad counters, as though Lightfoot is a salesperson trying to put one over on him.

"I said we were managing her symptoms," Lightfoot corrects patiently.

I'm not an expert in body language, but my mother is leaning away from me as if she's scared whatever I've got is contagious, as though having a family history can work backward as well as forward. Her legs are crossed so that her feet are pointing away from mine. She's wearing designer kitten heels, the kind of shoes that would be confiscated upstairs because even one-inch heels could do damage. Mom's beige blazer has trim that matches her navy-blue pants perfectly. Her pants are stylishly cropped above the ankle. When I was little and she still dropped me off and picked me up from school, I always thought that my mother's outfits were so much more stylish than what the other mothers wore. She might technically have been wearing the same thing as the other moms—a pantsuit, a pair of well-pressed slacks—but she invariably added something extra to her outfits: a brightly colored silk scarf, perfectly applied eyeliner, shoes with embellished heels. When we went shopping together, we'd share even the tiniest dressing room so we could show each other every single thing we tried on.

Now, I wonder if my mother will ever want to be close to me again.

I shift in my chair. When I got dressed this morning, I had a choice of what to wear: the new outfit my mother bought me for the hearing, or the leggings and tank top I was wearing when they brought me here months ago. I chose the new clothes, but put the leggings on beneath the skirt because I worried I'd be cold on the plane with bare legs. Lightfoot helped me roll the left sleeve up over my bandage. Now I wish I'd gone without the pants. I might have been cold, but at least it would've been an outfit my mother approved of.

I find myself thinking about Cassidy. She's somewhere in this building. In group therapy, maybe, or art class. If I stayed, maybe I could usurp her. Better to be a Queen Bee in here than a freak outside, right?

"We'll always have to keep watch for Hannah's symptoms." Lightfoot says *we* again as if she's still part of all this, but after today I'll probably never see her again. They must have taught her that in medical school: *Include yourself in the treatment plan to make parents feel less alone when they're about to take their newly diagnosed offspring home with them.* "A disease like Hannah's ebbs and flows. Think of cancer that goes into remission and then, seemingly out of nowhere, metastasizes, sending a patient back to the hospital."

"But if you catch cancer early, you can stop it from spreading," Dad interjects. "You said you caught this early."

Dad wants Lightfoot to tell him she *nipped this thing in the bud*, but Lightfoot won't (can't) give him the satisfaction.

"Over the years, Hannah's medications will need to be adjusted. You may consider new treatments. Your doctor in New York will help you weigh the benefits against the possible side effects." I wonder if my parents have noticed the sudden shift in Lightfoot's pronouns: *your* doctor, not *our* doctor, but not *Hannah's* doctor either. Maybe they taught her that in medical school too: *Before they leave, remind parents this is their responsibility now. You won't always be around to help.* "As I said, there is no cure. But it can be managed."

Even though our brains work differently, I'm positive my parents hear the same implication in Lightfoot's statement that I do: *Hannah's disease is under control now, but flare-ups may send her back to places like this from time to time.* (Maybe I will see Lightfoot again after all.)

I can't tell if the idea of sending me back to a place like this horrifies or comforts my parents. It must upset them to hear that I might need to be institutionalized again. On the other hand, sending me away whenever things get bad will give them a chance to spend time away from me. They could drop me off at an institution and head for a luxury resort in Europe. Instead of taking vacations from work like other people, they'll take their vacations from *me*.

Not so long ago, I couldn't have imagined that. I spent most of my life certain that my parents wanted me with them as much as possible—that's what they said, and I never doubted it.

But maybe they didn't forego babysitters because they wanted me with them. Maybe they simply couldn't be bothered. Maybe I fit into their lives—expensive travel, fancy restaurants—not because I was *born mature*, but because it never occurred to them to raise their child any other way.

And maybe they'd been looking forward to being empty nesters when I went away to college next year. Maybe after all these years of taking me with them everywhere, they were excited to be on their own again. Is that why Dad wanted me to apply for this summer program in the first place—not to *broaden my horizons*, but so he and Mom could have a couple months to themselves?

Maybe they'll never want to bring me with them anywhere ever again.

"You're sure she's well enough to go home?" Dad asks finally.

He's standing behind me so I can't see his face, but I can see my mother's. There's hope in her expression. They don't want to take me home.

Lightfoot nods. "With the right help, patients with Hannah's disease live rich lives—go to college, work, get married—just like the rest of us."

I wonder how many parents she's had to give this speech to over the years, how many mothers and fathers she's tried to keep from imagining their daughters like one of those homeless ladies in Central Park, wearing wool coats when it's ninety-five degrees out, carrying on full conversations with people only they can see.

Lightfoot continues, "People with diseases like Hannah's have gone on to write books, to practice law, medicine, psychology—you name it. Her path may be rockier than some, but it can still lead to extraordinary places."

Lightfoot smiles, and I wonder if she's remembering how worried I was about falling behind in school. I was convinced being held in this place would keep me from doing all the things I wanted to do. My doctor looks not at my parents but at me and says, "This isn't the end of all your plans."

Lightfoot shifts her gaze back to my parents. "Let me remind you," she continues patiently (she's said everything patiently this morning), "none of this is Hannah's fault." She pauses. "What happened to Agnes isn't Hannah's fault."

"But you said she was hallucinating. Who knows what she might have done…" Dad trails off.

Oh.

My parents aren't ashamed of me. Or anyway, they're not *only* ashamed of me. They're also *scared* of me. The day of my hearing, it wasn't just the judge or even Agnes's parents Lightfoot was trying to convince.

Lightfoot said that people with my disease are *more likely to hurt themselves than others.*

More likely isn't a promise.

More likely isn't a guarantee. "I know this is overwhelming." Lightfoot stands. Her patience has finally run out. Our time is up. I stand too, but my parents remain still. They're in no rush to get going.

"Hannah isn't the only one who has to adjust to the reality of living with this disease." Lightfoot walks around the desk to shake my parents' hands, a gesture which seems to finally make them move toward the door. "But I assure you, she doesn't need to be here anymore."

My parents do not look assured.

PART THREE

outside

forty-seven

Leaving the property today feels different than it did the day of my hearing. I'm still alone in the back seat, but my parents' rental car is a black SUV with smooth leather seats rather than an inexpensive sedan like the car Stephen drove. The gate at the end of the driveway swings open to let us leave (we don't have to punch in a key code; whoever controls the gate must have known we were coming). I crane my neck after we drive through, watching the gate swing shut behind us. I gaze up at the Santa Cruz Mountains. The sun is out, but the tops of the mountains are covered in fog, like it's waiting to roll back down later.

I wonder how long it will be before another patient moves into my room. Maybe some new girl is already there. Maybe they've already taken her clothes and given her a fresh set of papery green pajamas. Maybe she's counting her steps, gazing out the window, already wondering how long she'll be trapped inside.

Lightfoot told me that not all the girls at the institute are there by court order. Some are sent by their parents or teachers. Some even commit themselves voluntarily because they know they're sick. I asked if Cassidy was one of those volunteers, but Lightfoot wouldn't tell me. Doctor/patient confidentiality and all that.

I said that I used to think she didn't care about doctor/patient confidentiality. "You know, since we had our sessions with Lucy in the room."

Maybe one day I'll look back and realize that so much of what I thought about my stay at the institute was wrong.

"We talked to your teachers. You'll be able to go back to school soon," Mom begins. She doesn't turn to face me when she speaks. I'm sitting behind the driver's seat and my father is the one driving, so I'm able to see Mom's profile.

"But I missed a month." September seventh seems like so much more than a month ago.

Mom shrugs. She still doesn't turn. "You're such a good student that they're confident you'll be able to catch up. And they'll take your illness into account when calculating grades."

Mom says the word *illness* carefully, like she planned this conversation days ago and took some time to decide the best wording.

"Do they know what's wrong with me?"

"The teachers do, but they've assured us of confidentiality."

"They're not worried that I might…" I pause. "Have an episode?" I finish finally.

"Of course not. You heard what the doctor said." I suspect she wants to sound more confident than she actually does.

I wonder where my classmates think I've been. It's not the first time I've missed the beginning of the school year. I could say that my parents and I were on vacation again. I could come up with a good story: We were hiking in the Alps and an avalanche cut off the route back to town; there was no cell service, no way to get in touch. We lived in a cabin for nearly a month, eating roots and grubs that we dug out from under the snow. We collected wood to build a fire. We nearly froze to death.

No. That's the kind of story a five-year-old would tell. And it'd be too easy to disprove. Someone could easily Google the weather in Switzerland and discover my lie.

I should be more mysterious about my absence. Drop hints about the "place" I was "sent," the "treatment" I received. People would probably put the pieces together and guess I was in rehab. Some of my classmates would even think it's cool.

Of course, there's one way my classmates could find out the truth: I could tell them. I could make an example of myself—the young patient fighting to remove the stigma that surrounds mental illness. It's the kind of crusade my mother would pick up with gusto. But then, why does she sound so pleased that my teachers have been sworn to secrecy? Maybe it would be easier for her to take up this cause if it were someone else's daughter.

Lightfoot's voice: *Hannah isn't the only one who has to adjust to the reality of living with this disease.* (Not a hallucination; a memory.)

"And you still have plenty of time to get your college applications done," Mom adds. "Though, of course, the doctor thinks it would be best if you limited your search to universities closer to home for now."

"Lightfoot or the new doctor?"

"Lightfoot?" Mom echoes with concern.

"That was my nickname for the doctor at the institute," I mumble. I want to tell her that giving someone a nickname isn't a symptom—in fact, it's the sort of thing Mom would have found amusing before—but I'm not sure she'll believe me.

"In any event," she says, smoothing nonexistent wrinkles in her pants, "both doctors agree that staying nearby will be best for you."

I nod. Maybe they (the doctors? my parents? the university administrators?) won't let me live in the dorms, so I'll have to be a commuter student. Maybe the new doctor will suggest I keep my course load light, take an extra year or two to graduate if I need to.

Her path may be rockier than some.

I glance at Dad, but all I can see is the back of his head. I imagine his gaze is focused on the road ahead. Mom reaches out and pats his leg reassuringly.

Watching her touch him, I feel like an outsider. I close my eyes and pretend to sleep. I don't want to see them comforting each other, and I don't want Mom to go on talking as though I can pick up where I left off. The sling forces me to keep my left arm folded across my chest. It almost feels like being held.

The day of my hearing, Agnes's parents held hands while their attorney spoke. They were still holding hands while Lightfoot spoke. I thought I could see each of them tighten their grip when the judge cleared her throat before she announced that I wasn't responsible for what happened. They only let go when Agnes's mother dropped her face into her hands.

Would they have looked *happy* if the case had gone to trial instead of being dismissed? If I'd been found guilty and sentenced to a few years in prison? They still wouldn't have gotten their daughter back the way she was before.

I open my eyes just a little. My father's hand is resting on top of my mother's on his leg. Do I seem like a stranger to them now, even though they made me?

Technically, I made Lucy. Does that make me like a parent?

No. I didn't *make* Lucy, I *invented* her.

Like God invented Adam, if you believe in that sort of thing.

I let my eyes flutter shut. I think of our old inside joke: I was *born mature*. It always made us laugh, but now I don't think it was ever all that funny.

I hear Mom whisper to Dad, "There are studies that suggest solitary confinement induces hallucinations. I know she was hardly kept in solitary, but you saw that tiny room they gave her—for all we know, *that place* exacerbated her hallucinations, made her even sicker. We should never have let her stay there."

I imagine Dad nodding rather than reminding Mom that they hardly had a choice about where to send me, determined as he always is *to stay on the same page* with his wife.

"I'm going to look into it," Mom continues, her voice a little louder, charged with righteousness. She sounds almost like she did when she used to talk about the nurse's strike. "How can

315

they claim to make objective observations when they keep their patients in such an abnormal environment?"

If I weren't pretending to sleep, I might smile and tell Mom that I said almost the exact same thing to Lightfoot once.

My own voice: *This is hardly a* normal *environment.*

"It'll be better when we get her home," Mom continues. "The doctor we've lined up is the best in the business, highly recommended. Who knows? He might have a more promising diagnosis."

I'm not surprised my parents have lined up a well-known doctor. My parents trust people and places with good reviews. When they host parties, they only hire acclaimed caterers, and when they travel, they only stay at five-star hotels. They believe in following expert advice, taking expert suggestions. It's not as though the institute or Dr. Charan came *highly recommended.*

I think that's the first time I've ever thought of Lightfoot by her real name.

Dr. Priya Charan.

forty-eight

It's a long drive, but my father doesn't offer to stop for a snack or a bathroom break. Finally we drop off the rental car at the airport Hertz and get on the elevated train to the terminal. I stare out the windows. From here, the airport looks enormous. Every time the train stops (at a parking lot, at the BART station, then at one or another terminal), an automated female voice directs us to *hold on*, to watch for rolling luggage. I tug at the waistband of my leggings. I think about asking to change my clothes, but it seems like too much trouble.

With my right hand, I hold one of the poles in the center of the car, but I still stumble every time the train stops and starts. I worry that my parents are taking this as evidence of my instability rather than proof of the forces of gravity and inertia and whatever other scientific law from last year's physics class might apply.

My elbow throbs beneath the bandage. It's less swollen than it was but still bigger than it's supposed to be. Dr. Charan warned my parents to keep an eye on me since the antidepressants probably haven't kicked in yet.

The sun streams in through the train's windows. On one side of the San Francisco airport is the bay and on the other is Highway 101 and the foothills above it. For the first time in months, I'm not in a cage: Not inside the eight-foot-by-seven-foot room with its ugly green walls and plaster ceiling. Not in the three-story building built into the mountainside, not walking the grounds cloaked in fog. Not even in the car Stephen drove or the conference room where the hearing was held. I'm out from under Dr. Charan's care. I finally understand that expression—to be *under* someone's care.

I should feel free now.

"Terminal 2," the automated voice announces, listing which airlines are located there. My parents step off the train. They didn't tell me which airline we were flying, so I have to rush to make it off the train after them before the doors slide shut.

My parents and I have been to dozens of airports together. Even when I was three or four or five years old, with my small feet and short legs, I didn't have this much trouble keeping up with them. And my legs are longer than my mother's now.

I get in line behind my parents as they check their luggage. Mom hands me a tote bag that I recognize as my own. I had it with me when they brought me to the institution, but it was confiscated. I reach inside and there's my wallet with my driver's license so I can get through security. (Dad insisted I take driver's ed and pass the test before coming to California for the summer. We spent hours, just the two of us, in my parents' Range Rover practicing parallel parking and three-point-turns.) I find my cell phone, though of course the battery's dead, and the charger must have been shipped home with the rest of my things back in August. There's even a copy of the book I was reading before Agnes fell, a history of Tudor England. I was like that back then. It was only a few months ago, but it already feels like a distant *back then*, back when I read about history for fun. If anyone had asked me at the time, I would've said that the real lives of the Tudors were every bit as juicy as any romance novel. Of course, that was before I read any actual romance novels.

Now, the book feels heavy as I follow my parents to airport security. Now, I don't think I'll be able to concentrate on words like *peerage* and *courtiers* and *excommunication*. Now, I hope there will be a bookstore by the gate where I can pick out something less dense to keep me entertained on the flight.

I reach into the bag for a large barrette, sliding my arm momentarily out of its sling so I can pull my hair into a ponytail for the first time in months.

It's hard to keep my balance with one arm in a sling and my other arm holding this heavy bag. Instead of looking where I'm going, I keep my gaze trained on my feet to make sure I don't trip. I'm surrounded by dozens of people. I'm not used to being around this many people anymore.

Someone bumps into me, offering a muffled *excuse me*. I look up and see a woman with long dark hair.

"Wait," I say before I can stop myself.

She pauses, looking me up and down and then at the ground by my feet. "Did I drop something?"

No, I think. *It's just that for a second there you looked like my friend Lucy.* I shake my head, and she walks away. I wonder if she thinks I'm strange. Maybe she assumes I'm a confused tourist.

We make our way through security—shoes off, shoes on, bags on the conveyor belt, et cetera—and walk toward our gate. An announcement rings through the air, "Final boarding call for Flight 13 to Seattle-Tacoma."

Seattle is (was, wasn't, never was) Jonah's hometown.

"Hurry up, Hannah." Mom's trying to keep her voice light, like I'm merely dawdling (something I never did before, always determined to get from one place to the next efficiently like my parents taught me), but I can tell she's anxious. She and Dad want to get to the gate and sit down, stay put. I pick up my pace. I train my eyes on my parents' backs like a little kid who's scared of getting lost. I feel a flutter of adrenaline in my belly, as though I'm scared of flying.

I don't mean to lose track of my parents, but suddenly I can't see Mom's beige blazer, Dad's tweedy sport coat. I glance around nervously, trying to find them.

It's okay, I tell myself, taking a deep breath. *Just remember the gate number and follow the signs.* But I can't remember the gate number.

My ticket's in my bag. It says which gate to go to on the ticket.

I stop and drop the tote bag to the floor, crouch down and rifle through it.

I'll show Mom and Dad that I'm capable of getting to the gate by myself. They'll see that I'm not so different from the daughter they remember.

They probably miss that girl, the same way I miss Lucy.

My father's voice: *How long until she forgets about these imaginary friends?*

My heart pounds. I concentrate on my breaths—*in, out, in, out*—but no matter how hard I try, they come out short and ragged, not steady and calm.

I don't know when I start crying, but soon my vision is so blurred with tears that I can't find my ticket. I wipe my eyes and stand. My foot slips out of the slightly-too-big ballet flats (the stylish kind, not the Lightfoot kind) my mother bought me.

I slide my foot back into my shoe and take a tentative step. People rush past me on either side. They've got places to go: planes to catch, families to get home to, meetings to attend, but I move slowly.

If I just keep walking, I'll see my parents waiting at one of the gates.

My gaze lands on a poster advertising the San Francisco Ballet Company: a pretty Latina girl captured in mid-leap against a gray background, her long hair floating around her face.

Is this where I first got the idea for Lucy? Maybe I saw that poster when I got off the plane in June (was that same poster here in June?) and the image stored itself somewhere in the recesses of my brain.

Or maybe Dr. Charan's ridiculous ballet slippers gave me the idea to make Lucy a ballerina.

Or maybe none of the above.

I twist my left arm from its sling and close my eyes so tight I see spots. I press my hands to the sides of my skull as if I think I can squeeze out an explanation.

But there's only the bustle and hum of the airport around me.

forty-nine

I slide the lock into place and press my back against the metallic silver door.

Was there a line to get into the ladies' room? Did I cut the line? I don't know. I wanted to find somewhere quiet, some place away from the crowd where I could be alone. The bathroom seemed like the closest available option.

But I can still hear the women talking outside the stall. Discussing their upcoming trips, or how happy they are to be home. Chatting on their phones to pass the time while they wait in line. Will I ever get used to being around noise and chatter again?

My elbow hurts. I can feel my pulse under the tight bandage. I undo the metal teeth holding the bandage in place and start unwinding, letting the stretchy tan fabric pool on the linoleum floor. It's gray here too, but darker than the institute's floors. The bruise on my arm has gone from pink to red to purple to green, though it's still plum-colored at the center. I unroll the sleeve of my blouse so I won't have to look at it.

I slide my back down the door and sit, my legs straight out in front of me, my feet resting on either side of the toilet. I wish Lucy were here to tell me I'll be okay, it's all going to be okay. I wish Jonah were here to take my hand and pull me close and kiss the top of my head. Of course, wishing for them isn't the same thing as *hearing* them, *seeing* them, *feeling* them. I open my eyes and look at my hand, empty with no one to hold it. I wish my brain could give them back to me just long enough to make me feel better.

Would they make me feel better? They were so imperfect. Lucy might go on and on about Joaquin, and Jonah would probably refuse to hold my hand in public. Why didn't I invent better people?

It was Jonah who made the first move when we hooked up. It was Jonah who planted the idea of playing Truth or Dare with Agnes in my head. And Lucy pushed another girl for being effortlessly thin.

Was my brain just trying to give me some company? Did it invent Lucy to make me feel better about myself? After all, Lucy *knew* she pushed Rhiannon, she *wanted* to hurt her competitor. (How unoriginal, by the way: a dancer pushing her competitor to get ahead. For a second, I wish my brain had invented something more unexpected, but then I remember I should be wishing that my brain hadn't invented something at all.) Maybe it was Lucy who made me bad since it was *Lucy's* voice I heard telling me to push Agnes. But no. That's making Lucy too real, giving her too much credit. My brain made her, so the badness must have come from *inside* of me. It must have been there already. Lucy gave me a place to put it.

I'm not just crying anymore—I'm sobbing. I bend my legs and rest my forehead on my knees. The tears drip down my face and mingle with snot and spit. My entire body is shaking. I can't remember the last time I wept like this. I'm crying so hard I can barely breathe.

I've never been this scared before, never felt so panicked. (Is this a panic attack? Something new to add to my growing list of problems?) Not when I called the ambulance for Agnes and saw the blood beneath her head, not when the police questioned me and sent me to the institute, not when they replaced my real clothes with paper ones and locked me in.

Someone knocks on the stall door. "You all right in there, honey?"

This total stranger can't even see me, but she knows something's wrong. Can she tell I'm sick? Maybe everyone in this bathroom has guessed that I need medicine in order to see what's real. Maybe they all think I'm a freak.

I shake my head. All they know is that I'm crying, gasping for breath. And being sick doesn't make me I'm a freak. At least, that's what Dr. Charan would say.

A loudspeaker announces that a flight to New York is boarding.

A few minutes later, there's another announcement: "Hannah Gold, please report to gate 8A."

Someone knocks on the door again. I wait for another stranger to ask me if I'm okay, but instead my mother's voice says, "Hannah, open the door."

I get up slowly, open the door, and immediately wish I hadn't. Mom looks mortified. She steps inside the tiny stall and grabs a handful of toilet paper, roughly wiping my face. I can feel her nails through the thin material.

She leads me out of the stall. She doesn't stop to pick up my discarded bandage, whether because she doesn't want to touch something that's been on the dirty floor or because she can't be bothered, I don't know.

"I'm so sorry," she says to the women waiting in line. "My daughter is sick." She pauses, then adds, "Food poisoning. Can't trust anything you eat at the airport."

The strangers look unconvinced. People with food poisoning don't usually sob.

My mother has her fingers wrapped around my left arm. She's pressing on the edges of my bruise. "Mommy, you're hurting me."

She stops and faces me. I don't think either of us remembers the last time I called her *Mommy*. She stares at me like I'm a stranger.

fifty

We're sitting in business class: Mom and Dad are next to each other, and I'm one row behind them in a window seat. Even though the bandage and sling are gone, I keep my left arm folded across my chest. My elbow is tender. I'm still crying. My shoulders are shaking, my breaths ragged. The man sitting in the aisle seat next to me pretends not to notice, keeping his gaze focused on an article in the *Wall Street Journal*. I reach into my bag and take out my book on the Tudors (I never had a chance to buy something less dense), open it to the chapter I flagged with my bookmark months ago. The words swim on the page in front of me, but at least I look more normal like this. After a few minutes, I turn the page even though I haven't read anything. And again a few minutes after that. And again.

I saw my reflection in the bathroom mirror before my mother dragged me to the gate. My hair had fallen out of the barrette. Strands stuck to my face, and my skin was red and blotchy and wet. My eyes were open wide, too wide. It must have been a panic attack. I remember the quiet girls in the institution's cafeteria. I didn't want to be like them, but at least their glazed eyes weren't so frightened.

The plane begins speeding down the runway. I hold my breath when we leave the earth behind. I look out the window and watch California fade beneath the clouds. The farther we get from this ridiculous state, the more easily my breaths come, the more relaxed my pulse. The lump in my throat is shrinking.

I lean my head back against my seat. Maybe none of this would've happened if I'd stayed home this summer.

Mom twists around in her seat to face me. "Here," she says, reaching out. She's holding a plastic water bottle in one hand and a blue pill in the other.

Lightfoot—no, Dr. Charan—told us about the possible side effects of my medication: weight gain or loss; lethargy or trouble sleeping; increased or decreased appetite; mood swings. (I wondered if anyone else noticed that my medication could cause the same potential side effects as a severe traumatic brain injury.) Dr. Charan also said over time the medication might become less effective, and my new doctor would have to adjust my dose, try different medications, different treatments. (Different side effects.)

I should've asked *what* different treatments.

Electroshock therapy? (Supposedly humane now, but who do they think they're kidding?)

A lobotomy? (Do they still do that? Anything is possible.)

More padded walls? More sedation and more restraints? More seven-by-eight-foot rooms? More vacations for my parents?

"For your headache," Mom says loudly, as I reach up and take the water and medicine from her hand.

Mom settles herself back in her seat, and I stare at the chalky pill in my palm.

I never had a panic attack before I started taking these pills.

There was no reason to panic because I never questioned who was right or what was real.

I wipe my tears with my left hand, even though bending my elbow makes it ache. I never tried to hurt myself before I took these pills. What is that, if not proof positive that they're bad for me?

Maybe I should skip this dose. Just to be safe.

The doctor my parents have lined up in New York is an expert, top of his field. He won't be anything like Dr. Charan. After all, when I first met her, I guessed that she worked at the institute only because she was too incompetent to find a job anyplace else, and now I'm sure I was right: Why else would someone take a job at place like that? (Her name even sounds like *charlatan*.) Mom's hoping for a *more promising diagnosis*, but I bet that this new doctor will realize I'm not sick at all. He'll call Dr. Charan's methods inhumane. She kept me locked in a room, and even if she claimed it was for my own safety, a good doctor like my new doctor (*best in the business*, like Mom said) would never do such a thing.

Then, again, I can't be sure Dr. Charan actually kept me in isolation like I remember. If I really was in the throes of a psychotic episode at the time, then my memory of those weeks isn't exactly reliable. Maybe I spent my afternoons weaving baskets in art therapy, maybe I took group showers, maybe I ate in the cafeteria as often as not.

When I complained about being stuck in the room, Dr. Charan had said, *I'm sorry you feel that our interactions are so limited.* At the time, I hated the way she made it sound like we might be having additional interactions I didn't know about.

But now I wonder—were we?

In the car on the way to the airport, Mom said I was *hardly* kept in solitary. How does she know? Was she getting weekly reports about my performance in group therapy, my interactions with other patients?

Then there's the fact that I hadn't yet stepped foot inside the institute when I heard Lucy's voice tell me to push Agnes.

And six weeks before that, my brain invented Jonah.

I shake my head. If I'm not sick, there's got to be an explanation for those symptoms, too. It's easy to assume that Dr. Charan lied to cover up her shoddy medical work. But why did my brain invent Jonah and Lucy? I close my eyes and concentrate until I'm certain I know exactly why: I was *bored.* The summer school classes were too easy. I got A's without so much as cracking a book. I was like the girl in the Roald Dahl book I read when I was eight: Without enough stimulation, Matilda had magical powers. Once her brain was properly occupied, the magic disappeared.

That must have been what happened to me! The world wasn't complicated enough, so my brain invented Jonah because

I needed a challenge. Otherwise, why not make a perfect boyfriend instead of a cheating boyfriend?

And then when I was bored to tears in *that place*, my brain gave me Lucy. (Mom's voice: For all we know, that place *exacerbated her hallucinations*.) The medication Lightfoot prescribed dulled my brain enough to make Lucy disappear, but I don't really *need* it because I'm not really *sick*.

When I get home, I'll have to be careful to keep myself occupied. I'll take more classes—AP classes. No, college-level classes. I'm already signed up for that Russian literature lecture at NYU, but now I'll add another class or two to my schedule. It'll look great on my applications, and my brain will be too busy to make mischief. I'm not sick, I'm just smart. My brain isn't *broken*; it's actually so advanced it invented puzzles to keep itself busy. And people like Dr. Charan don't understand that because they're not intelligent enough.

My new doctor—expert, top of his field, *best in the business*—will un-diagnose me. He'll say that clearly, Dr. Charan made a mistake. You know, crazy California doctors and all that.

My parents will be happy. They won't be embarrassed by me, and they won't be scared of me. We'll go back to the way our lives used to be.

I take a deep breath. The lump in my throat shrinks and then vanishes completely.

When I get back to school, I'll make a new best friend. I already know whom I'm going to choose: April Lu, Rebekah's former best friend. We were in the same physics class last year.

April could be pretty if she wore the right makeup, if someone helped her pick out her clothes, if someone urged her to cut her jet-black hair into a short and edgy style. She'll be grateful for my guidance, just like Agnes was. Just like Rebekah was when I offered to help her get her first kiss. Just like Alex was when I laid our sleeping bags side by side.

I roll the pill across my right palm, then close my fist over it. Yesterday's dose is probably already leaving my body. I imagine my metabolism hard at work to get rid of whatever remains. Eventually, the medication will come out in my sweat, in my urine, in my saliva. Maybe one skipped dose will be enough. Maybe by the time we land in New York, the medication will be completely out of my system. Maybe Lucy and Jonah will be waiting at the gate. No, not at the gate, security won't let people greet you at the gate anymore. They'll be waiting for me in baggage claim.

Jonah will tell me he never believed I hurt Agnes, and he always wanted me more than he wanted her. He'll tell me Dr. Charan lied—of course she lied!—about his classes and his dorm room, and he's so sorry he disappeared when I needed him most. He had no idea what I was going through over the past few months. He'll smile like a fox, and his hazel eyes will narrow, and he'll wrap me in a warm, reassuring hug.

And Lucy...Lucy will say *To hell with the San Francisco Dance Academy!* She's decided to apply to school in New York. Julliard or the Joffrey, somewhere close so she can be near me.

They'll both be there when April and I start playing the same old games—Light as a Feather, Stiff as a Board, Never Have I Ever, Truth or Dare. In fact, maybe I won't take all those advanced classes after all. Maybe I'll let Lucy and Jonah stick around to keep me company, just in case my friendship with April doesn't progress as planned. But it will, of course it will. I've never had problems making friends before.

I lean back into my seat and exhale calmly. My eyes are dry and a smile spreads across my lips.

The flight attendant asks me if I'd like anything to drink. Before I can answer, Mom twists in her seat again.

"No, she already has water."

I feel my smile start to fade. There's something in Mom's voice that I don't like.

"I didn't see you take your pill, Hannah," she says slowly, evenly.

"You weren't looking."

"I can tell you didn't open that bottle of water." She gestures to the bottle wedged between my thigh and the seat, its plastic cap still sealed shut.

"I was just about to—"

"So, let's see it."

"But I—"

"*Hannah.*"

Mom's never used that tone with me before. It's the tone other parents use on their naughty toddlers. It's not the tone of someone who believes her daughter was born mature.

It's not the tone of someone who thinks her daughter might not be sick.

She was hoping for *a more promising diagnosis*, not no diagnosis at all.

I open my right hand and look at the blue pill. I squeezed it so hard that it cracked in two. Crumbs of it stick to my skin.

I put the pieces of the pill in my mouth. I even lick the powdery crumbs off my palm. I lift the water bottle to my lips and swallow. The pill's jagged edges scratch the back of my throat.

I look around the plane. The door to the cockpit is locked shut and behind us, a curtain divides business class from economy.

I estimate that it would take me ten steps to walk from the cockpit to the curtain, three steps to walk from one side of the plane to the other. The walls are smooth and cream-colored and curved, not green and bumpy, and there is a long row of oval windows on either side of the plane, instead of a square-shaped one up in the corner. These windows don't open either.

"Good girl," Mom says as I take another swig of water to speed the pill on its way. Mom resettles in her seat, facing forward.

The plane is just another room.

I'm still a girl in a room.

They'll never let me see Jonah or Lucy again.

I'll never make best friends with April Lu. She's hated me since eighth grade. Even at my best, I couldn't overcome that kind of dislike.

I close my eyes and sigh. It was easy with Agnes. She liked me from the start. It was later, apparently—according to her parents, their lawyer, and the months-old messages he played at the hearing—that she started to think I was strange.

Agnes was in a coma for two weeks.

Will they think I'm strange when I go back to school?

The doctors didn't know if she would ever wake up.

Maybe one of my teachers has already let the truth slip.

A neurosurgeon had to drill burr holes in her skull to relieve the pressure on her brain.

Soon, everyone will know.

She appeared to have lost all verbal function.

They'll stop talking when I walk into a room.

Eventually, she was able to communicate through blinks and grunts.

They'll look at me differently. They'll treat me differently.

She needs assistance to leave the bed to perform her bodily functions.

No one will want to be my friend.

She will have years of physical therapy, speech therapy, and occupational therapy ahead of her.

I'll be all alone.

It's not yet clear how much care Agnes will need going forward.

I said I was sorry.

She may still be different in ways the doctors can't predict.

I meant it, at the time.

After vigorous therapy, Agnes finally said the first word she's managed since the accident.

I take another swig of water. The last traces of the pill slide down my throat.

Mama.

I open my eyes and look through the gap between the seats in front of me. My mother rests her head on my father's shoulder, and he kisses her hair.

I'm not a magical girl whose brain needed more stimulation.

I'll never play Light as a Feather, Stiff as a Board again.

Agnes Smith's life will never be the same.

Neither will mine.

AUTHOR'S NOTE

Authors are often asked which is their favorite character—I've always found that question nearly impossible to answer, but I have to admit, Hannah Gold has a special place in my heart. She's imperfect and even unkind, but I loved writing her. I loved writing her intelligence and wit, her confidence, and her belief (at the beginning of the novel, at least) that she's the smartest person in the room. She starts this story certain she's the heroine in a thrilling mystery about being wrongly accused, only to discover that she's the subject not of a thriller, but of a story about coming to terms with a mental illness diagnosis.

In chapter thirty-nine, Dr. Lightfoot—er, Dr. Charan—says that people with Hannah's disease are more likely to hurt themselves than others. In fact, while researching this book, I read that rates of violence *against* people with mental illness are much higher than for the general population, especially those with complex mental illness and psychotic illnesses, and people with mental illness are also more at risk of homicide, suicide, and self-harm. At the end of the novel, Hannah isn't sure whether she meant to hurt Agnes. But one thing that *is* certain is that

Hannah hurt herself and might have done a lot more damage if the orderly hadn't gotten to her room when he did.

Dr. Charan also says that Hannah is lucky to have been diagnosed so young—lucky that she'll benefit from treatment (and, though the doctor doesn't mention it, lucky to have parents who can pay for treatment not covered by insurance). Some people suffering from mental illness go years without a diagnosis or are misdiagnosed and therefore mistreated for years.

This book is a work of fiction and is not meant to educate readers about mental illness or institutionalization. No doubt I granted myself some creative liberty to tell Hannah's story: it's unlikely that any proper doctor would keep Hannah confined to her room the way she is (or rather, believes she is) for much of the story, and Hannah might not be sent home quite so quickly following her diagnosis. Additionally, I read that antipsychotics may take effect after a few days, but following acute episodes, they can take as long as four to six weeks, so it's hard to say how long Hannah would have been medicated before she discovered Lucy was a hallucination.

If you or someone you know is struggling
with mental illness, please reach out to:

National Alliance on Mental Illness (NAMI)
Helpline: 1-800-950-NAMI (6264)
Email: info@nami.org
www.nami.org

ACKNOWLEDGMENTS

Many thanks to my wonderful agent, Mollie Glick, and to Emily Westcott, Joy Fowkles, Jamie Stockton, and the entire team at CAA.

Thank you to my lovely editor, Annette Pollert-Morgan, and to the Sourcebooks team: Chris Bauerle, Sarah Cardillo, Sara Hartman-Seeskin, Cassie Gutman, Nicole Hower, Sarah Kasman, Kelly Lawler, Katy Lynch, Sean Murray, Beth Oleniczak, William Preston, Dominique Raccah, Jillian Rahn, Stefani Sloma, Todd Stocke, Heidi Weiland, Shane White, Christina Wilson, Christa Desir, and thanks to Jennifer Heuer for the stunning cover.

Thanks to Samantha Schutz, and many thanks to Hannah's early readers: Rachel Feld, Caroline Gertler, Jackie Resnick, Danielle Rollins, Julie Sternberg, and Melissa Zar. Thanks also to Jocelyn Davies and Anne Heltzel.

Thank you to my sister, my parents, my friends, and my teachers. And once again, thank you JP Gravitt, for everything.

"Because of the dog's joyfulness, our own is increased. It is no small gift."

—Mary Oliver, "The Summer Beach"

ABOUT THE AUTHOR

Alyssa Sheinmel is the *New York Times* bestselling author of several novels for young adults including *Faceless* and *R.I.P. Eliza Hart*. She is the coauthor of *The Haunting of Sunshine Girl* and *The Awakening of Sunshine Girl*. Alyssa grew up in Northern California and New York and currently lives and writes in New York. Follow Alyssa on Instagram @alyssasheinmel and Twitter @AlyssaSheinmel or visit her online at alyssasheinmel.com.

FIREreads

 #getbooklit

Your hub for the hottest young adult books!

Visit us online and sign up for our
newsletter at FIREreads.com

 @sourcebooksfire

 sourcebooksfire

firereads.tumblr.com